MY KIND
OF
Beautiful

A Finding Love Novel

NIKKI ASH

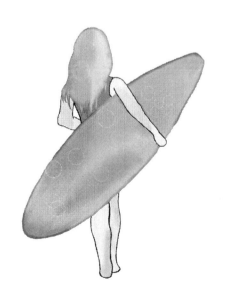

MY KIND OF BEAUTIFUL'S PLAYLIST

Your Song- Rita Ora

Perfect Storm- Brad Paisley

You and Me- Lifehouse

Say You Won't Go- James Arthur

Broken-Lifehouse

Breakeven- The Script

Battle Scars- Lupe Fiasco & Guy Sebastian

Don't You Wanna Stay- Jason Aldean

Stay- Rihanna

Let Me Go- 3 Doors Down

It Will Rain-Bruno Mars

How to Get the Girl- Taylor Swift

Rumors- NEFFEX

There's No Way-Lauv

I Loved Her First- Heartland

Somebody-Natalie La Rose

All I Want- Daniel Skye

I Don't Want to Miss a Thing- Aerosmith

As Long as You Love Me- Justin Bieber

Sweet but Psycho- Ava Max

Too Close- Next

Let Me See Ya Girl- Cole Swindell

Leave Her Wild- Tyler Rich

Replay- Lyaz

Nightmare- Halsey

FRIENDS- Ann-Marie & Marshmello

Halo- Beyoncé

What Ifs- Kane Brown

Heaven-Kane Brown

Love You Like I Used To-Russell Dickerson

Nobody but You-Blake Shelton

To my daughter, for showing me every day how beautiful life is.

One

ALEC

"It's your turn to cook, bro, and I'm thinking burgers." Chase grins wide and throws two packages of ground beef into the shopping cart. "I'm also thinking baked potatoes." He pushes the cart over to the produce section and grabs several potatoes, tossing them into a produce bag and then the bag into the cart.

"Yeah, yeah. Why is it when it's your turn to cook, you buy pre-made meals, but when it's my turn, I actually have to cook?" I pick out a few tomatoes and onions and add them to the cart.

"Maybe because you can actually cook. Trust me, I'm doing everyone at the station a favor." He chuckles, throwing a head of lettuce into the mix. "Who'll put out all the fires in Los Angeles if all the guys are sick with food poisoning?"

I throw a couple cans of baked beans into the cart. "Maybe you should give those words of advice to Lexi. The woman is determined to learn how to cook, and I'm pretty sure it's going to end with her killing all of us."

"Food poisoning doesn't kill." Chase laughs.

"No, but fires do." I shake my head as I think about the last few times my best friend and roommate has attempted to cook and failed. "I'm telling you right now, if that damn fire alarm goes off one more time while I'm trying to sleep, I'm going to find a way to padlock the oven so she can't cook."

"When are you going to admit you have the hots for Lexi Scott?" Chase shoots me a knowing look, which I choose to ignore, instead grabbing a package of buns from the shelf and throwing them at him.

"Oohhh, that hurt." Chase groans dramatically. "Seriously, though, in the last year, since I was transferred to this station and have gotten to know you, not once have I seen you treat the women you're talking to the way you treat that woman."

"That's because I'm not *talking* to Lexi." And if I'm honest, I'm barely talking to other women. But when the guys and I go out, it tends to send up a red flag when they're all trying to hook up with various women, while I'm wallowing in my drink, trying to fight my feelings for a woman I'll never make mine. It'd probably be smart to actually hook up with one of those women—fuck my feelings for her straight out of my system. But the few times I tried ended with me walking out the door, leaving the woman hanging—sexually frustrated and pissed—so I decided to take a short hiatus from sex, get my shit together, and then try again.

Only that hiatus has lasted way longer than I planned. I've been abstinent so long now, my dick has probably disowned me. If it could, it would detach itself from my body and find another guy to get it laid.

"She's my friend," I tell him for the millionth damn time, hoping this time he'll believe me. "Just like Georgia is my friend. And if you want to stay friends with women, you don't *talk* to them."

"I'm not buying it. I've seen you with both of your roommates. You don't give Georgia the same look you give Lexi."

"And what look might that be?" I regret the question the second the words come out of my mouth. I thought I've been good about hiding my feelings, but it's hard when we share a living space. When she flits around in her tiny little cutoff shorts and bikinis. When she lays her legs across me on the couch, begging me to give her foot massages. Or when she snuggles up next to me to watch a movie, and her tiny, perfect body rubs up against mine. I try so damn hard to ignore the way my heart clenches in my chest, or the way my dick stands at attention at her touch. If Lexi's noticed, she hasn't said anything. So, she's either blind to my feelings, ignoring them, or I'm doing a good job at hiding them— at least from her.

"The look that says you want to lock her up in your room and fuck her until the sun comes up," Chase says. "Then, when all the condoms run out and she can't take any more, you cook her breakfast in bed." He waggles his eyebrows.

"Chase, you're seeing shit that isn't there," I deadpan, lying through my teeth. "And speaking of breakfast in bed, when are you planning to sleep in your own bed?" I give him a pointed look.

Without answering me, Chase pushes the cart into the checkout line and starts loading the items onto the conveyer belt. I could push him to answer, but I don't. For one, Chase sleeping on my couch when he has his own home and a wife can't be a good sign, and if it means he's having marriage troubles, the last thing I want to do is make him feel like he can't crash at my place. And two, it might cause him to further push the subject of me hooking up with Lexi, and the last thing I need is to visualize my best friend in my bed: under me, on top of me, me fucking her from behind. Pulling her long blond hair while she calls out my name. *Damn it!* I look around to make sure nobody is watching me, then adjust my pants.

Chase pays the cashier while I bag the groceries and then we head back to station one-fifteen, which is located in Los Angeles near UCLA. We're one shift away from having three days off, and once we're off, I plan to spend at least one of those days in my bed asleep.

We get back to the station and the guys are all hanging out in the workout room. Chase and I work shift B with four other guys. This shift consists of two twenty-four-hour shifts every other day and then four days off. Chase has been a firefighter for ten years and was recently promoted to Battalion Chief—he's in charge of the guys on our shift. He took the place of a guy who was promoted to Fire Chief when ours retired. I've been working as a firefighter-slash-paramedic for the last five years at this same station and was promoted last year to Lieutenant. The other guys on our shift are Luke and Thomas, who are both firefighters-slash-paramedics like me, Carter, who is the Driver Engineer—he drives the fire truck and manages the equipment—and Scott, who just recently finished the academy and is still working on his EMT license.

"What's for dinner?" Carter yells from the treadmill.

"Burgers," I yell back, throwing the bags onto the counter while Chase lights the grill.

I've just finished putting everything away and am in the middle of prepping the burger patties when the tone goes off throughout the station. It doesn't matter how long you've been working as a firefighter, when the ridiculously loud ringing hits your ears, you cringe. Then you jump into action. Because all of our bunker gear is kept on the truck, all we have to do is jump on once Chase comes out with the information from the dispatcher to let us know where the fire is.

"Westwood Village condos," Chase calls out, looking straight at me. "Alec's address," he adds with a smirk. The guys all groan. *Dammit, Lexi.* Even though the fire probably isn't anything to be too concerned about, we still treat it how we would treat any fire that's called in.

We arrive at my complex in less than two minutes and head up to the second floor. The door is already open and you can smell the smoke leaking from inside. The smoke alarm is blaring throughout the house, and is Lex in the kitchen trying to put the fire out? Nope, her ass is standing on a chair with a broomstick in her hand, jabbing at the smoke alarm to shut it off. Chase and a couple of the other guys head into the kitchen to make sure the oven fire is under control while I go straight for Lexi.

Grabbing her by her waist, I pull her off the chair. She shrieks in shock, until she sees it's me, then her eyes go wide. I lower her to the ground before I reach up and press the button to silence the alarm. When the room goes quiet, Lexi sighs, and I can see it in her face that she's trying not to laugh.

"Lex," I groan, about to lay into her, but then her deep blue eyes meet mine and I shake my head. It's damn near impossible to be mad at her. "This is the third time this month. Maybe you could...I don't know...practice cooking at your parents' place." At least then it would fall on another station.

"I wasn't cooking." She shakes her head emphatically, and several strands of her blond hair fall from her loose ponytail. I give her a pointed look and she grins wildly, reminding me of a rose: beautiful to look at from afar, but filled with thorns, making her impossible to touch. And if you do attempt it—thinking you can somehow get around them, so you can experience her beauty up close—there's no doubt she'll prick you, leaving you bleeding and in pain.

"Happy Birthday to you! Happy Birthday..." The guys begin singing, and I turn around to see a charcoaled cake in Chase's hands, a huge smirk splayed across his face. The guys are all shaking with laughter as he sets down what I'm assuming was Lexi's attempt at baking me a cake for my birthday. They finish singing and start clapping, thinking they're fucking hilarious.

"See? I wasn't cooking. I was baking." Lexi shrugs innocently. "It's your favorite...white cake."

Her eyes go to the black cake that could pass for burnt brownies, then back to mine, her top teeth biting down on her bottom lip. "Sorry about Ms. Holden calling nine-one-one." She rolls her eyes. "She could've just come over and asked if everything was okay. She doesn't have to be so dramatic all the time."

I throw my arm across the back of Lexi's shoulders and pull her into a side hug. "Lex, you know I love you, right?"

"Yeah..." She tilts her head up to look at me, and I ignore the stirring in my gut at the sight of her. Of her plump, kissable lips, of the way her blue eyes remind me of the deep ocean—full of life, yet mysterious and uncertain.

"You've gotta stop trying to cook and bake. Paint, surf, go graffiti the hell out of some of those abandoned buildings." I give her forehead a kiss to lighten the blow. "But for the love of God, woman, don't touch our oven, please."

"Ugh... fine. I did find some crock pot recipes I've been wanting to try out. Maybe I'll ask my mom if I can borrow hers." The guys start to chuckle, but when Lexi glares at each of them, they all stop laughing at the same time.

"Lexi, I'm home." The door slams closed and in walks Georgia, Lexi's sister and my other roommate. "Please don't tell me that firetruck outside is for..." Her feet and mouth come to an abrupt halt when she sees all of us standing in the kitchen.

"Hey." She shyly waves at the guys. "I guess it is..."

"Lexi, here, was baking me a birthday cake." I point to the cake pan.

"I was gone for less than an hour." Georgia sighs. "How do you even burn a cake in that amount of time?"

"Well...I..." Lexi looks at her sister sheepishly.

"You what?" Georgia grabs the pan and throws the entire thing into the garbage can, not even bothering to try to clean it out and at least save the pan. "I wasn't even gone long enough for you to burn a cake. What did you do?"

"Well, Ricco may have called and said the waves are killer. There's a storm brewing, you know. But I had already put the cake in, and you were gone. I just thought if I doubled the temperature, I could cut the bake time in half. It makes sense, right?" Lexi's shoulders shrug and her head tilts to the side.

I cover my mouth from laughing, knowing it will only encourage her. But holy shit, she's so fucking adorable. She's just so lost in her own world. Chase's gaze meets mine, and he raises one knowing brow.

"Anyway," Lexi continues when nobody answers her. "I figured while I was waiting for the cake to finish, I could paint some, so I put my earbuds in and got to work. The next thing I know the fire alarm is going off and the condo is all smoky."

"It's okay, darlin'," Carter says. "You know..." He approaches

Lexi, who eyes him speculatively. "I've been known to make a mean omelet"—he nods slowly—"the morning after." He shoots her a flirtatious wink, and the guys' gazes go to me, and it's in that moment I realize they *all* know my feelings for Lexi. I thought I've been doing a good job of hiding them over the years, but apparently not. Does that mean Lexi knows too? If she does, and hasn't said a word, wouldn't that mean she doesn't return my feelings?

Lexi scrunches her nose up in disgust, and I bark out a laugh. "And on that note, let's go." I give her a kiss on her cheek. "Be careful surfing."

"Always." She beams.

The guys all say goodbye to the women and then we head back to the station to finish our night.

Two

LEXI

"How's it going?" I throw myself onto my sister's bed and peek over at her computer screen. She's working on designing a new website for Jumpin' Java—our favorite coffee shop in Larchmont Village, where our mom has a painting studio and our dad owns a UFC training facility. While we both take after our mom creatively, I'm more of a paintbrush-in-hand kind of artist, and Georgia is all about the digital. Technically, Georgia is my stepsister. Her mom married my dad when we were little and they each adopted us. But to anyone who doesn't know that, we're sisters—and she's my favorite person in the entire world.

"It's going." She smiles softly, pushing a wayward strand of brown hair behind her ear. "Finishing this up." She points to the screen.

"Want to come watch me surf tonight?" Georgia's made it

known she doesn't particularly care for the people I hang out at the beach with, but I hate that she almost never goes anywhere, so I invite her everywhere. She's either at school, at our mom's studio helping with the children's parties, or at home working behind her computer.

"Max is coming to take some pictures," I add, knowing if I say our younger brother is going to be there, she might actually go.

Georgia gives me another smile—the one that tells me she loves me and doesn't want to hurt my feelings, but she doesn't want to go. When I look up at her, her bright green eyes are dimmed, and my heart hurts for my sister. Somewhere in there I believe there's a woman who's begging to come out and be carefree, but that woman is being pushed down by another part of my sister who shies away from the public and all social situations. She's more comfortable sitting behind a computer than hanging out with living, breathing people—except for me. Georgia is the yin to my yang. She's more than my friend, more than my sister. She's the other half of my soul.

"I received a weird email today," she says.

"Oh yeah? From who?"

"She said she's my grandmother. She emailed my business page."

I sit up, confused. We only have one grandma and grandpa, and they're currently traveling through Europe. "Did it sound like Grandma?"

"No, she said she was my biological father's mom."

"Oh my God!" I push the laptop away from Georgia. "Did you tell Mom?"

"Not yet. She never talks about my bio dad. I never thought about the fact he could have siblings or parents out there."

"Did she mention why she's emailing you now?"

"All she wrote was that she would like to meet with me to discuss some matters. I replied not to contact me again. I didn't know what else to do... and please don't mention anything to Mom. You know she gets upset at any talk about her old life."

"Okay," I agree. "But if she emails again, you should ask her why she wants to meet with you. I doubt she just wants to get to know you. You're about to turn twenty-one. She's had years to contact you."

"Maybe."

"So, no to the beach tonight?"

"Not tonight. Have fun and ride all the waves."

"Fine. Want to watch some more of *The O.C.* when I get home?" Binge watching older shows is Georgia's and my thing.

"Sure."

Grabbing my surfboard and art supplies, I throw it all into the back of my Jeep and head over to Santa Monica Beach. When I get there, several people are already out in the water. There is only about three hours of light left, and most people prefer not to night surf because it can be dangerous and not worth it. But with the storm heading this way, the swells are coming in between ten and fifteen feet compared to the normal surf of three to five feet.

Usually, in order to get bigger waves, we have to drive a couple hours south.

Before I head over to my friends, I stop at the taco stand and buy a bunch of tacos, then drop them off to my friend Aiden. He wasn't expecting me, so he's not there—probably going for a walk along the beach. I leave them for him in his tent, knowing he'll be surprised and happy when he returns and finds them there.

"What's up, Lexi!" Shane, a surfer and friend of mine, calls out as I make my way over to him and set my stuff down. Taking my clothes off, leaving me in just my bikini, I pull on my Roxy wetsuit and zip it up from the back. Then I cover my art stuff with my towel, so it doesn't get dripped on.

"Lexi! How's my sexy little artist doing today?" Jason, another friend of mine, stabs his board into the sand and pulls me in for a hug.

"Chilling... How long have you guys been out here?"

"Long enough to see all the Barneys about kill themselves. Already seen two guys break bones and had to call an ambulance." Shane shakes his head.

"Ugh! Why does everyone who owns a surfboard see big waves and think they can all of a sudden surf?" I ask through my laughter.

"I don't know, but these waves are seriously bitchin'. I swear some of them have hit a good twenty feet." Jason reaches into his bag and pulls out a joint, lighting it up and taking a drag. Then he passes it to me. Not wanting to be fucked up while on the waves, I decline.

"Later... Right now I want to hit the waves." I grab my board to head down the sand, but before I can walk away, Jason grabs my cheeks and pulls me in for a kiss. The smoke he was holding in transfers from his mouth to mine.

I push him away with a cough of laughter. "Jason," I whine, making him laugh. "Don't be a douche. Let's go!"

He takes one last hit then pinches the joint between his fingers to put it out. After throwing it back into his bag, he grabs his board, and we run down the beach. Just as my feet hit the water, I hear my name being called. When I look back, I spot my brother, Max. I wave to him, and he waves back. Then he throws a blanket down on the sand and has a seat, camera in his hand. Max is sixteen and a sophomore in high school. His true love is photography, and you'll never see him anywhere without a camera.

Jason, Shane, and I paddle out, and once we're far enough, we meet up with several other guys and a few girls, who are all watching the waves. Some I don't recognize and others I've grown up surfing with. Everyone's talking and bullshitting, but I'm not here to gossip. I'm here to surf. I watch each wave, and when I spot the one I want, I drop to my belly and start paddling. The wave hits and my back arches as I'm lifted. Just as the wave begins to pick me up, I pop up and catch it, riding the wave all the way back to shore.

I spend the next few hours riding wave after wave, taking the occasional break to talk to my brother and to give Ricco a hug when he shows up. When the sun is almost all the way down and nearly everyone has headed home, I drop my board into the sand and peel my wetsuit off my body.

"You staying to paint?" Max asks.

"You know it." I drop onto the blanket and grab my bag of supplies and canvas.

"Want me to stay?" he asks, looking around. There are still a few straggling surfers, including Jason and Sean, who'll be here for hours night surfing.

"No, I'm good. I just want to paint the storm that's brewing."

"Text me when you get back to your Jeep, yeah?"

"Of course."

The storm breeze is a perfect mixture of humid with a hint of coolness to it. It has me grabbing the orange and blue paints. My hair whips around my face, so I throw it up into a messy bun and begin painting. The waves are gorgeous. Dark blue with white crests roll into the shoreline. The sun is now a faint yellowish-orange in the background peeking out from behind the now black ocean. I get lost in my painting, until I hear my name being called. When I look up, I find Ricco, Shane, and Jason standing to the right of me, drinking and getting high—a typical night for them.

"Damn, that painting looks like the real thing." Jason glances from my canvas out to the sea. "One day, when you're a famous artist, will you still find time to visit us lowly surfers?" he jokes.

"Shut up." I throw my paint brush at him and he catches it. He lunges toward me and wraps his arms around me. I've known Jason's had a crush on me for a while, but I ignore it. There's only one guy on my mind—*one I don't stand a chance at being with.*

My phone dings, giving me the perfect excuse to pull away from him. *And speak of the devil...*

Alec: How are the waves?

I type back a quick response: **Awesome! I wish they were like this all the time.**

I snap a picture of my painted canvas with the ocean in the background.

Alec: Looks beautiful. We should hang it in the hallway.

I smile to myself. There isn't a picture I've painted that Alec hasn't found a spot for in our home. At this point, it looks more like an art gallery than a home.

I notice it's already nine o'clock, so I start packing up my stuff.

"Heading out?" Shane asks.

"Yeah." I stand and shake off the blanket.

"Here, we'll help you to your car," Ricco offers, taking my still-wet painting from me.

"Thank you, but I'm perfectly capable of carrying my stuff." I laugh at how crazy my friends are acting.

"We know," Ricco says, "but did you hear about that girl who was attacked on the beach the other night?"

"No." A shiver runs down my spine. Sure, the beach is filled with homeless folks, and the city is riddled with crime, but it's not often you hear of someone being assaulted on the beach where I surf and spend a lot of my time.

"They haven't caught the guy yet," Shane says. "But the girl didn't make it..."

"Damn, well, thanks for looking out for me." I give the guys a grateful smile. I'm lucky to have so many people in my life who love me and care about my well-being.

We carry all our stuff up, and they help me load everything into my car, refusing to leave until I'm safely inside and driving away. When I get home, I text Max to let him know I'm home safe. Georgia's sitting at the kitchen table, working on something on her laptop.

"Hey you," I say, walking over to her.

"Hey! Good night?"

"The waves were perfect."

Georgia sniffs the air then glances up at me. "Were you smoking tonight?" she asks, disappointment laced in her tone. I hate when she acts like this. For one, smoking weed is common on the beaches of LA. Hell, doing harder drugs is even more common. But also, because I hate the thought of Georgia being disappointed in me, and let's be real, I'm pretty much a walking disappointment. Sure, I'm in college, but what exactly am I going to do with that degree? No fucking clue. While Alec has known he's wanted to be a firefighter since he was a kid, and Georgia has always wanted to follow in our mom's footsteps and do web design, I have no clue what I want to do with my future. I love painting, but the thought of having to do it to earn a living makes me cringe. I do it because I love to do it, not because I need to. And if I had to do it to earn money, I fear I would resent it.

"No, the guys were," I tell her, already making my way down the hall to jump in the shower. Once my body is clean and rid of the saltwater, I get out and get dressed in a pair of pajama shorts and a tank top.

When I come out, I find Georgia in her room. She has the next episode of *The O.C.* ready to play. I cuddle up in her bed next to her, and my head falls onto her shoulder. I'm not sure how many episodes we watch before we both pass out.

ALEC

"You're more than welcome to crash at my place," I tell Chase as we walk to our vehicles. It's finally eight in the morning, which means we're off for the next four days. "I was only fucking with you yesterday about squatting on my couch."

"I know, man, and I appreciate it, but... I need to go home." Chase shrugs. "I'll see you tomorrow night."

Because my birthday is today, I'm celebrating with my family tonight and my friends tomorrow night. Both parties were completely their doing and not mine. It's funny, when you're little, you can't wait to get older, but then once you're older, you want time to stop. Not that I'm old. I'm only turning twenty-five today. But I'm pretty sure I'm too old to still be having multiple parties. I laugh when I think about Lexi arguing with me, insisting she throw me a birthday party at Club Hectic. We both know the party is more for her than me, but I'll let her have it. Lexi loves finding any reason to party, and I love watching her party.

I'm pulling up to my house, when my phone rings. Seeing that it's my dad, I answer the call.

"Hey, old man."

"Don't talk shit, Son. You're getting up there in age, too."

"If I'm getting old then that must make you ancient," I joke.

"Not ancient, just wiser. I wanted to be the first to wish you a Happy Birthday."

"Thanks, Dad. I'll see you tonight, right?" My mom and stepdad, Mason, are having a dinner party at their house to celebrate my birthday. I'm one of the lucky kids whose parents are divorced and actually get along, so everyone, including my dad and my stepmom, are invited.

"Of course. You just getting off your shift?"

"Yep, I'm off for the next four days." My eyes are already starting to close of their own accord—we were up all night putting out a house fire and didn't get any sleep—but I will them to stay open so I can finish this conversation with my dad and then head upstairs to bed.

"I was wondering if you'd like to have brunch with me on Sunday."

"That sounds great." Every year for my birthday we always go to brunch just the two of us. Even if it didn't fall on his weekend with me, he would come and pick me up for the day.

"Eleven okay?"

"Yeah, and, Dad?"

"Yes?"

"How about this year you bring Lacie? I know it's always just been the two of us, but she's part of our family too now." They've been together for a few years and were married last year. I don't know her well, since I'm older and don't live with my dad, but she's sweet and good to him.

He's silent on the phone for a beat before he says, "Thank you, Alec. That means a lot to me, and I know it'll mean a lot to her."

"I'll see you guys tonight."

"I love you, Alec."

"Love you too, Dad."

I open the door and the place is quiet. The girls must be sleeping. Because they're on summer break, they don't have any classes, which means they'll sleep until noon. I spot them both sleeping in Georgia's room, and after getting changed out of my uniform and taking a quick shower to rinse off, I slip into bed with them. Lexi must feel me, because she rolls over and lays her head down on my chest.

I dip my head to give the top of her head a kiss. I can smell her coconut-scented shampoo mixed with saltwater. It doesn't matter how many times she showers, I think she'll always smell like the ocean, and I'll never be able to go to the beach without thinking of her. As my fingers run up and down her back, my thoughts go back to last year, right after Georgia and Lexi finished their sophomore year at UCLA and Lexi insisted it was time for them to live on their own. Of course, she had to bring it up during a barbecue when everyone was there...

"It's time for Georgia and me to move out," Lexi says nonchalantly.

Tristan, Lexi and Georgia's dad, chokes on his beer. "Excuse me?" His eyes are wide, and he looks like he's about to lock his daughter up in her room without a key.

"It's time, Dad. We talked about this a while ago. I'm going to be twenty-one in October and Georgia will be twenty. We're both adults and need to spread our wings. Right, Georgia?" She looks at her sister like she always does when she needs her on her side. Of course, Georgia agrees, just like she always does.

"And how are you paying for this apartment?" Tristan argues, which has everyone grinning because we all know he's going to be paying. Lexi and Georgia are his little girls, and he would sell his kidney to make sure they were happy.

Of course, Lexi wouldn't be Lexi if she didn't have all the answers. "Well, I was thinking we could get a roommate. There are plenty of apartments near campus, and we could split the bills. Georgia makes money working at Mom's art studio, and I have money in my savings from the surfing lessons I've given and the competitions I've won." She smiles sweetly, and Tristan groans.

"You're not using your savings," Charlie says.

Lexi beams, knowing if she's got her mom on board, Tristan is screwed.

"I don't know," Tristan says. "We live in LA. It's a scary world out there beyond this gated community. We would have to find you somewhere safe with a gate, and we would need to have an alarm system installed. I don't like the idea of my girls being alone in an apartment, nor do I want you moving in with some stranger."

"Dad, we're not babies anymore." Lexi pouts. "We're perfectly capable of living on our own."

"Weren't you just calling me to come over because you couldn't figure out how to open the oven?" I ask.

"How was I supposed to know when you press clean on the oven, it locks it to clean it!" Lexi yells.

"You thought the oven was on fire." I laugh. "You called me at the fire station freaking out."

"I thought when I clicked to clean it would shoot out cleaner! I didn't know it locks and heats up!" Lexi growls.

"And what about the time when you clogged the vacuum and couldn't get it to work?" I chuckle.

"I didn't know it fills up!"

"Where did you think it all goes? Back into the ecosystem?" I taunt. "Oh! And remember the time when you clogged the toilet and—"

Everyone laughs.

"Aleczander Sterling, if you don't shut up right this second, I'm going to tell everyone about the time I caught you—"

"Whoa! Okay, chill, woman." I hold my hands up in surrender. Because no one needs to know what she caught me doing when we were younger. And no, I'm not saying—you can use your imagination.

"I was just trying to point out maybe you aren't as ready to live on your own as you think." I shrug a shoulder.

"And you are?" Lexi argues.

"I'm a grown man, Lex. I'm a firefighter and a paramedic," I point out smugly.

"Oh, whatever, Mr. Paramedic. Remember when you choked on that pizza cheese?" Lexi giggles. "Your hands were flailing everywhere, and I had to reach over and do the finger sweep to save your life!" Her hands flail through the air as she mocks me. "You wouldn't eat pizza for like a year after that!"

Everyone cracks up laughing.

"That was before I became a paramedic. Now I'm a trained professional. Just the other day my neighbor had an emergency, and luckily I was there to help her."

"Are you referring to that ditsy, slutty neighbor of yours? What did she need help with? Locating her panties?" Lexi's hand goes to her hip, and I stifle my laugh, not daring to answer that question. If there's anything my dad, stepdad, and Tristan have taught me over the years, it's not to walk into traps like those.

"Ha!" Lexi yells. "Not answering because you know I'm right." Damn, woman...

"Okay, okay," Tristan says with a laugh. "While this has been extremely entertaining, it's given me an idea. While I have to accept you and your sister want some freedom, I also want to make sure you're both safe."

"Okay..." Lexi says slowly.

"What if you move in with Alec?" Tristan looks at me. "You mentioned you're looking for two new roommates since yours got married and moved out. It would be perfect. And I would make sure their part of the bills is paid."

Is he fucking crazy? There's no way I'm living under the same roof as Lexi. It's hard enough being best friends with her while living in separate homes. Now he wants me to share a small area with her? My mom might've raised me to be a gentleman, but that still makes me a man, and I'm not sure how the hell I'll be able to hide my feelings for her if I have to share a roof with her. Every day, coming home to her, knowing she's naked in the shower, watching her lounge around in her tiny fucking pajamas...

I glance toward my stepdad, Mason, and he cringes, knowing the feelings I have for Lexi. He also knows I would never go there. Her friendship is too important to me. She's too wild and carefree. She's never been in a relationship that's lasted more than a couple months. She does what she wants, when she wants, and she doesn't like to answer to anyone. She's the most independent woman I've ever known. I love all of that about her, but it also scares the shit out of me, because I'm not sure, if I told her how I feel, I could be the man she needs. I'd like to think I could since I know her better than anyone—aside from her sister. But what if I couldn't be? It would end with us breaking up, and then I would lose her completely—because everyone knows, couples who break up rarely remain friends. And that's just not a chance I'm willing to take. Maybe in the future, when she's older and has calmed down a bit...

"Yes!" Lexi squeals, throwing her arms around me. "That would be so awesome!"

I hug her back, and my eyes meet Georgia's, who's grinning from ear *to ear. When I cringe, she smirks. Georgia might be soft-spoken and shy around people she doesn't know, but that doesn't mean she isn't paying attention. And based on the look she's giving me, it's safe to bet she knows damn well how I feel about Lexi.*

"Georgia, what do you think?" Lexi asks her sister.

Georgia smiles. "I think it's the perfect plan."

"It's settled then. We'll move into Alec's condo!" Lexi jumps up and down, her hands clapping in excitement, which causes my palms to sweat in nervousness. My gaze meets Mason's again, and he's grinning a knowing smile, certain there's no way I'm going to tell Lexi no.

My eyes close, remembering what it was like the first few months of living with Lexi. I took so many cold showers, she thought I had mysophobia—fear of germs—and was trying to get me to see a therapist. When she mentioned it one night while we were all out to dinner, Mason cracked up laughing, and the next day showed up at the station with several pornos and a bottle of lube as a joke.

I WAKE UP TO SOMEONE KNOCKING ON THE DOOR. When I look around, the bed is empty, and the condo is quiet. The girls must've left. I grab my cell phone to check the time and see there's a piece of paper on top of it.

Happy Birthday! See you tonight! Xoxo Lexi and Georgia

I open the door and find Mason standing on the other side

with a coffee in his hand and a smile on his face. "Happy Birthday, Son." He hands me the coffee then pulls me in for a hug.

My mom and Mason married when I was eight years old, and while my biological father is in my life, Mason has become just as much of a father figure over the years as my dad. Mason is now a retired UFC fighter who trains other fighters at Tristan's gym, but when I was younger, Mason was my idol. I worshipped the ground the man walked on, in and out of the ring, and while I might've tamed down my obsession with him the older I got, he's still someone I look up to. And not just because he was a UFC fighter, but because of the way he loves my mom, my sister, and me. I couldn't have asked for a better stepdad than Mason.

"Thanks, man, but you didn't need to come all the way over here to say it. Aren't we meeting up tonight?" We walk back into the condo, and that's when I notice Chase is sleeping on the couch. One of the girls must've let him in.

"We are, but I was thinking we could get a workout in."

"Sounds good." I check my phone and see it's already three in the afternoon. "Let me get dressed and grab a change of clothes. I'll just shower at the gym."

"Is there a reason Chase is sleeping on your couch?" Mason asks when I come back out.

"He's having marital issues. Hasn't really said much."

"Wanna wake him up to go?"

"Nah, let him sleep. I don't know what time he got here."

We get to the gym, and the place is packed. There are fighters practicing in the octagons, several using the weights. Even the treadmills are all taken.

"Alec!" Tristan yells from over near one of the octagons. "Get over here!" He gives me a hug. "Happy Birthday, kid."

"Thanks."

"You here to get a workout in?"

"You know it." The octagon we're standing next to is empty. "Hey, Mason, wanna spar?"

Mason grins like a fucking Cheshire cat. "I'd hate to beat your ass on your birthday."

A bunch of the guys who are standing around laugh.

"Well, I'm okay with beating your ass on my birthday," I volley.

"All right, Bruiser," Mason says, calling me the nickname he dubbed me with years ago, when I knocked him to the ground and busted his lip open. "But when you show up to dinner tonight all bruised up, make sure you let your mom know it was your idea."

"I'm a grown ass man," I scoff. "I don't need to explain shit to my mom."

All the guys crack up.

"Yeah, okay." He laughs. "Keep telling yourself that. Get some damn gear on."

Four

LEXI

"Mom, Dad!" I call out when Georgia and I walk through the door.
"Max!" I yell. "Where is everyone?" I ask Georgia.

"Their cars are in the garage, so they must be here," she says.

We head out back and find our parents in the pool. Mom is wrapped around Dad, and they're making out like a couple of horny teenagers right in the middle of the pool. When I look closer, I notice Mom is topless!

"Oh my God! Please tell me you guys aren't seriously fucking in the pool!" I screech, covering my eyes with my hands.

Georgia lets out a snort-laugh. I can't see her, but I'm sure she's covering her eyes as well.

"Young lady, watch your mouth!" Mom scolds me through her laughter.

"If you don't want to walk in on your parents fornicating,

maybe you should call first," Dad adds.

I hear the pool water shift, and then wet feet padding across the pool deck.

"We're decent." Mom giggles a minute later. I lower my hands from my face and find them both in towels. "And to what do we owe this pleasure?" She gives me a kiss on my forehead, then heads over to Georgia to give her one as well.

"We had to pick up Alec's birthday present before the dinner tonight, so we thought, since we had time, we'd stop by here to see you guys," Georgia says. "Sorry." She smiles apologetically.

"Don't apologize. It's not our fault our parents can't keep their hands off each other." I give my dad a kiss on his cheek.

"Did you hit the waves last night?" Dad asks.

"I did! You should've seen them! Max took some pictures. Wanna see?"

"You know it." He puts his arm around my shoulders, and we all head inside. "Just let us change into dry clothes and then we'll meet you in the living room."

When Georgia and I walk into the living room, Max is now sitting on the couch with his laptop open. "Did you just get home?" I ask.

"Yeah, I was hanging out with Anna, but she needs to get ready for tonight." Anna is Alec's sister and my brother's best friend.

"Can you show Mom and Dad the pictures you took last night?" I plop on the couch next to him. When he clicks on a file, several photos come up, but they aren't of me. They're of Ricco—

my brother's unrequited love interest. Max smiles sheepishly before scrolling down to the ones he took of me surfing. Then he turns the laptop around for everyone to see, as our parents walk in fully clothed—thank God.

"Wow! That sunset is gorgeous!" Mom gushes. "That's a beautiful image, Max."

"Umm... hello, look at me on the surfboard." I point to the perfect image of me barreling deep in the hollow of the wave.

Dad chuckles. "Oh, sorry, we didn't see you there, front and center."

Max and Georgia laugh.

"I signed up for the Vans Surf Classic at Huntington Beach. It's in July this year."

"That's awesome, Lex," Mom says. "Will you have time to practice, though, with school?"

"I was actually thinking I would take the summer off. I was only planning to take a couple classes anyway. I can start back up in the fall. It's not like I have to graduate by a certain date, so I could take a couple extra classes in the fall or spring or finish in the summer..." I hold my breath, waiting for my parents to freak out.

"Have you figured out what you want to do yet?" Dad asks.

"Aside from illegally tagging the walls all over LA," Max adds with a laugh.

Mom and Dad glare at him, and Georgia groans.

"I think it's time to head to the Street's house," I point out.

There's no way I'm touching that subject with a ten-foot pole.

Since Alec's parents only live one street over from my parents, we walk over there. With the storm having passed through earlier this morning, there's a gentle breeze. We get to their house and Anna answers the door with a huge grin.

"Alec totally told you, didn't he?" I huff.

"You burned a cake!" She cracks up laughing, and both my parents' eyes dart over to me.

"You didn't." Mom tries to stifle her laugh, but fails.

"She did, and the chief said they're charging her this time." Alec shakes his head. "Three hundred and fifty-three dollars." He chuckles.

"You would've been better off just buying the cake," Max says.

I shoot daggers his way, but he isn't fazed.

"Hey, leave your sister alone." Alec pulls me into his side. "It's the thought that counts." He gives me one of his panty-dropping winks, and my insides turn to mush. Why couldn't my best friend be ugly? Like seriously? Did I do something in another lifetime where God decided I needed to be punished? Or maybe Alec just did something really good. It had to have been something amazing, though. For him to have been given those gorgeous milk chocolate eyes, that strong nose and chiseled jawline. Not to mention, his perfect, silky smooth hair that has my fingers always twitching to run through the strands. And let's not forget his hard, muscular body that has every woman drooling when they see him. Ugh! And that ass! My God, I hate the gym with a passion, but sometimes I go just to watch the guy run from behind. His tight, muscular ass bouncing as he runs on the treadmill.

Sigh.

In another lifetime, he must've saved tons of kittens who were stuck up in trees, or maybe he cured some crazy disease that, if not for him, we'd all be dead. Something. Because there's no way God just makes someone that damn beautiful for no reason. It just doesn't make sense. And not only is he beautiful, but he's seriously hung. I'm talking about huge! Like when he goes to the store, he's definitely buying king size, and I'm not talking about candy bars. And in case you're wondering, no, I've never gone there—not that I haven't fantasized about it. But you can't live with someone for close to a year without accidently—or on purpose—walking in on them naked at some point.

Oh, and did I mention he has tattoos? Yep! The man's bulging biceps are covered in them! And not shitty ones like most guys get. Nope, all sexy, meaningful ones. His body is literally the equivalent of a perfect canvas that I just want to paint—or lick—my way across.

Unfortunately, there will be no licking—I mean painting—for me. I just get to be the best friend. You know the one I'm talking about. The girl who gets to meet all of the other girls he dates, while cursing each one to hell while smiling way too brightly. Luckily, Alec isn't a manwhore, so it doesn't happen often. Actually, now that I'm thinking about it, it hasn't happened in a long time, but when it does, it takes everything in me not to kick them out and beg him to take me right there on the coffee table, and on the couch, on the kitchen counter, in the shower. Oh hell, if Alec were mine, I would make him take me on every inch of every surface in our condo.

And I know what you're thinking: why not just beg him now? What could you possibly lose? Well, I've obviously thought about that, and the answer to your second question is *everything*. I'm only twenty-one years old. Alec isn't much older. The odds would be stacked against us, and if it didn't work out, I would lose him. I don't care what people say. You can't fuck your best friend then go back to being friends once it doesn't work out. I would rather have Alec as my best friend long-term than as my boyfriend temporarily.

The truth is I kind of suck at relationships. Being Tristan and Charlie's daughter has made it easy for me because in their eyes I can never do any wrong. Their rose-colored glasses probably stem from the fact I was abandoned by my mother at birth—from the little bit my father told me, Gina was a drug addict who felt I was better off with my dad. She walked out the door of her hospital room without looking back, caring more about her drug addiction and drug addict boyfriend than me. Eventually, she overdosed and died.

My parents would never say it, but I'm almost certain I take after Gina in several ways, including my 'free spirit' as my parents like to put it, which is really just a nice way of saying I'm a hot fucking mess. Sure, my parents say they love how carefree I am, but I see the worry in my dad's face every time he asks me what I want to do with my life. Or there was the time when Max let it slip that I occasionally smoked cannabis while hanging out with my friends at the beach. My dad nearly lost it, afraid I would end up just like Gina—which is how I found out the truth about her.

My mom says the way I am is just the artist in me, but if that's the case then why is she so put together? Both my parents went to college, started their own businesses, and years later are still successfully running them. Georgia is a year younger than me, and she's already running a successful web design business. Me? The only reason I'm in college is because it was the only way I could keep slacking off—painting and surfing—and make my dad happy. If it wasn't for Georgia keeping me on track with my classes, I would've failed out my first semester in.

Aside from my parents, I've had three successful friendships in my life: Georgia, my pseudo cousin Micaela, and Alec.

Georgia is my sister and, just like our parents, she wears beautiful rose-colored glasses when it comes to me. She doesn't always agree with my choices, but she never judges me, and she always supports my decisions.

Micaela probably only remains my friend because she's long-distance and doesn't have to deal with me on a daily basis. She grew up in Las Vegas, but now lives in San Diego with her husband, Ryan, and their son, RJ.

And then there's Alec. I've been in love with him for God knows how long, and every relationship I've been in was doomed from the get-go because of it. Not that it took much for them to fail. All I had to do was be myself and they practically ran for the hills. The truth is, Alec deserves more than I could ever give him. A woman who knows what she wants in life. A woman for him to get married to and have tons of babies with. She'll be as put together as Alec is—as put together as my parents are—and they'll live happily ever after. And she won't be able to cut him out of my life because I can honestly say that Alec and I were never anything more than friends.

"Hey, you okay?" Alec asks, his arm still slung over my shoulders, snapping me out of my thoughts.

"Yep, just thinking about what an old man you are now." I stick my tongue out, and Alec laughs.

The doorbell rings, and Alec lifts his arm up, leaving me to go answer the door. I sit next to Georgia on the couch. She's talking to Alec's grandma, Denise, about the program she runs: *Keeping Kids off the Streets*. It's a non-profit organization that helps to keep single moms and their children off the streets and in safe homes. Georgia is in the middle of updating their website for them.

Alec walks back into the living room with his dad, Gavin, and stepmom, Lacie, by his side. Mason and Mila come out of the kitchen and give each of them a hug, then Mila announces that dinner is ready. Everyone finds a seat at the table and starts passing the delicious food around. Alec's favorite is stuffed shells, so that's what Mila's made, along with a huge salad and garlic knots.

"How's work going?" Gavin asks Alec, who smiles wide.

"Good, it's been pretty busy lately, but with the rain finally coming through, it's quieting down. Aside from the occasional oven fire, that is." Alec smirks at me, and I shove his shoulder playfully.

"Leave Lexi alone," Gavin chides playfully.

"Thank you." I smile at him.

"I can't help it." Alec laughs. "It's just too easy to rile her up." Alec's hand comes up to my hair, ruffling it, and I'm sure messing it up.

"Oh my God, you're so annoying!" I duck and swat his hand away.

"It's like he's still ten years old," Gavin says with a wink. "Saying he wants nothing to do with you, yet messing with you to get your attention."

Mason laughs. "Remember when Alec used to tell everyone how much he hated Lexi?"

"I didn't say I hated her," Alec says defensively. "I just said she was annoying." He shoots me a wink that makes him look like his father, only younger and more handsome.

"Whatever." I roll my eyes. "You were just as annoying, and you still are." I take a bite of my garlic knot and swallow. "That's why you're still single." I poke my tongue out, and Alec chuckles.

"You are too," he points out.

"Yeah, but I'm still young. You're practically an old man now." Everyone laughs, and Alec groans.

"He's still young," Gavin says. "He has plenty of time to find the love of his life." His arm goes around his wife. "I didn't find mine until a couple years ago." He presses his lips against Lacie's cheek.

"I was thirty when I met Mila," Mason adds.

"Love knows no age," Mila says. "You don't find love... it finds you."

"I love that," Anna says, raising her glass of water. "To love finding you."

"But not too soon," Mason adds, giving his daughter a pointed look.

She rolls her eyes, and everyone laughs.

"Are you enjoying your summer?" Gavin asks Anna, changing the subject.

"Yes," Anna says with a smile. "I'm catching up on my sleep. It's been fabulous."

"And," Max adds. "When we go back, we won't have to ride the bus anymore since I'll be driving." He looks at my dad, who laughs. Max turned sixteen recently and got his license. He's been begging Dad to get a vehicle. Anna is the same age, but she isn't a fan of driving, so she has no desire to get her license.

"Real subtle, kid. Maybe, if you're lucky, I'll let you borrow one of my vehicles." Dad laughs.

"Yeah right, Tristan." Mom cackles. "We both know you'll be buying him a car simply because you won't want him to touch your precious Ford truck."

When I turned sixteen, Dad reluctantly bought me my jeep.

And I say reluctantly because he wanted me to drive a Ford, but I wanted a jeep. He gave in and bought me my baby. It's the same jeep I drive today. Georgia, on the other hand, let Dad have his way, and she drives a Ford F-250. The thing is huge! Dad had to have a side-step installed, just so she could get into the damn thing, but she loves it, and she loves that it made Dad happy to buy her a Ford.

"FYI," Max says, "I'm totally okay with a Ford." He looks at me and laughs.

"Whatever, I'm okay with being the black sheep of the family. I love my jeep. It holds my surfboard perfectly."

"As long as it holds your books perfectly," Dad volleys.

"You girls only have about a year left, right?" Gavin asks.

"Yep, we both have one more year to go." Even though Georgia is a year younger than me, she's so smart, she took extra classes in high school and graduated early, with me.

"Actually," Georgia says. "I met with my advisor and since I've been taking extra classes every semester, she told me if I go full-time this summer, I can graduate early."

"How early?" I ask.

"At the end of the summer," she admits.

Everyone congratulates her, and she blushes, not keen on all the attention.

"I'm really proud of you, Georgia," I tell her. "It sucks we won't walk together, but at least once you're done, you'll have more time to help me with my classes." I wink playfully, and she rolls her eyes.

"Any plans for after college?" Gavin asks.

"I want to expand my graphic and web design business," Georgia says.

"Great goal," Gavin says before he turns his attention to me. "How about you?"

"I've actually been thinking about doing a little bit of traveling," I blurt out, having no clue where the hell that even came from. I feel everyone's eyes hit me, and I immediately want to take it back, but it's too late now.

"Really?" Lacie asks. "I did quite a bit of traveling in my twenties. Where are you planning to go?"

I think about this for a second. Where would I go if I could go anywhere? My mind goes to what I love most: surfing. "I would like to visit all the best places to surf: Sydney, Ireland, South Africa, Bali... I could check out the different cultures and art..."

"I heard Tahiti and Fiji are known for their surfing waters," Lacie says.

"Yeah," I agree. "The only places I've surfed are here and Mexico."

It doesn't get past me that my family and Alec haven't said a word. They're all just staring at me, most likely in shock since I've never once mentioned wanting to travel after I graduate. Well, that's because I never thought about it. But now that I'm thinking about it, it actually sounds like a really great idea.

"Traveling can be expensive," Lacie points out. "If you need any tips, let me know."

"Thank you," I say, not bothering to tell her that when I graduate my grandparents on my dad's side will be giving me my trust fund. They've set one up for each of their grandchildren to receive once they graduate from college or turn twenty-five. It's not enough to live off of, but it's enough to buy a house, or in my case, go traveling. They set it up to help us start our lives. My dad used his to open his own gym.

Nobody else says anything, but I can feel Alec's searing glare on me, as well as Georgia's hurtful stare.

Finally Mason, who must sense the tension, speaks up. "We've decided to finally purchase a cabin in Breckenridge," he says. "Mila and I are going to be heading up there for winter break with Anna."

"Sounds good," Alec says. "I'll put in for it. It's been a couple years since we've been."

After dinner, Alec's birthday cake is brought out and we all sing Happy Birthday. Then everyone gives him his gifts, while he whines that he's too old, but thanks everyone. I save mine and Georgia's for last.

"Here you go." I hand him the small box. "It's from Georgia and me."

He opens the box and inside is a Casio Men's G-Shock Solar Atomic watch. Georgia and I searched online for the perfect watch for a firefighter after Alec's got messed up while on a call a while back.

"The guy at the store says it's the perfect watch for a firefighter.

It has a digital compass, a barometer, a thermometer, an altimeter, five different alarms, and is solar powered."

"Thank you." He leans over and kisses my cheek, then gets up and hugs Georgia.

Everyone stays for a while afterward, talking and hanging out, until it gets late and we all say good night. Georgia rode with me in my jeep, so we head back home together, Alec following.

"I'm going to head to the beach," I tell her once I pull up into my parking spot.

"It's late," she points out.

"I know. I'm just going to go paint."

"You're just trying to leave so you don't have to explain yourself... It's okay if you want to travel, Lex." She looks over at me, a sad smile splayed across her lips. "I just wish you had said something."

"Honestly, I wasn't sure until Alec's dad asked me about my plans."

"So, when are you planning to leave?"

"I don't know. I still have a year of school left. I was thinking next summer, if I graduate on time."

We're both quiet for a couple minutes, and I know I need to make this right between Georgia and me. Explain to her where I'm coming from, so she'll understand.

"Hey, sis," I start. "Sometimes I feel a little lost." My words come out as a whisper. I'm not good with being vulnerable, and Georgia is great about accepting me the way I am, which is why we're not only sisters but best friends.

"I do too," she agrees, her green eyes meeting my blue ones.

"It's like we have this amazing life. The perfect parents. The sweetest brother." Hot tears burn behind my lids. "We're so blessed."

"We are."

"But sometimes I feel like I don't fit in."

"And I do?" She laughs softly.

"At least you know what you want to do in your life. I have no clue what I want to spend my life doing after graduation."

"Oh yeah, my life is looking so glamorous. My goal in life has been to make sure I have a job where I can hide behind a computer screen," she says, her words throwing me for a loop. I always assumed Georgia just preferred to stay behind the scenes. But now she's making it sound like she's unhappy *not* putting herself out there.

"I'm afraid," I admit.

"Of what?"

"Of ending up a loser like my real mom."

"That's not possible. You're like the most beautiful, coolest person I know." She grins, trying to lighten the mood. "I don't think it's possible for you to be a loser."

"My mom was pretty too. She was actually pretty freaking gorgeous. And she was the life of the party." One day, without my dad knowing, I found her on social media and stalked her pictures. Even though she's not alive, pictures never go away. Her pages are still up, but nothing has been added to them in years.

"That doesn't mean anything."

"I think I would feel better if I knew what I wanted to do with my life."

"I think it's okay to not know," Georgia says. "After listening to you, I'm definitely questioning everything."

"What do you mean?" I bring my hand down on top of hers.

"When you said you wanted to leave, it hit me that all these years I've been hiding from life, using you as a crutch."

"Why have you been hiding?" I feel bad that I've never asked that before. Georgia's always been the way she is, and the same way she accepts me without question, I accept her. But maybe I should've asked...

She quickly averts her gaze, something I've only seen her do when she would lie to Mom and Dad to cover for me. They eventually caught on and it became a joke in our family. "When I was younger and we would go places, I would get nervous. I would feel like I was going to have a panic attack."

"I remember." She would go quiet and hide behind our parents or me. Mom would tell people she was just shy.

"When I'd be at home, or it would be just us, it wouldn't happen. So, eventually I made it a point to not leave." Something in her voice, in the way she's refusing to look at me, tells me there's more to this than she's admitting. But I don't call her out on it. When she's ready, she'll tell me.

"Maybe if you put yourself out there, you can overcome it. I mean, I'm not a doctor or anything, but I can be with you. If you don't want to be stuck behind a screen, then you shouldn't be."

"You're right. I think it's time I get out of the house."

"Really?" I grin, so proud of her for wanting to take this step.

She nods. "If you can be brave enough to travel the world on your own, I can be brave enough to put myself out there. Instead of saying we're lost, how about we just say we're looking down each road for the perfect path to take?"

"Finding our perfect path... I love that."

"Me too. And I was thinking I could borrow something a little sexier for Alec's birthday..."

"Really?"

"Yeah... Maybe I'll... I don't know. Dance with someone besides you." She smiles shyly. Georgia has been to the club with me on quite a few occasions. She's never missed anyone's birthday celebrations, but she tends to dress more formal, so as not to get noticed. Even though she's so gorgeous she could probably wear a garbage bag and get noticed.

"I bet we can find you the perfect dress in my closet." I lean across the middle of my jeep and give my sister a hug. "I love you, Georgia, and I'm so proud of you."

"I love you, too."

Five

ALEC

I'm sitting in a booth in Club Hectic, surrounded by several of my friends, as well as some of the guys I work with who have tonight off. I'm pretty sure between Lexi and Chase, everyone I know has been invited to celebrate my birthday. I'm watching Lexi and Georgia shake their asses on the dance floor to an old-school remix. Right now "Hypnotized" by Plies is pumping through the speakers, and my eyes are stuck on Lexi's sexy-as-fuck body. When she and Georgia came out of their rooms dressed in tiny—way too fucking tiny—black dresses and fuck-me heels, I about lost my shit. For one, Georgia doesn't dress like that. In all the years I've known her, I've never seen her in anything that shows off every damn curve she has.

When I asked what the hell was going on, Georgia smiled and said, "We're finding our perfect path." I have no clue what she meant by that, and I didn't ask because I was too focused on Lexi, and how gorgeous she looked. She tends to be a ripped jean shorts and tank kind of girl, so when she dresses up, it makes it all the more special.

"Holy fuck, man." Chase comes over and sits next to me. He grabs a shot off the tray and downs it. "When the hell did she get so hot?" He nods toward Lexi and Georgia, who are now grinding up against each other to "Me & U" by Cassie, completely oblivious to the fact every fucking perv is staring at them. If this is how they plan to find their perfect path, I'm about to be getting into a lot of fights.

"Who's *she*?"

"Obviously Georgia. I wouldn't dare talk about your precious non-girlfriend. But she's definitely looking good as well."

"Aren't you a married man?" I might not have the same type of feelings for Georgia as I have for Lexi, but I'm just as close to her as I am with her sister. I've known her almost as long as I've known Lexi, and she's just as much of a sister to me as my own is. I'll be damned if any guy is going to fuck with her—friend or not.

"Not for long." Chase downs another shot and slams it down.

"Damn, man, I'm sorry."

"It's all good." He shrugs. "I found out she's been fucking around with another guy. I think it's time I do a little fucking myself."

"That's rough, bro." I take a shot then look Chase dead in the eyes, so he knows what I'm about to say is serious. "I don't blame you for wanting to get laid, but it won't be with Georgia."

"Are you seriously cockblocking me?" Chase asks incredulously.

"Call it whatever you want. There are hundreds of women in this club. Go fuck 'em all if you want, but Georgia is off-limits, *especially* since you're still married."

Chase opens his mouth to argue, but whatever he sees in my face must tell him I'm not playing, because he just nods. "All right, but can I at least dance with her?" He points to the women who are now surrounded by a bunch of men.

"Yeah, let's go." We take one more shot before we head over to Georgia and Lexi, not so subtly pushing through the guys. Chase makes eye contact with Georgia, his hands going to her hips. At first, she looks like she's about to hyperventilate just from his simple touch alone, but when he leans down and whispers something to her, she smiles and nods, then wraps her hands around his neck.

When I know Georgia is okay, I pull Lexi's back into my front. She spins around, her hand coming up about to slap me, but when she sees it's me, her hand lowers and a beautiful smile appears.

"I thought you were one of those guys." She nods toward the guys who're moving on to other women now that they see Georgia and Lexi aren't available.

"Good to know you would've handled yourself." I take her hand in mine and bring it up to my lips. Lexi's eyes go wide. I should really stop the flirting. I know my boldness is thanks to the tequila, and tomorrow morning when I'm no longer buzzed, I'll regret what I've done. Not because I don't want Lexi, but because I've worked hard to keep that thin line neatly drawn and in place.

"Damn right, I would've." Her arms snake around my neck, and she continues to dance seductively, using me as her own personal dance pole.

I'm not sure how long we dance, but when the club lights and music lower, I realize I've spent my entire night with Lexi in my arms, and it feels so damn good that, when she removes her hands from my body, I almost pull her closer, not wanting her to let go. And that thought has me sobering because Lexi isn't mine to hold on to. No matter how much I wish she were.

"I'm meeting my dad and Lacie for brunch later. Want to join me?" I ask Lexi when we're back home and heading to bed.

"Sure, just wake me up," she says before heading into her room. "Good night, Birthday Boy."

MY ALARM GOES OFF ALL TOO SOON, AND AFTER hitting snooze several times, I finally drag myself out of bed. *What the hell was I thinking agreeing to go to brunch the morning after going clubbing?* Knowing Lexi will need some time to get ready, I make my way to her room. Her door is partly open, so I don't bother to knock, instead quietly entering. She's sleeping on the left side of her bed like always. I constantly joke with her that she has a king-sized bed for no reason since she never sleeps on the entire thing.

Georgia says she's waiting to share a bed with someone.

With her eyes closed and her face free of her makeup, she looks all natural and even more beautiful. Her body is snuggled into her blanket, and she's snoring lightly. I look at the time on my cell phone. Maybe I have enough time to lie with her for a little while...

Setting my alarm for a little later, I drop it onto the nightstand and climb onto the right side of the bed. Lexi startles slightly when she feels the bed dip, but when her eyes open and she sees it's me, a small smile makes its way upon her lips. She groans softly and edges closer so that her neck is snuggled in the area where my shoulder meets my chest. She throws her arm over my stomach and immediately falls back asleep. I should close my eyes and get another hour of sleep, but all I can think about is how perfectly her body fits with mine.

"ALEC, IT'S TIME TO WAKE UP." I OPEN MY EYES AND LOOK around. I must've fallen back asleep after all. "Your alarm was going off, but I hit stop." Lexi's chin rests on my arm as she smiles up at me. "Did you have trouble sleeping?"

"No, I came in here to wake you up, but you looked so adorable sleeping and snoring, I decided to join you." My comment earns me a swat to my arm.

"You don't tell a woman she snores." Lexi sits up and pouts.

"Now get out, so I can get ready. What time do we need to leave by?"

"Ten thirty."

After I get ready, I head out to the living room to wait for Lexi. Chase is lying on my couch, scrolling through his phone.

"Have a good night?" he asks.

"Yeah, it was a good birthday. You?"

"Yeah, until Georgia—"

"Until Georgia what?" Lexi asks, stepping into the living room.

"Left me hanging for another guy," Chase finishes, shocking the hell out of not only me but Lexi.

"What?" Lexi gasps. "What are you talking about?"

"Last night... You two were too into each other to notice, but while I was dancing with Georgia, some asshole asked to cut in, and she let him."

"Well, you *are* married," Lexi points out.

"And he's not an asshole," Georgia says, joining the conversation. "His name is Robert and he's very sweet."

Lexi's mouth falls open. "You got his name?"

"And his number." Georgia smiles. "I figured it was a good first step to find my perfect path."

"What the hell is up with you and these paths?" I ask.

Georgia blushes and Lexi actually looks at me shyly.

"It's none of your business," Lexi says. "It's a sister thing." She walks over to Georgia and envelops her in a hug. "I'm so proud of you. I think that's a great first step."

I'm not sure what they mean by a path, but so far, it's involved Georgia dressing sexy and getting a guy's number. I have a feeling this path bullshit isn't something I'm going to like. Especially if it involves Lexi getting a guy's number.

Lexi and I arrive at the restaurant at eleven on the dot, and I spot my dad and Lacie already seated. I texted him before we left to let him know that Lexi would be joining us, so he could get us a table for four.

"Good morning, you two." Dad stands and gives me and Lexi a hug. Lacie does the same. The waiter comes over and we order our drinks.

"How was your night out?" Lacie asks after the waiter walks away.

"Good, but I don't think my body is able to handle those long nights out like it used to," I groan.

Lexi laughs. "You're twenty-five, not sixty, and we were home by three."

"You'll understand when you're my age," I joke.

We spend the next hour or so enjoying our meal. My dad talks about a new client he and Lacie have picked up at their real estate firm. He's one of the majority stakeholders in a large investment firm, so it's a huge deal for their firm. Lexi gushes about a storm she heard is coming in soon and can't wait to get out on the water. My dad, of course, warns her to be careful.

"You sound just like your son," she says, right before she shoots a playful glare my way.

"That's only because I love you and can't imagine what my life would be like if something happened to you," I tell her truthfully.

Her glare softens. "I know. That's why you're my best friend."

My dad gives me a knowing look, but I just laugh it off. My family will forever be rooting for Lexi and me, but like I've said a million times, I'm not about to risk losing our friendship just to have a chance at something more with her. Lexi is wild and untamed. She isn't meant to be tied down. She's meant to soar and be free.

While we're finishing our meal, Lexi's phone dings with a text. When she checks it, she frowns.

"Everything okay?"

"Yeah, that guy Georgia met at the club last night..."

"Robert?"

"Yeah, he asked her to meet him for lunch."

"What's wrong with that?" I ask.

"Nothing, I guess. It's just that Georgia has never dated before, and now she's going from zero to sixty. She should take her time and get to know him first, before meeting with him."

"You've hooked up with guys with less conversation," I point out. I'm not trying to judge, but I'm surprised she's being so judgmental toward her sister.

Lexi's eyes meet mine. "Exactly, and I know how empty it feels. I don't want that for my sister."

It takes everything in me not to pull her into my arms and beg her to let me show her how meaningful it can be. I haven't personally experienced meaningful sex, but I know without a doubt if Lexi and I were to get together it wouldn't be without emotions.

Instead, I nod. "You're a good sister."

When the bill is paid, my dad and Lacie walk out with us to my truck.

"Thank you for brunch," I tell my dad, giving him a hug.

"Anytime. You know this new client I have? He's offered me tickets to some country music festival next weekend. Apparently, the company he owns has ties to the Empire Polo Club." The Empire Polo Club is a large concert venue in Indio. "Lacie and I thought about going, but to be honest we couldn't even tell you who half the bands are that are playing at the festival. I'm starting to realize I'm no longer the cool guy I used to be."

"It's okay, Dad, you're still cool in my book." We both laugh. "I'll see if Lexi wants to go. She loves country music, so I'm sure she'll be down." I glance over at her chatting with Lacie, giving my dad and me a minute to talk alone.

"He said he'll have four tickets for me at will-call. I'll let him know you'll be the one picking them up."

"Sounds good." I give my dad another hug. "Thanks."

Six

LEXI

"This feels soooo good," Georgia groans, dropping her head against the back of the salon chair. "Aren't you glad you drove up for a girls' day?" She glances over at Micaela, who has her eyes closed, also thoroughly enjoying her pedicure.

Even though my toes end up getting ruined from the sand and saltwater, every two weeks, Georgia and I go to get pedicures. She loves them, and I love spending time with my sister, so it's a win-win. This morning, Micaela drove up to join us. After going to breakfast, we came to our favorite salon to get pampered.

"I am," Micaela gushes. "Summer classes start Monday, so it's nice to relax for a little while."

"How are Ryan and RJ doing?" I ask. Ryan is staying home with RJ while Micaela goes to school full time. He posts the most adorable pictures on social media, but I really should make my way down to visit soon. RJ is so cute and growing up too fast.

"They're good." Micaela smiles. "I can't wait to be done with school so things will slow down a little. Between school and interning at Scripps... and being a wife and a mother..."

"You're like superwoman," Georgia tells her.

"Hardly. I couldn't do it without Ryan, that's for sure."

"You're both amazing parents," Georgia says.

"I can't even imagine having a baby," I admit. But then I picture a brown-haired, brown-eyed little boy who looks like Alec, and my belly flip-flops. I bet he would make a wonderful dad, what with his big heart and all his patience. He would teach him how to fight and I would teach him how to surf...

"What are you thinking about?" Micaela asks.

"What? Nothing." I shake myself from my ridiculous thoughts.

"Bullshit. You got this goofy look on your face," Micaela accuses.

"I was just thinking about my adorable godson and how glad I am you're the one with the baby, so I can spoil him rotten and then hand him back when it's time for him to be fed and changed." I poke my tongue out and Georgia and Micaela both laugh.

"This color?" the nail tech asks me, holding up a bottle of blue nail polish.

"Yes, please."

After we finish getting our toes done, and Georgia gets a manicure, we get our eyebrows threaded and then each get a facial. Once we're completely pampered, we head over to the Santa

Monica Pier to have lunch. I stop at the taco stand and order some tacos, then tell Georgia and Micaela I'll be right back.

"Hey, Aiden," I say when I approach. He's sitting in the sand and drawing in his sketchpad, something he does often.

"Hi, Lexi," he says back, his brown eyes meeting my blue ones. "Did you bring me tacos?"

"I did." I hand him the bag.

"Thank you. I'm drawing a picture. You want to see?"

"Of course, but then I have to go. My sister and cousin are waiting for me."

"Okay." He turns his sketchpad toward me.

The drawing is of the ocean with several dolphins swimming around. It's in pencil and the details are flawless. Every line, every shadow done with perfection. "Did you see these?" I ask, pointing to the dolphins.

"Yes, they were swimming right there." He points out toward the water.

"It's a beautiful picture," I tell him, hating that nobody but me ever sees his art. He deserves to have his art hung up where everyone can see it.

"Thank you, Lexi," he says, opening the bag so he can eat his food.

"You're welcome. I'll see you soon."

I head back up to the pier and find Georgia and Micaela sitting at a table with our food and drinks.

"How's Aiden?" Georgia asks when I sit down. She's only met

him once, when she came with me to the beach, but she knows I feed and visit him on the regular.

"Good... drawing."

"Who's Aiden?" Micaela asks.

"A friend of mine who's homeless and has lived in a tent under the pier for the last several months. I brought him something to eat." I met Aiden one day when walking by him. I offered him some food I had packed and, even though at first he was reluctant, he accepted my offering. Now, every day I'm here I either buy him tacos, which is his favorite meal, or bring him food from my house.

"That's so sweet of you," Micaela says.

I shrug. "I wish there was something more I could do."

We eat our lunch and then Micaela takes off back home. Georgia and I spend the rest of our afternoon getting ready for tonight's music festival.

"THIS LINEUP IS AMAZING!" I YELL AS LUKE BRYAN thanks everyone for coming out tonight, and the crowd screams and shouts their love for the man.

"It is!" Georgia sports a wide grin that tells me she's enjoying herself. I was shocked when she agreed to come to the music festival with Alec, Chase, and me. I know she's already made steps toward finding her perfect path, like going to the club and dancing with Chase and Robert, and then meeting Robert for lunch the next day—which she told me went really well and they're planning to go out again soon. But I kind of expected her to say the music festival was too much too soon. However, when I told her about it, she squealed in excitement, shocking the hell out of me and making me proud at the same time. It probably helps that she's a huge country music fan and it's just the four of us in the owner's box, so while it's loud all around us, we're not actually in the middle of the craziness.

I can't deny that her willingness to find her perfect path has me thinking about mine. Since we made that pact in my jeep, she's made a pointed effort to get out of her comfort zone, while I haven't done anything. I think my issue is that I don't even know what path I'm looking for, what getting out of my comfort zone entails. Georgia's issue has always been that she's shy and isn't comfortable around a lot of people, so finding her path seems so cut and dry: put herself out there in crowds. I'm not saying it's easy for her, but at least she knows what path she's looking for.

Me? Not so much... I know I'm lost, unsure of what I want for my future. I've thought a lot about how I said I want to travel, and I have to wonder if maybe it's my way of trying to escape. But at the same time, maybe traveling will mean finding my path. I guess, for right now, I'll just keep moving forward and hope to eventually see that perfect path.

Rodney Atkins makes his way out onto the stage, and a couple minutes later, we're singing our hearts out to "These are My People" while we wait for the guys to return with our drinks.

"You better drink every damn bit of this," Alec says when he hands me the most adorable drink I've ever seen. I don't even know what's inside of it, but the cup is shaped like a fish bowl and it lights up. I saw someone else walking with it and begged Alec to find it for me.

"Twenty-five dollars," he adds with a groan.

"Thank you!" I grab the drink from him and take a sip. It tastes like lemonade with a bit of a kick to it.

Chase hands Georgia the bottle of water she asked for, and then both guys have a seat, with their beers in their hands, in the chairs behind us. Georgia and I sing and dance to several songs, but when Kane Brown hits the stage with "What Ifs", a song that always makes me think of Alec, I set my drink down and pull Alec out of his chair to dance with me.

Turning around so that his front is flush against my back, I start shaking my ass. I sneak a glance back and see he's shaking his head, but his eyes are silently laughing. His hands grip my sides, and his face dips down. He's so close, I can feel his cool breath hit my overheated skin. I assume he's leaning in to tell me something, so I'm shocked when his lips brush up against the curve of neck, sending shivers straight down my spine. He places several kisses along my sensitive flesh, and I find myself tilting my head slightly to give him better access as I get lost in Kane Brown's words about being made for each other and Alec's touch.

Needing to see his face, I twirl around in my spot. His dark brown eyes, filled with lust and want, lock with mine. I recognize the look because it's exactly what I'm feeling. The sexual tension in the air is so thick it's almost suffocating. My heart picks up speed and my brain screams *abort!*

Afraid the moment is getting too deep, I take his hat off his head and place it on my own with a playful smirk. In return, his hands glide down my sides and land on my ass, and then he shocks the hell out of me when he lifts me up. My legs wrap around his waist and my arms snake around his neck. We sway to the music, our eyes never leaving one another. No words are spoken, and I haven't the slightest clue what any of this means. This is Alec. The guy I've had a crush on since I was old enough to understand boys don't really have cooties, and it's just something dads tell their daughters to keep them from chasing the boys. I've seen him date various women. I was there the day he decided to join the fire academy. I can remember the moment I realized my crush wasn't just a crush, but actual love. He's my roommate, my best friend. And as good as it feels to be in his arms, I can't let myself get lost in him. Whatever is happening between us will end in destruction, heartbreak. I'll lose him. And I *can't* lose him.

Needing to put some distance between us, I open my mouth to ask him to set me down, when he leans in and softly brushes his lips against mine. It's barely even a kiss, more like a sensual whisper that leaves me wanting more. His tongue darts out and slowly licks across the flesh of my lips before it finds its way into my mouth. My lips curve around his and our tongues swirl around each other. My arms tighten around his neck and his fingers massage circles into my ass cheeks. Everything and everyone around us fades away as we get lost in our kiss, in each other.

The kiss ends, and I faintly hear the current song fade out and a new one begin. It's slower, more sensual, and I can't handle being in Alec's arms like this, without knowing what that kiss means to him. I was just thinking we can't be together, I can't risk losing him, but with that one kiss, all I can think is how much I want him and need him. Fuck the risks. Fuck the consequences. What if *he's* my perfect path?

I stare into his smoldering gaze, as both of our chests heave like we've just run a marathon. I silently beg him to say something, anything, but he remains quiet, the look on his face a mixture of lust and confusion. Reluctantly, I release my legs from around him. Understanding what I'm silently asking, he gently sets me onto my feet. I turn back around to face the concert, but Alec doesn't sit back down. Instead, he wraps his arms around my waist from behind and nuzzles his face into my hair, his scruff tickling my neck. My body sways to Kane Brown as he sings about lying next to the woman he loves, comparing it to what heaven must be like.

I don't realize my butt is rubbing against Alec's crotch, until he pushes my hair to the side and whispers into my ear, "That's not wise, Lex." His fingers dig into my hips, stopping my body from moving, and that's when I feel it—his hard erection pressed up against my ass. Before I can react to it, he snatches his hat off my head and sits back down. I glance back at him and see the hat is covering his crotch. I throw my head back in a loud belly laugh, and he rolls his eyes.

When I look over at Georgia, I see her and Chase standing next to each other, laughing and swaying to the music. Her eyes meet mine and she shoots me a knowing wink, telling me she didn't miss what happened between Alec and me.

The rest of the concert goes by way too quickly. The four of us dance and sing and Georgia even drinks some of my drink. Before we know it, everyone is making their way back onto the stage to say good night, and then we're piling into my jeep. Alec only had one beer, so he drives us home.

We all go our separate ways once we're inside. Georgia says she's exhausted and is going straight to bed. Alec says he's jumping in the shower, and I do the same. When I get out, I throw on a pair of boxers I stole from Alec years ago and a comfortable tank top and pad into the kitchen to grab a bottle of water. I'm on my way back to my room when Alec steps into the hallway in nothing but a pair of loose sweats hanging low on his hips. His hair is still wet and beads of water are dripping down his taut muscles. His tattoos are shining bright from being wet. I watch, mesmerized, as the tiny droplets of water glide down his torso. *Damn, I'm thirsty. I wonder if he'd let me lick him...*

If Alec notices me staring like a damn perv, he doesn't point it out. Instead he says, "I had a good time tonight."

I give him a small smile. "Me too."

There's so much going through my head, but I'm afraid to

voice my thoughts. If I say the wrong thing... if I'm overthinking what happened tonight, it could potentially ruin our friendship. Everyone witnessed what happened between Joey and Dawson on *Dawson's Creek*. You don't date your best friend unless you're okay with ruining your friendship. Their experience should be a warning for everyone.

"Listen," Alec says, stepping toward me. The way his brows are furrowed has my stomach twisting into a knot. This can't be good. Nothing that begins with *Listen* is ever good. "Tonight, what happened between us..."

"Yeah?" I hold my breath, waiting for the blow to come, but praying it doesn't.

"It shouldn't have happened," he says, knocking me right onto my ass.

"Okay." I nod robotically. There's more I want to say, but I don't. The moment is already awkward, which is exactly why he's right... Tonight shouldn't have happened. All we did was kiss and everything's changed. What would happen to us if we hooked up, or if we decided to give a relationship a chance?

"It's just that—" he starts to explain, even though he doesn't need to, because I get it. I do. No matter which way we go, we'll end up at a dead end, and then nothing would ever be the same again. I would lose my best friend. Georgia would have to pick sides. Family get-togethers would be weird.

Alec isn't my perfect path. And I need to accept that and stop trying to make this into something it's not. Something it can never be.

"Sorry," Chase mutters, cutting off Alec. "I'm just going to take a quick shower." He slips by us and into the bathroom, shutting the door behind him.

Alec's eyes never leave mine. His lips part, about to continue, but I can't deal with whatever he has to say, so like the coward I've apparently become, I speak first. "I'm going to head to bed. Good night." And without waiting for him to respond, I slip into my room, closing the door behind me.

Seven

ALEC

I wake up to my phone ringing, and when I look at the time, I see it's already ten in the morning. I rarely sleep in this late, but between the late night at the club and then last night at the music festival, I was exhausted. The phone stops ringing then starts again. When I look at my caller ID, I see it's Lacie. She's probably calling to see how the concert was.

"Hey, Lacie."

"Alec." When she doesn't say anything else, I'm immediately on alert.

"Lacie, is everything okay?"

"Oh God, Alec," she cries out. "No, everything is *not* okay. Your father has been in an accident."

I sit up, trying to focus on what she's saying, but my entire world feels like it's being shaken.

"He didn't make it," she adds, and I was wrong, my world hasn't been shaken—it's been blown to pieces.

"What happened?" I whisper, the lump in my throat too big to allow me to speak properly.

"It's all my fault. I told him I was hungry." She sobs through the phone. "We hadn't been by the store, so we didn't have anything to make for breakfast." She cries harder. "He offered to go pick us up breakfast at the diner. The paramedics believe he had a heart attack while he was driving, and by the time the ambulance got there it was too late."

"Fuck!" I feel the burning behind my lids and know I'm crying. "Where are you?"

"I'm at the hospital. I-I don't know what to do," she admits softly.

"I'll be right there." I jump out of bed and quickly throw some clothes on. I step out of my room and the house is quiet. My hand presses to Lexi's door to tell her what happened, but I quickly back away, instead heading down the hall to the living room. Chase is passed out on the couch, and I consider waking him up but don't. If I have to say the words out loud then they'll be true. My dad will really be dead. And right now, I'm still in denial.

The entire drive to the hospital, I come up with a million different scenarios where my father is still alive—from Lacie being misinformed, to my dad playing a sick joke on me. But deep down I know none of the scenarios are going to pan out. I can feel the heaviness in my chest. My dad is gone.

I arrive at the hospital and find Lacie sitting in a waiting room chair by herself. Her head is resting in her hands, her quiet sobs racking her body. Sitting next to her, I slide my arm around the top of her shoulders. She looks up, her eyes swollen and her cheeks blotchy.

"Oh, Alec," she cries. "I'm so sorry. I didn't know. If I had known that—"

I shake my head and pull her into my embrace. "Don't do that. It's not your fault. People leave the house every day. Don't blame yourself." I see this happen all the time. A husband leaves the coffee pot on by mistake, or a wife forgets to turn a burner off. The house burns down, and they blame themselves, blame each other. It doesn't matter, though, who did what. It happened, and no matter who you point your fingers at, it's not going to change the outcome.

"They said they're doing an autopsy to confirm how he died, and once they're done..." She can't finish her sentence, her cries now coming too hard for words to form. She holds me tighter, and I rub her arm in a soothing gesture in an attempt to comfort her.

When she finally stops crying, I notice her breathing has evened out. I dip my head slightly and see she's cried herself to sleep. The nurse sitting at the desk across from me gives me a sad smile.

"Sometimes our bodies and minds just need a small break," she says. I nod in understanding. I haven't shed a single tear since I arrived, and I'm almost positive I'm still in denial. My mind and body are numb, refusing to acknowledge my dad is gone.

Instead of calling anyone, I drop my head back against the wall and just sit here while Lacie sleeps. When she wakes up, we're going to have to deal with this. We'll have to speak to the medical examiner, have my dad's body moved to a funeral home, then, we'll have to plan a fucking funeral. We'll have to tell each and every one of our family members, friends, and his employees that he's dead. But for right now, while Lacie is asleep, I can pretend for a little longer that my dad isn't gone.

Lacie eventually wakes up, and when she does, for a brief moment, I can see it in her eyes that she's confused. She's wondering if this was all a horrible nightmare. She's looking around and wondering why she's in my arms and not my dad's. She's disoriented, curious as to why we're sitting in a hospital waiting room. I can see the moment when she remembers. Her throat bobs as she swallows thickly, her top teeth biting down on her bottom lip. Her eyes widen and fill with devastation, and her head tilts slightly to the left in a silent attempt of asking me if what she's remembering is indeed real.

"It really happened," I confirm, saying the words out loud for the first time. "He's gone."

She shakes her head back and forth and closes her eyes. The tears race down her cheeks, and she drops her head into her hands. "No, no, no, no..." She continues to repeat the same word over and over again, not wanting it to be true, and I know exactly how she feels.

Eight

LEXI

"Oh, man, those waves!" I yell over the music blaring from someone's speakers as I jab my board into the sand. I drop onto the blanket, grabbing a cold bottle of water from my cooler, and down the entire thing. It must be ninety-five degrees outside right now, and the saltwater may cool my body down, but it does nothing for my thirst. "Adulting seriously gets in the way of my surfing time."

"Hell yeah, it does," Jason agrees with a laugh, grabbing a water as well. He flops onto my blanket, soaking the entire thing. I've known Jason for about a year or so now, but I don't know a lot about him. From the little he's mentioned, he's a trust fund kid who spends the majority of his time fucking off and surfing. According to him, when he's not at the beach, it's because his dad is making him learn the company he owns, so he can one day take over. He doesn't seem too thrilled about the idea.

"I told my parents I'm taking the summer off to train for the Vans Surf Classic."

"The winners get a sponsorship for next year's world tour," Jason says. "If you win, you would have to quit school. You prepared to do that?"

Before last night, I would've said no. Surfing has always just been for fun. I wouldn't give up school, something that's important to my parents, to leave here—*leave Georgia and Alec*—and travel the world surfing. When I had mentioned traveling at dinner the other night, I wasn't really one hundred percent sure. I was just lost and wanting to escape. And then Alec kissed me, and if he had told me right then and there he wants to be with me, I would've given up anything in the world to be with him. But he didn't. Instead, he told me it shouldn't have happened. Which means if I stay around here, one day I'm going to have to watch Alec fall in love with another woman. Get married, have kids, create a life together. And I can't be around for that.

Alec was right. That kiss shouldn't have happened, because it changed everything for me. It was one thing to love him from afar, but to actually feel his body against mine, to know how his mouth tastes when entwined with mine, changes everything. Because now I've had a glimpse of how good it could be with Alec, and it hurts to know I can never have that—to know he doesn't want that.

He once told me he wants what his mom and Mason have, what my parents have. Maybe the reason why he doesn't want me is because I'm nothing like them. I'm too wild, too carefree—too unpredictable. I don't know what I want for my future. I live in the moment. I've always been the black sheep of my family—even if my parents swear they love me the way I am. I've always worried I'm too much like my biological mom, that my dad wants me to go to college so I don't end up like her. But what if finding our own perfect paths isn't possible? What if my path has already been decided, and I'm just fighting the inevitable?

"I saw your recent tag," Jason says, snapping me from my thoughts. "On the abandoned building near Luciano's." Luciano's is an authentic Italian bakery in the rougher part of LA. It's the only business in its neighborhood that hasn't been shut down yet. The city has been shutting down or buying out each business, so they can tear the buildings down to create condo developments.

"I've never admitted to anything." I give Jason a side-eye, and he rolls his eyes. Everybody who knows me knows I've been graffitiing all over the abandoned buildings in LA for years. Everywhere I graffiti, I leave my tag: a silhouette of a surfer chick holding a surfboard. In a city that's filled with so much darkness and chaos, I've always been drawn to adding my own color and brightness. People think LA is so glamorous, so beautiful, but those people have never lived here. It's not like what you see in the movies or on TV. There's a small percentage of wealth and the rest is poor. The beach is beautiful but filled with homeless people. The businesses are thriving but too expensive for the common folk to shop at. For every fancy restaurant, there's fifty people who can't afford to even eat. They fill the alleyways, the beaches, the sidewalks, and I fill the walls with hope and beauty.

"You don't have to admit to it." Jason laughs. "I would know your work anywhere. It's beautiful... just like you."

"Thanks," I say, my cheeks heating up from his compliment. Jason is a good-looking guy. He can be a huge flirt, and I know he sleeps around. I also know he's interested in me. He's made it known on several occasions without actually saying it. And if I weren't completely in love with my best friend, I would probably give in to his advances, but I am, and no matter how many times I've tried over the years to get under someone else to get over Alec, it never works. Eventually I stopped trying. Too many meaningless one-night stands led to me giving up. Now, it's been so long, my vagina would probably go into shock if it was touched by anything other than my fingers or vibrator.

"So, I was thinking..." he begins.

I bite down on my bottom lip, praying he doesn't ask me out. Things are already awkward with Alec. The last thing I want is for things to be awkward with another one of my friends.

Then I remember why things are awkward with Alec. *It shouldn't have happened.*

"...maybe we could go out sometime," he finishes.

I expected him to say something sexual, like he wants to hook up. I wasn't expecting him to actually ask me out. Maybe this is my path: moving forward, finding a nice, good-looking guy who wants to go out with me.

I'm about to tell him okay, when my phone rings.

Alec's name appears on the caller ID, and I take a deep breath, worried as to why he's calling. Maybe he feels the need to finish telling me why our kiss shouldn't have happened... *Or maybe he's changed his mind...* I tamper down that thought, refusing to get my hopes up.

"Hey," I say nervously, jumping to my feet. Jason is still on the blanket, watching me intently, so I lift a finger, silently asking him to give me a minute.

"Hey," Alec echoes softly.

The silence between us is awkward, and I know right away, he isn't calling because he's changed his mind. I'm suddenly very thankful the only thing that happened between us was a kiss. Joey and Dawson were still okay after their kiss. It wasn't until after they decided to take the leap from friends to a couple that everything changed between them. Which means Alec and I will get through this. We'll get past this awkwardness and go back to being best friends.

"Alec? Is everything okay?" I ask slowly, when he remains quiet on the other end of the line.

"It's my dad... He was in an accident." My hand goes to my mouth with a gasp. "Lacie and I just left the hospital, and we're heading to the funeral home. He's gone." He chokes out the last word, and my heart feels like it's just imploded inside my chest. Leaving everything where it is, I grab my keys and take off, running to my jeep. My only thought is that I need to get to Alec. The kiss, the unrequited feelings, the awkwardness, none of it matters anymore.

"Which one?" I ask, turning my ignition. "I'll be right there."

Alec gives me the name of the place, and I tell him I'll see him in a few minutes. On my way, I call my parents and then Georgia to let them know. When I arrive at the funeral home, I see Alec's silver truck parked in the front. Remembering I'm still in my wetsuit, I strip out of it and throw on a pair of cutoff jean shorts and a tank. I look like shit, but this will have to do. I'm not driving all the way home to change.

I get inside and immediately spot Alec speaking to an older gentleman. His stepmom is sitting in the corner with her face in her hands, her shoulders moving up and down while she cries quietly.

"Hey," I say softly, making my presence known but not wanting to interrupt the two guys conversing. Alec stops talking and turns to me. His eyes are bloodshot, and when they meet mine, a single tear falls. If I had to guess, I would say that, up until now, Alec's refused to acknowledge his grief. Not knowing what to say in this situation, I do the only thing that comes natural and wrap my arms around him and hug him tight. Alec's body sinks into mine, his face nuzzling into my neck. His hot tears hit my skin as he cries over the loss of his father. I don't bother speaking. There's nothing I can say that will make this better.

When Alec's body calms down, and he goes still, I lift my head up slightly to meet his eyes. "Tell me what you need."

"You here is all I need."

WHEN I WAS FIVE, MY BIOLOGICAL MOM DIED. THERE was a funeral, but my dad said he felt it was best for me not to attend. We visited her grave once, but I don't remember it, and I haven't been back since then. When I was eight, my great-grandma passed away, but once again, wanting to shelter me, my dad and mom insisted Georgia and I stay home. So, at twenty-one years old, I've just attended my first funeral, and if this is part of growing up, I must admit, I'm not a fan of getting older. To say it was sad would be a gross understatement. Gavin's wish was to be cremated, so Alec and Lacie picked out a lovely wooden urn that was placed for everyone to see. Georgia created the most beautiful slideshow of images and videos Lacie and Mila gave her. I had some images blown up, and since I couldn't sleep, I painted a portrait of Alec and his dad, which Alec insisted be shown. His stepmom read a poem, and Alec spoke of fond memories he had with his dad.

When the funeral was over, everybody went back to Mila and Mason's home. I'm not sure what the point of it was. Maybe to reminisce? I don't really know. Food and drinks were brought in, but most people didn't eat. Everyone gave their condolences to Alec and Lacie, and eventually one by one people trickled out.

From beginning to end, Alec's had me by his side. Even the last four nights he's slept in my bed with me. He holds me close until he thinks I've fallen asleep, and then he cries softly into my chest for hours. Alec has taken some personal time off work and hasn't said when he plans to return. We haven't discussed what happened between us the night of the concert. It's as if, with the death of his father, everything between us went back to normal. It solidifies why we can't ever be together. We need each other too much, and we can't gamble what we have, in hope of something more.

Now, the funeral is over, the meals everyone made for Lacie are in her fridge, and we're back home. For the first time in days, there's nothing to do. No funeral to plan, no pictures to create. It's done. Gavin is gone, and he isn't coming back. All that's left is for everyone to start living their new life, one without Gavin in it.

Alec has been quiet since we got home, and I imagine he's struggling with this next part. Now that everything is calm, there's nothing for him to do to keep busy. He excused himself to shower the second we walked through the door, and when he got out, he went straight to his room to get dressed, closing the door behind him. I thought about knocking to see if he's okay, but if he wanted or needed me, he wouldn't have shut the door, or he would've opened it back up after he got dressed.

Chase is sitting on the couch—which now seems to be his new, permanent bed—messing with his cell phone, and Georgia's next to him texting on her phone—probably with Robert.

Unable to take the silence another second, I stand, needing to get out of here. "I'm gonna to head to the beach." I haven't been since Alec called me with the news of his father passing away. I left my board there, and Jason texted me to let me know he would hold onto it for me.

"You're going to leave Alec?" Georgia asks, her brows furrowed in confusion.

"He obviously needs some time to himself." I nod toward his closed door. "I'll be back in a few hours."

After changing into my bikini and grabbing my wetsuit and keys, I head to the beach. I send Jason a text, and he replies that he's already there and has my board.

With the daylight limited, when I get to the beach, after getting Aiden some food and bringing it to him, I don't waste any time putting on my wetsuit and getting my board from Jason. He tries to bring us up, but I shake my head, telling him I can't do this right now. Thankfully, he doesn't push. I spend the next couple hours in the water. Paddling out and riding in. The waves are good, but it wouldn't matter if they weren't. I needed this. To feel the saltwater against my skin. To be out in the Pacific Ocean with nothing but the water and my board.

When I finally decide to take a quick break and grab a drink, I notice Alec is sitting in the sand. His knees are bent with his arms around them. His sandals are next to him, and his toes are digging into the wet sand.

"Hey," I say, shocked that he's here. "What are you doing here?" When I get closer, he stands, shaking the sand off him. He's in a plain white T-shirt and khaki cargo shorts. His face is freshly shaved, and his brown hair is messy.

"You look amazing out there, Lex." He smiles, but it doesn't reach his eyes like it usually does. I wonder how long it will take for him to smile like he used to before his dad died. It's probably selfish, but I hope it doesn't take too long. It's only been four days and I already miss his real smile.

"Thank you." I push my board into the sand.

"Can we go for a walk?" He worries his bottom lip nervously.

"Sure." I reach behind me and pull the zipper on my wetsuit down, shrugging out of it and leaving me in only my bikini.

"Do you have clothes?" he asks, his eyes raking down the front of my body.

"Oh, yeah. In the car."

Alec's hand rises behind him, and he grabs the back of his shirt, pulling it up. My eyes dart to his muscular torso and up to his hard chest as his shirt rises higher and higher, until it's off his body. He hands it to me, and I take it, throwing it over my head. Immediately, the signature cologne Alec wears hits my nostrils, and I force myself not to bring the material to my nose to inhale it like a crazy person.

I drop my board onto the ground and throw my wetsuit on top of it, then call out Ricco's name. "Can you keep an eye on my board?"

He's sitting on a blanket with a bunch of our friends, smoking a blunt and listening to some oldie's rock. He nods once and smiles, taking another hit. My eyes land on Jason, who's also sitting there, only he isn't smiling. He's shooting daggers my way. At some point

I'm going to have to speak to him, but right now Alec needs to come first.

Alec looks like he wants to say something, but he doesn't. Instead, he starts walking in the opposite direction toward the pier. Nervous as to why he came here to talk to me, I stay quiet and wait for him to speak first. When we reach the pier, he stops in his tracks and faces me. The sun is just about gone, and the only light shining on us are the pier lights.

"The last few days have been hard," he starts. I simply nod in response, letting him speak. I can't even imagine what he's going through or how he feels, and I'm not going to pretend like I do. "When we got home today, my first instinct was to push you away." Now him shutting his door makes sense. "I called Lacie to see how she's doing, and she's a mess. She's pushing everyone away: my mom, me, her sister..." He stops speaking, and I'm not sure if I'm supposed to say anything, so I don't. I have no clue what's going through Alec's head right now, but he obviously drove over to the beach because he has something he needs to say to me.

Taking a deep breath, his eyes meet mine. "I called Mason, worried about Lacie, and he said when his father died, his mom did the same thing. She pushed him away, not knowing how to deal with the grief. Then he said something that made me think." Alec takes my hand in his, and I look down at our fingers intertwined. His large, masculine hand swallows my smaller one whole.

"He said the dark, ugly moments, like death, have a way of pushing people together or tearing them apart." Alec's voice cracks, and in the faint light I can see his eyes are glossy with unshed tears. "I don't want my father's death to tear us apart, Lex."

I start to shake my head because there's nothing that could tear us apart. Before I can voice my thoughts, though, Alec presses two fingers against my lips, stopping my words from coming out. He runs them across my lips then smiles softly.

"Life is too short. Too uncertain. My dad didn't find his soul mate until he was in his forties, and his time with her was cut short because of a clogged artery he didn't know about. He left to go get breakfast and will never return home. Now, only a few years after meeting my dad and falling in love, Lacie is alone again."

Alec's grip on my hand tightens as he pulls me closer to him. "I don't want to one day die with regrets. I'm in love with you, Lex, and I'm done pretending that I'm not."

"Alec," I breathe. He's saying the words I've longed to hear for years, but I'm scared he's only saying them because he's grieving over the loss of this father. He just told me the other day the kiss shouldn't have happened.

"I mean it, Lexi. I want you. I want to be with you. I want to hug you, kiss you, make love to you. I want to spend every day of our lives loving you up close, instead of from afar like I've been doing for years."

His hands lock behind by back, and he pulls me closer to him, our bodies flush against one another. "Tell me you want that too. Tell me you need me the way I need you. I've seen the way you look at me, the way you touch me. The other night at the concert, the way your body fit perfectly against mine. The way your lips molded against mine. It's like you were made just for me."

I want so badly to say yes. To wrap my arms around him and tell him I want him the way I want to spend my days surfing. I need him like I need to paint, to create. I love him like I love the smell of the saltwater. He's my addiction. I crave him every day. But I can't tell him any of that. Because when the grief lessens and he realizes I'm not what he needs, I'll lose him. He thinks he needs me as his girlfriend, but what he really needs is me as his friend. And that's exactly what I'm going to be—his friend.

"I love you so much," I tell him, wrapping my arms around his neck. I breathe in his scent and my eyes momentarily close, getting lost in everything that is Alec. "But I can't be with you."

He tightens his hold around me before loosening his grip so he can back up slightly and make eye contact with me. "Lex, please."

"You don't mean this. You're hurting. You just lost your dad and your heart has a gaping hole in it. But I can't be the one to fill it. I love that I'm the person you turned to for comfort. It means the world to me. And I'm here for you. But we both know we can't have anything more than friendship."

His gaze sears into mine. "What I *know* is that losing my dad made me realize how short life is, and I don't want to spend it in denial. I'm in love with you. And yeah, maybe it looks bad admitting that right after my dad died, but it doesn't make it any less true."

God, I want to believe that, so damn badly. But I can't chance it. If he changes his mind... If he regrets it later... He's hurting and not thinking clearly, and I have to be the clearheaded one for both of us, so we don't make any decisions we'll regret later. Decisions we can't take back or come back from.

I cup his face with my hands. "I'm sorry, but you're my best friend and it can't be anything more."

Alec sighs, shaking his head. "There already is something more. I was part of that kiss we shared *before* my dad died."

"The kiss you told me shouldn't have happened?"

"Because I was scared," he barks. "Just like you are."

"Hey, Lexi," Jason calls out. "Everything okay?"

Alec tenses, tilting his head slightly to the side. "Everything's fine."

"I asked Lexi," Jason says.

"I'm okay," I yell back. "I'll be over there in a minute." I turn back to Alec. "I'm supposed to be practicing for the upcoming surfing comp, but if you want to go somewhere—"

"No," Alec says. "Go surf." He grips the curves of my hips and pulls me into him until our bodies are flush. His face is so close to mine, I can feel his warm breath on me when he whispers, "This isn't over, Lex." He kisses the corner of my mouth, and a shiver runs down my spine. "I know you feel the same way I do, and I'm going to prove it to you."

He walks me back to where my stuff is and then takes off. Once he's gone, Jason walks over. "Your boyfriend?"

"No, just a friend." But as the word friend leaves my lips, I know that's not entirely true. Alec is so much more than that, even if I don't want to admit it.

"Let me take you out," Jason says. When I hesitate, he closes the distance between us. "Please. Just one date."

I should tell him no, admit that I have feelings for someone else, but does it matter what feelings I have for Alec when I refuse to act on them? Maybe going out with Jason will help me force the idea of Alec and me from my head—and heart. At the same time, I want Jason to understand...

"I'll go out with you, but I'm not looking for anything serious right now."

"Got it," he says with a nod. "Just one date."

ALEC

It's been almost a week since I made it clear to Lexi, I'm not giving up on us. The problem is, since then, she's been avoiding me like the plague. Most days and nights, she's at the beach surfing. The few times I've tried to hang out there, she's made it a point to act like she's too busy to spend time with me. And when she's home, instead of watching television in the living room, she stays in her room. At night, when she goes to bed, she shuts her door. I'm trying to be patient. I know this is her way of fighting the inevitable, but I'm getting a little antsy.

Especially since I overheard her talking to Georgia earlier about going on a double fucking date with that dick Jason. I've seen him hanging around her, and if I thought for a second that Lexi really liked him or that he would be good for her, I would throw in the towel and let her be happy. But I know damn well he isn't her type. For one, he has no ambition. He literally just hangs around the beach, drinking and getting high. Lexi might hang out with them, but she wants more in life, even if she's a little lost right now. She paints the walls to spread her hope and beauty because she sees the good in everything. She's in school—even though she hates it—because she knows it will better her future. And she's not your stereotypical surfer, looking to get high and party, like the idiots she hangs out with. She surfs because it's her passion.

"We're going out," I tell Chase, who's in his usual spot on the couch, watching TV.

"Seriously?" He pops his head up and quirks a brow. I haven't been out in some time, not since my dad died.

"Yeah, but don't say a word." I gesture my head toward the hallway, silently indicating I don't want the girls to know. They're currently in Georgia's room getting ready. They don't know I overheard, and I don't want them to. I heard Lexi mention she doesn't want Jason to pick her up here—probably because she knows I'll lose my shit—so they're meeting the guys at the bar downtown. I considered busting in there and demanding she not go, but decided to take a different approach. Show her it's me she wants.

"Be ready to go after they leave."

Before the girls come out, I make myself scarce, not coming back out until I hear the front door close, indicating they left.

"Where're we going?" Chase asks, once we're in my truck.

"To The Black Sheep. Georgia and Lexi are going on a double

date there."

Chase laughs. "Well, this just got interesting."

We walk into The Black Sheep and my eyes immediately go in search of Lexi. I haven't the slightest clue how this is all going to play out. I have a few options: I can stay hidden, watch and see how her date goes. I can make my presence known but keep a distance, or I can—

"Holy shit! Look who's here," Chase exclaims, taking the choice out of my hands. "Lexi, Georgia, what the hell are you guys doing here?"

Chase grabs a chair from another table—without even asking—and drags it between Georgia and Robert. With a smile plastered on his face, he plops his ass into the chair and sits back, crossing his arms over his chest.

I stifle a laugh and follow along, only I sit between Lexi and Georgia, since Lexi's date, Jason, is sitting too close to her for me to move in between them.

"What are you guys doing here?" Lexi stiffly asks.

"We heard this place has great burgers," Chase answers, dropping his arm onto the back of Georgia's chair. Robert notices and shoots him a possessive glare that Chase either doesn't pay attention to or doesn't notice. Georgia snorts a laugh, knowing Chase's full of shit, and her eyes dart between Lexi and me, at the same time Robert turns his glare on her. Call me an overprotective friend, but that move just added him to my shit list.

"Well, in case you didn't notice," Jason speaks up, leaning over so his eyes meet mine, "we're on a date."

"Oh, shit," Chase says like he wasn't aware. "Our bad. But you guys don't mind us joining, do you?" He glances at Georgia, who covers her mouth to stop herself from laughing.

"Alec, can I talk to you for a second?" Lexi asks, already standing and grabbing my arm before I can respond. She drags me down the hallway, until we're hidden in a darkish corner, away from prying eyes and ears. "What the hell are you doing?" she shrieks, jutting out her cute-as-fuck chin, like the little badass she is.

"As Chase said—"

"No." She covers my mouth with her hand. "Don't you dare lie to me. We don't do that, ever." Her plump lips form a flat line. She removes her hand and crosses her arms over her chest. She's wearing a formfitting tank top and it takes everything in me not to dart my eyes to her breasts I know are peeking out of the top.

"I warned you I wouldn't give up." I grip the curves of her hips and gently push her until her back is against the wall. "You don't like that guy, not like you like me. And you're wasting all of our time by going out with him. If I learned anything from my dad's death, it's that we should never waste our time because we don't know how much time we have."

"You can't do this, Alec," she begs, her eyes shining with raw emotion.

"Can't do what?" I place a palm above her head and lean in, so she's forced to look up at me. In this position I could easily take her mouth, but I won't do it, not until she agrees to be mine. "Can't show you that I'm in love with you?" I tuck a blond hair behind her ear, and she visibly shivers. "I know you want me, *you* know you want me, hell, everyone at that fucking table knows you want me. You want to fight this, fine, but I'm not going to make it easy for you, and I'm not going to give up until you're mine."

Lexi closes her eyes and takes a deep breath and for a second, I think maybe she's going to give in. But when she opens her eyes, I instantly see the defiance in her irises. "I'm on a date, Alec. You and I are friends, and if you keep this up, you're going to ruin that friendship."

She turns to walk away, but before she can, I tug her toward me, so her back is against my front. I dip my face so my lips are right at the shell of her ear. "I get that it's going to take you a bit longer to get on board with the idea of us, and I'm okay with that because I know in the end we'll be together, but I need you to promise me something."

She sighs. "What?"

"Until you're one hundred percent sure he's the man you love, please don't sleep with him."

Her breath hitches, and then a few seconds later, she nods before she walks away.

I follow after her, but instead of sitting, I nod to Chase that it's time to go. I'd like to say I'm a good enough guy to wish them a good date, but I'm not. With a squeeze to Lexi's shoulder and a smile to Georgia, I do the hardest fucking thing and walk out of the bar.

"I WANT TO BE WITH HER, AND I KNOW DAMN WELL SHE feels the same way." I'm sitting at a local diner having lunch with Mason and Chase. It's been damn near two weeks since I told Lexi how I feel and almost a week since her date with dick-face. Since I walked out of the restaurant, we've barely spoken, let alone seen each other. She swears it's because she's busy surfing, getting ready for her competition in July, but I know her and she's definitely avoiding me. "How the hell do I get her to admit her feelings for me?"

Mason laughs, and Chase shakes his head.

"Maybe it's for the best," Chase says. "I married young and look where I ended up... divorced."

"You signed the papers?" I ask. Chase was served divorce papers a couple weeks ago. After throwing them on the table, he took off and didn't come home for a few days. When he returned, he didn't say a word about them and I didn't want to pry. I figured when he was ready to talk, he would bring them up.

"Yeah. Since neither of us really has any assets, it'll go through quickly," he says, taking a sip of his coffee. He looks like shit, like he needs to take a long as fuck nap, but I don't point that out. No need to kick the guy while he's down.

"I'm sorry, man," Mason adds.

"It's all good," Chase says. "She was a cheating druggie. The more I tried to get her help, the more she pushed me away. I should've known how it would all end."

"Maybe you're right." I sigh, crossing my arms over my chest. "One of the reasons I didn't pursue Lexi before is because of how young we are. My parents married young..." I swallow thickly, trying to keep it together. Any time I bring up my dad, I lose it. It's been almost three weeks since his death, and it doesn't hurt any fucking less.

"You aren't your parents," Mason points out. "Sure, as people grow, they change, but plenty of people who get married young last. And you can't not be with someone because there's a chance it won't work." He glances at Chase. "Did you love your wife?"

Chase nods once.

"Did you have good times with her? Create memories?"

"Yeah."

"Then you don't regret it. Every moment, every situation happens for a reason," Mason says. "I had a shit life growing up, but I would go through it all again if it meant it would lead me to right here—with your mom, you, and your sister." He quirks a brow. "And I know your parents feel the same way. Had your mom not been with your dad, they wouldn't have had you. And I know damn well neither of them could ever regret their time together *because* it gave them you."

"Yeah, well, I'm just glad Victoria and I didn't have any kids," Chase says, referring to his soon-to-be ex-wife. "I didn't grow up in a perfect home where my parents got along and we all sat around having meals together like you guys do. My parents barely got along. And after..." He clears his throat, his face all of a sudden looking pained. "After my sister died, it only got worse, until my dad drank himself to death."

"You had a sister?" He's never mentioned having a sibling.

Chase nods. "It's not something I like to talk about. We grew up in a shitty neighborhood, surrounded by shitty people, and it led to her making shitty choices. Now she's gone. Where I come from, that elusive happily ever after people talk about is only found in those bullshit Disney movies." His sad eyes meet mine. "And since we were so poor, we couldn't even afford to watch them anyway." He shrugs.

"I didn't get it at first either," Mason says. "I actually came from a similar home. It took me finding Mila to understand what real love is all about."

"Oh, I know what it's all about," Chase says bitterly. "I loved Victoria with every ounce of my being. But look what loving her got me: ten years wasted, homeless, and sleeping on my best friend's couch. I think I've had enough of that love bullshit to last me a lifetime."

"You're too young to be this bitter," Mason says. "Take it as a learning experience and move forward."

"Oh, I am." Chase chuckles. "Every night since I signed those divorce papers I've moved forward." He waggles his brows, and Mason and I both groan.

"Well, I'm not trying to move forward," I say, wondering how the hell we went from me trying to convince Lexi to be with me, to Chase transforming into a manwhore. "I'm trying to figure out how to get Lexi to admit she wants to be with me."

Mason grins. "That's easy. Do what I did when I needed to convince your mom to stay married to me... Show her how good it can be with you."

"It's kind of hard to do when she's avoiding me." *And going out with another guy...* Thankfully, from what I've seen, she hasn't been out with Jason again, and the night she did go out with him, she got home only an hour after me, so I know she didn't go with him back to his place.

"You're just going to have to try harder." Mason smirks.

The waitress drops off our food and we eat in silence. I think about what Mason said. Maybe he's right. Maybe the key to getting Lexi to give in, isn't to beg her but instead to show her.

After we finish eating, we talk for a little while, then head to the gym to get a workout in. Afterward, I stop by Lacie's place to check on her. She's finally starting to come around. She's not back to work or even leaving the house yet, but she's at least showering. I bring her some food from one of her favorite restaurants and she thanks me. When she stands to take it, I notice something is different... her stomach has a bump.

"Lacie?" My gaze darts between her face and her stomach.

Her eyes well up with tears. "I'm thirteen weeks."

"Did my dad know?"

She nods. "It wasn't planned, and because I'm almost forty, we were worried about the possibility of a miscarriage, so we were waiting to tell everyone." Tears slide down her cheeks. "I can't believe I have to do this alone."

"Hey, you are *not* doing this alone. You have me and my parents. Your sister... I know it's not the same, but I promise you, you aren't doing this alone."

She chokes out a sob. "Thank you, Alec. That means a lot to me. Your brother is going to want to know all about his daddy, and you know him the best."

"Brother?"

"Yeah. I had a blood test done. It's a boy."

"Congratulations." I give her a hug. "My brother will know exactly who his dad was. I promise."

After Lacie updates me on her pregnancy, I head home. On the way, I call my mom to let her know about Lacie, and she promises to stop by to check on her. While Lacie and I were talking, she mentioned possibly moving in with her sister. She lives a couple hours north, and she felt bad for leaving and taking my brother with her. But I assured her that no amount of distance would stop me from being part of their life, and if moving in with her sister is what's best for her, then that's what she should do.

I get home and find Chase on the couch, texting on his phone. "Want to go out tonight?" he asks. Tonight is his last night off before he's back on shift.

"Nah, tonight starts Operation Get Lexi."

Georgia walks out of her room and laughs. "Operation Get Lexi?" She shakes her head. "Only my sister would require an actual operation to get her to see what she already knows." She grabs her purse off the end table. "I'm heading over to Robert's. Be back later."

"Things are moving a little fast with him," I mention, making Georgia roll her eyes.

"Not everyone waits twenty years to admit they like someone. Bye!" she yells, closing the door behind her before I can say another word.

Ten

LEXI

I open the front door and tiptoe inside. It's late—I stayed out surfing later than I planned. Okay, let's be honest, I did it on purpose. Ever since Alec told me he wants more, I've been avoiding him. And since the night he showed up to my date, I've been double-y avoiding him. I know it's immature, but I don't know what else to do. I almost gave in that day at the beach, and again, when he cornered me in the restaurant, and I know if he keeps pressing it, I'll eventually give in. My plan is to stay away long enough that he comes to his senses and realizes he's not actually in love with me, but in love with the idea of being in love. Then, once he admits it, I'll tell him it's all good and things will go back to normal between us.

But then why did you tell Jason you needed to hold off on going out with him again?

Pushing that thought away, I set my surfboard against the wall and notice Chase is lying on the couch, texting on his phone.

"Hey," he says, without looking up. "You can sneak in all you want, but Alec is on to you."

I glare at him. "Shouldn't you be out screwing your way through LA?" I immediately regret my snippy comment. Chase is a good guy. He's just hurt over his wife cheating. I can't really blame him for wanting to get lost in other women to get over his wife. I'm not sure how I would react if I were in his shoes.

"Leaving soon," Chase volleys, as I walk down the hallway toward my room.

"There she is," Alec says, appearing out of nowhere.

"Jesus, you scared me." My hand clutches my chest.

"Sorry, I heard you talking to Chase."

"Is he like officially living with us?" I whisper.

"I'm not really sure." He shrugs. "He's got a lot of shit going on. Are you okay with him crashing here? Because if you aren't..." I love that Alec would be willing to kick his friend out if it makes me uncomfortable, but I would never ask him to do that, and truthfully, I don't mind Chase here.

"No... He's fine staying here. I was just thinking that maybe you should offer to share your bed, so he doesn't have to keep sleeping on the couch." I smirk playfully.

"Men don't share beds like you women do. The couch is all he's getting." He steps closer, invading my personal space, and I suddenly find myself backed up against the wall in our hallway.

"But I wouldn't mind sharing a bed with you." He waggles his eyebrows, and the butterflies that were dormant in my belly take off. This is exactly why I've been avoiding Alec.

"I don't think that would be a good idea," I breathe out.

"On the contrary." Alec rests his palms on either side of my head. "I think it would be a great idea." He runs his nose along my cheek and down my jawline. "What do you say, Lex?" He presses his lips to the rapidly beating pulse point on my neck. "Share a bed with me, and we can give Chase his own room."

"Shit, sorry, guys," Chase says, walking past us and snapping me out of the moment. "I'm jumping in the shower and then I'll be out of your hair."

"Actually," I say, ducking under Alec's arm. "Alec and I were just talking."

"We were?" Alec says, his voice perking up.

"Yeah. We were saying, instead of you sleeping on the couch, you can have one of the rooms."

Chase's brows go to his forehead. "You don't have to do that."

"We know, but we want to. I have to talk to Georgia, but I'm sure she'll agree. I'll move my stuff into her room and then you can have my room."

"You sure?" Chase asks.

"Yeah."

"Thanks." He smiles appreciatively. "Let me know how much the bills are, and we'll split them," he says before he disappears into the bathroom.

Once he's gone, Alec is back in my space. "Georgia has a new boyfriend. Don't you think she'll want her own space? You can share a room with me."

"Good one." I pat his chest. "Not happening."

He chuckles. "Oh, it will definitely happen. You *will* be sharing a bed with me soon enough." He lowers his head and brings his lips to my ear. "And when it does, it's going to be fucking amazing."

After I shower, since I'm not tired but don't want to leave my room, I lie in bed and pull up surfing videos on my laptop. With Alec on my mind, it's hard to focus on what I'm watching. A few videos in, there's a knock on my door. I consider pretending I'm asleep in case it's Alec, but worry it might be Georgia. She's been hanging out with Robert a lot lately. I need to make it a point to hang out with her soon so we can talk about him.

"Come in," I call out.

Of course it's Alec who steps through my doorway. Dressed in a pair of red basketball shorts hanging low on his hips, a white T-shirt stretched across his chest, and a knowing smirk on his lips, he saunters into my room like he owns the place.

"What do you want?" I groan.

"I thought we could watch TV." He shrugs, nodding for me to scoot over. When I ignore his silent request, his mouth quirks into a lopsided grin. "Have it your way."

Before I can protest whatever he's thinking of doing, he's scooping me into his arms. He plops onto my bed and settles me across his lap, his arms encasing my body tightly, so I can't try to crawl off him.

"Alec!" I shriek, wriggling to get free.

"I wouldn't do that if I were you," he warns.

Confused, I continue wriggling, until I feel something hard against my ass, and then it hits me—I'm grinding against his crotch. My neck and cheeks warm in embarrassment, and Alec barks out a laugh.

"Fuck, you're so adorable."

When I glare at his choice of words, he sobers. "Hey, there's nothing wrong with being adorable."

"Little kids are adorable." I pout. "Puppies are adorable..."

"*You* are adorable," he repeats. "Ninety-nine percent of the time, you're this badass, wild little thing who takes no prisoners. Nothing bothers you; nobody fazes you. But then, every once in a while, you let a select few see the *real* you. The you that's vulnerable and insecure and shy." Alec runs his fingers through my hair and, stopping at the back of my nape, tugs softly so my chin is jutted out and we're locking eyes. "The way your skin turns the most beautiful shade of pink, giving away your true feelings. It's so fucking adorable, and beautiful, and sexy."

I swallow thickly at his words, trying to push the golf ball-sized lump down my throat so I can breathe. He warned me he wasn't going to give up, but I wasn't prepared for all this. His words, his touch...

"You're not playing fair," I whisper, my heart beating erratically.

"I never said I would," he murmurs. His fist tightens on my

hair and he pulls my face to his. "Your excuse for not giving us a chance is that I only want you because my dad died, but that's not the truth and we both know it. You're scared to let me in, and I get it, Lex. I was scared too. Hell, I still am. I told you the kiss shouldn't have happened because I was terrified of what it would mean to admit my feelings for you. But now, I'm more terrified of you never knowing how I feel. Of us never getting our chance." He brushes his lips against mine, and a shiver erupts down my spine.

"I'm in love with you, Lexi," he says against my mouth. "And all I want is to show you just how much..."

"Alec," I breathe, but the argument can't get past my lips.

"I love you," he repeats. "And I know you love me."

I should tell him it would be better to wait until he isn't so emotional to make a decision like this. Give him more time to grieve over his father. There's a chance he's going to wake up in the morning and want to take this all back, but he's right. I do love him. I've been in love with him for years, and what if he wakes up in the morning and still feels the same way? Sure, there's a chance we end up like Joey and Dawson, but what if we're not them? What if we're actually Joey and Pacey, and taking this chance means we'll get our happily ever after? It's a chance I have to take. Because if I don't, I know I'll always regret it.

"I do love you," I admit. "I've been in love with you for as long as I can remember. I don't even know when it happened. Maybe it was when we were younger and you would help me defend Georgia against the mean kids at school. Or it might've been when you would pick me up at five in the morning to take me surfing because you had your license and I didn't, and you would sit in the sand and watch me for hours without complaining. I don't know. I just never..." My voice wavers as I'm overcome with emotions I never thought I'd be able to express. "I never thought you would ever feel the same way, and now that I know you do, I'm scared shitless."

"Don't be scared," Alec murmurs, his lips now only mere centimeters away from mine.

"How can I not be? If we do this and it doesn't work out, I'll lose you." I twist my body so I'm straddling Alec, then push him so he's lying on his back, his head resting against my tall stack of fluffy pillows. "I can't lose you."

His hands come around and cup the backs of my thighs, grinding my center against him. "You're not going to lose me," he promises. "No matter what happens, we'll always be in each other's lives." His brown eyes plead for me to believe him, to believe *in* him, in *us*.

There are so many things that can go wrong. I'm not a relationship expert by any means, but I'm old enough to know the odds are against us. Every adult in my life didn't find their forever until they experienced heartbreak. If we give in to what we want, there's a huge chance we might end up breaking each other's hearts.

"Don't do that," Alec says, fisting the back of my ponytail. "Don't think of everything that can go wrong." He pulls my face down to his. "Don't set us up for failure before we've even begun. Let's just take it one day at a time."

"One day at a time," I repeat, taking a deep breath. I can do that. One. Day. At a time.

"One day," he murmurs against my lips. "One moment... One kiss..."

I wrap my arms around his head, and my fingers thread through his short hair. His lips part mine, and his tongue sinks inside. Warmth floods through my veins as his tongue strokes mine. He kisses me gently, with patience, proving through his actions that he really is taking it one moment at a time. And I have to say, this moment feels damn good.

Since I'm in only a tank and a pair of cheeky underwear, Alec massages the globes of my ass, gently grinding our bodies against one another, the friction hitting my clit in all the right ways.

Needing to feel more of him, I break our kiss and pull at the bottom of his shirt, silently telling him what I want. With eyes screaming of love and desire, he sits up and yanks his shirt over his head, revealing his perfect body. I rub my hands down his sculpted, tattoo-covered chest, then place open-mouthed kisses to each of his nipples, before I begin to work my way down each of his rippled abs. His skin is soft yet firm, only a sprinkle of dark hair running down the center. I've fantasized so many times about what Alec would feel like... taste like... but none of my fantasies did him any justice.

I pepper kisses down his happy trail, excited to be so close to the Promised Land. When I arrive at my destination, I lower his shorts and his dick springs free. It's thick with a single vein running from root to tip, and my mouth waters at the sight, wanting to taste him. I fist his hard shaft gently, then wrap my mouth around the swollen head. It's smooth and tastes clean, the scent of the soap he uses in the shower lingering on him.

I take him into my mouth, as far as I can go, dragging my teeth along his entire length. Alec hisses, gripping my nape, as I run my tongue along the same area, licking away the sting.

"Jesus fucking Christ," he growls, tugging my head off his dick. My mouth makes a popping sound and saliva drips down my chin.

Alec flips us over so I'm on my back and he's hovering above me. He licks his way up my chin then sucks my bottom lip into his mouth before releasing it.

"It's my turn," he murmurs, pulling my top down and exposing my breasts.

"But I didn't get to finish." I pout.

"Patience," he says, as he wraps his lips around my pebbled nipple and sucks on it. Electric waves shoot through my body, as if there's a direct path from my breast to my core. Wrapping my legs around Alec's waist, I clench my thighs together.

"I need—"

The door swings open, making us both jump. Alec's head swings to the side as my eyes pop open to see who's there, realizing when Alec came in to talk to me, he never closed the door.

"Hey, Lex, I—Oh my God!" Georgia squeals, at the same time

I shriek, "Georgia!" as I try to cover my breasts—which is really pointless since my sister has seen me naked plenty of times over the years. But in this moment, I'm not exactly thinking clearly...

"Sorry!" she yells, slamming the door behind her.

Alec glances back at me, his face a bit flushed, and his eyes wide in shock and embarrassment. Makes sense since Georgia probably got a nice peek of his butt since, at some point, he removed his shorts and boxers.

"Well, that was one way for her to find out about us," he finally says.

"Yeah." I laugh, covering my chest back up since the moment has been ruined. "I should probably go talk to her."

"Okay." Alec drops his hands to either side of my head and presses his mouth to mine. "But when you're done, we're moving your stuff into my room."

It takes me a second to understand what he's talking about, but when I do, I shake my head. "No way, it's too soon. I'm moving into Georgia's room with her."

Alec eyes me for a brief moment, as if he's trying to think of his argument.

"Fine," he finally says with a shrug. "You want to share a closet with her, so you can tell yourself we're taking this slow, have at it, but you'll be in my bed every. Single. Night."

Eleven

ALEC

"There." I drop onto the bed in Chase's new room. "Everything has been moved out and into Georgia's room." I shoot Lexi a mock-glare, and she giggles. She can laugh all she wants, but there's no way she's spending a single night in bed with her sister instead of with me—at least not on the nights I'm home. If she wants to share a bed with her when I'm on shift, she's more than welcome to. But the nights I'm home, her warm body will be wrapped around mine—just like she was last night.

"Maybe we should get him a more manly comforter," Georgia suggests, glancing around the room. Since Georgia already has furniture, we left all of Lexi's in here for Chase. All we did was move his clothes, which were shoved into the corner of the living room, into his new room. The girls hung them up and folded them neatly into the drawers.

"It's a room and has a comfortable bed. Chase won't give a shit about the color of the comforter." I stand and pull Lexi into my arms, fucking stoked that I get to touch her and kiss her and hold her whenever I want now. "Want to grab something to eat?"

"Sure," she says, pecking me on my lips. I want to drag her to my room so I can continue exploring her body, but I hold back— there will be plenty of time for that.

"Georgia, want to ask Robert to join?" she asks her sister.

"He's still at work," Georgia says. "And I have homework to get done before class tomorrow. You guys go ahead."

"You sure?" Lexi asks.

"Yeah, but if you want to bring me home something, I won't stop you." Georgia smiles, then exits the room.

"Since it's late, we can just grab something at the pier," Lexi suggests.

"Sounds good."

It's a nice night, so we jump into Lexi's jeep. The beach is only a short drive from where we live, and a few minutes later, we're parking.

"I'm starved," Lexi groans, taking my hand in hers. I glance down at our joined hands, loving how easy it was, once we gave in, for us to move from best friends to more. It's only been a few hours, but her taking my hand tells me she isn't second-guessing shit.

We place two orders of fish and chips then find an empty table. Lexi sits next to me and I pull her into my arms, kissing her while we wait. Now that I've knocked down that wall, and I know I get to have her this way, I can't fucking get enough of her.

"Lexi?" a gruff voice says from behind us.

We both turn and find Jason standing there with his board in his hands. He's in his wetsuit, the top half unzipped and pulled down to his waist. He must've just come up from surfing.

"Hey," Lexi says slowly.

"What's this?" Jason asks, nodding toward us. It's obvious by the way we're sitting what *this* is, so I'm assuming he's asking out of shock not ignorance.

Lexi tries to pull her hand out of mine, and when I tighten my grip, she whips her head back around and glares. "I need to talk to Jason real quick," she says, her tone even. "Can you give me a minute?"

Not wanting to be a possessive dick, I nod, but when my eyes land on Jason, who's glaring my way, I can't help myself.

Holding on to her hand, I pull her face toward mine and kiss her hard. My tongue pushes past her parted lips and I devour her. The kiss is short, but my point is made.

When the kiss ends, Lexi sighs in contentment, and then, as if her foggy head has suddenly cleared, she pulls her hand back and her mouth forms a flat line. "Not cool, Alec."

"Maybe not." I shrug. "But he needs to know you're mine." I lean in and press my mouth to hers. "And I'm yours."

"When you say shit like that, it's hard to be mad at you."

Without waiting for me to respond, she stands and approaches

Jason. Of course, at that moment, our order number is called. Figuring it's best to give her a minute, I get up and grab our food from the counter.

As I'm walking back over to the table with our food, my eyes find Lexi, who's still talking to Jason. Her back is ramrod straight and she's shaking her head. Jason's glaring at her, his eyes filled with anger. I don't want to interfere, but I'm not about to let him make her feel bad for choosing to be with me.

I set our tray of food on the table, then walk up to them, wrapping my arm around Lexi's waist. The second she glances over and sees it's me, I feel her instantly soften into my side.

"You mind?" Jason snaps. "We're talking."

"Not with that tone, you're not." I remove my arm from Lexi and step into Jason's space.

His glare moves from Lexi to me. "That isn't up to you."

"Lexi, you done?" I ask, without looking at her.

"Jason, I really am sorry," she says, her voice filled with remorse. "I didn't plan for this to happen..."

"You don't have to explain shit to him," I tell her, backing up from Jason and taking her hand. "Our food's getting cold." I pull her away from him, refusing to give him any more of my time. He's pissed he lost his shot with her, and I get it, but it's not my damn problem, and quite frankly, it's not hers either. And it sure as hell doesn't warrant him giving her shit.

"You okay?" I ask, when I notice she's eating her food in silence.

"Yeah." She shrugs a single shoulder. "I just feel bad."

"For what? You went out with him once and it didn't work out. That's called dating. It doesn't always end up in marriage."

"I know," she says with a sigh, "but he called me a tease, said I led him on. And maybe he's right..."

"Bullshit," I argue, refusing to listen to her put herself down. That guy is damn lucky he's already left. If I see him again, we're going to have some words.

"I did only agree to go out with him with the hope of knocking you out of my thoughts." She glances out at the water, her eyes full of guilt.

"Hey." I press my palm to her cheek, forcing her to look at me. "He's a grown ass man. No, you probably shouldn't have agreed to go out with him if you weren't interested, but it doesn't matter. You followed through and went on your date. You weren't interested in going out again, so you didn't. Some guys have trouble with being let down, but that's not your fault. It's his, and he needs to get over it."

"Okay," she says, twisting her mouth into a small smile. "I'm done. Want to grab Georgia something to eat and then head home?"

"Yeah." When my lips pull into a grin, Lexi's own smile widens.

"You're totally thinking about getting laid." She smacks my shoulder playfully. "I should make you wait..."

"Until when? Marriage?" I volley, imagining Lexi walking down the aisle in a beautiful wedding dress.

"Yeah," she smarts.

"Fine."

Her eyes widen. "Fine?"

"Yeah, I have no intention of waiting long to marry you anyway. I've waited years to be with you, what's a couple more months?"

"A couple months?" she shrieks. "You're crazy!"

"About you." I pull her into my arms. "I don't want to waste any time, Lex. I love you and you love me. I want to marry you... and soon."

"Are you proposing?"

I shake my head. "When I propose, I'll have a ring and it will be romantic. You deserve that."

"Well, that's good to know," she says with a soft laugh. "Now I'll be waiting and wondering when."

She snakes her arms around my neck and threads her fingers through my short hair, then climbs into my lap, not giving a shit that there are people surrounding us. "But until then, I don't want to wait. Like you said, we've both waited a long time to be together. With anyone else, it would feel like we're rushing, but you're my path, Aleczander Sterling."

"I don't know what the hell a path is, but I like that I'm yours, Alexandria Scott."

She giggles, and the sound does shit to my insides. "Georgia and I made it up. It's not a real path... It just represents us trying to find our way because we both feel lost."

"We're young, Lex, and we're not always going to know which

way to go, but I can promise you, no matter what, I'll be by your side while you're trying to figure it out."

"I like the sound of that," she says, softly pressing her mouth to mine. Her tongue slides through my parted lips, and I taste the lemonade she was drinking mixed with Lexi. We kiss for a few minutes, until she grinds her center against my dick, and I remember where we are.

Something prickles in the back of my neck, like a sense we're being watched. My eyes scan the area, not seeing anyone paying attention to us, but I still don't like it. "Let's take this back to the house," I murmur against her lips. "Where I can explore every inch of your body without an audience."

After getting Georgia's food, we jump into Lexi's jeep to head home. When we arrive, Georgia is sitting on the couch with Robert watching a movie.

"Hey," she says, jumping up to grab the bag from me. "Thank you. All that studying has me famished." She sits back down and opens the box. "Mmm... this smells so good." She takes a bite of the fried fish and moans. "And tastes just as good."

Robert scrunches his nose in disgust. "Yeah, if you're into clogged arteries."

"Not all of us can eat healthy twenty-four-seven," Georgia says, taking another bite.

"You're an adult, Georgia. A little discipline won't kill you," Robert replies with an eye roll. *Real fucking adult...*

Georgia laughs him off. "The movie just started." She points to the screen. "Want to join us?"

Lexi gives her sister a strained smile, and I can tell she's holding back from saying what's on her mind. We haven't discussed Georgia's boyfriend, but based on the glare she's shooting his way, I'm going to guess she isn't a huge fan.

"Actually, we have somewhere we have to go," I tell her.

Lexi's gaze swings over to me. "We do?"

"Yeah." When I had placed Georgia's food into the back seat I saw Lexi's backpack that I know is full of supplies—which gave me an idea. "We'll be home later."

Taking Lexi's hand in mine, I pull her out the door and back to her jeep.

"Where are we going?" she asks with a playful pout. "I thought you were going to explore me in your room."

I chuckle at how adorable and sexy she is. "When I explore you, I'm planning to be so thorough you'll be screaming my name. And that's not something I want to do with your sister and her *boyfriend* in the living room."

"Not a fan of his either?"

"Something about him just rubs me the wrong way."

"I agree. But Georgia is happy, and he's her first real boyfriend. I don't want to be a Debbie Downer."

"We'll keep an eye on him." I don't give a shit how excited Georgia is to finally have a boyfriend. If that fool doesn't treat her the way she deserves, I'll kick his ass to New York.

"So, where are we going?" she asks when I open her door for

her.

"I saw your art supplies in the back. I was thinking we could take a little field trip."

"You want to watch me graffiti a wall?" she asks incredulously.

"I've seen your work all over the city, but I've never actually seen you do it."

"If we get caught, we'll be arrested," she warns. "I don't have anything to lose, but you have a job you love, and..."

"I'm not worried." I dip my head and press my lips to hers. "Show me a night in the life of Alexandria Scott."

Twelve

LEXI

As I drive down the back streets of LA, Alec and I are both silent. I've never allowed anyone to witness my work firsthand. Sure, my close friends and family know which pieces I've graffitied, but it's always been something I do on my own. When I'm feeling down, and the world is feeling a little uglier than usual, it's my way of adding beauty to it, making my small little mark in the big bad world.

I was prepared to go home and have sex with Alec, something that is considered to be the most intimate act between a man and a woman, yet somehow the thought of him watching me paint feels as if I'm baring myself to him—cracking my chest open and pouring my heart and soul into his hands.

I find an abandoned building the city has bought but hasn't torn down yet and park around the corner. Reaching back, I grab my backpack that contains my spray paints, then hop out of my jeep. Wordlessly, Alec follows after me, over to the giant brick wall. There are already several tags littering the wall, but I find a good blank spot I can make my mark on.

Unzipping my bag, I grab the different colors I want to use and begin to create my picture. Tonight's image is Alec-inspired. He stands behind me, watching, but doesn't say a word the entire time. I get lost in my creation. With every spray of paint, a piece of ugly is transformed into something beautiful. A bit of darkness is brightened.

When I'm done, I draw my moniker on the bottom of it—a multi-colored silhouette of a woman holding her surfboard—then step back to check out the finished product. It's my signature night sky with bright, twinkling stars above the ocean, but tonight, I added a boy and a girl facing each other. They're small in comparison to the large sky, because in the grand scheme of things, we all are—just two people in a world filled with billions. Next to them is the quote Alec's mom recited at his birthday dinner: *You don't find love... it finds you.*

"Holy shit, Lex," Alec says, finally speaking. He snakes his arms around me and rests his chin on my shoulder. "Do you have any idea how fucking talented you are?"

"It's just graffiti." I shrug a shoulder nonchalantly. "Talent is Picasso or Van Gogh... Monet or Magritte."

Alec's hands grip the curves of my hips, and he twirls me around, backing me up against the brick wall. "I don't know who

half those people you named are, but I know that that painting"—
he juts his chin toward the wall behind me—"is fucking amazing.
How you were able to take something as simple as spray paint
and turn it into something so awe-inspiring blows my mind. It's
us, right?" His eyes bore into mine. "The boy and girl... love found
them."

"Yeah," I choke out, swallowing the lump in my throat. "It's
us." Tears prick my lids as I'm suddenly overcome with emotion.
Usually I draw a painting and then leave it behind. I'm not forced
to face what I draw or why I draw it. But standing here with Alec,
I want—no, I *need* him to know what this painting means to me.

"I have this amazing, beautiful life that's filled with supportive,
loving parents, a sister who is more like my soul mate, and friends
and family like you and Micaela. But even with all the good, I still
feel like something is off. Like something is missing. I don't know
if it's genetic..." I swallow down the raw emotions I feel when I talk
about the woman who gave birth to me and then abandoned me.
"My biological mom, Gina, was a druggie who was unhappy until
the day she died."

"You're not her, Lex."

"That's the problem. I don't know *who* I am, what I want to do
with my life. It's why Georgia and I made that pact about finding
our perfect path, so we could find our way." I raise my hands and
frame Alec's face—the scruff tickling my palms. "Georgia took off
out of the gate, making all these changes, and I was worried she
would leave me behind, but then you came along and found me—

love found me, found *us*, and now... I'm still lost. I have no idea what my future holds, but that dark, scary path just got a whole lot brighter because of you."

"I've always been here, Lex, and I always will be." Alec kisses the tip of my nose, and the simple act sends sparks through my body. "You *will* find your place in the world." He dips his face and brings his mouth to my ear. "Watching you in your element was the most beautiful thing I've ever witnessed, and I have no doubt that one day you will find exactly where you belong. But here's the thing..." He trails kisses down my neck and then suckles on my pulse point. "Life isn't about the destination, so while you're searching for where you want to end up, we're going to enjoy the beautiful journey we're going to take together to get there." His lips move up my neck and he peppers kisses along my jawline. "Every step..." He kisses the corner of my mouth. "Every detour..." He kisses my chin. "Every moment will be beautiful in its own way."

Our mouths fuse together and our tongues unite, stroking, teasing, caressing one another. Without breaking our kiss, Alec grabs the globes of my ass and lifts me. My legs wrap around his torso at the same time my fingers weave through his hair. Since I'm in a jean skirt, the denim scrunches up to my waist, leaving only the barrier of my thin panties between us. As we devour each other, I grind against his hard stomach, and it's almost as if we're skin to skin. My center rubs up against him, my clit receiving the perfect amount of friction to send me souring, as my orgasm rips through me. He deepens our kiss, swallowing my moans of pleasure. My legs are shaking, my breathing erratic. My clit is overly sensitive. But I want more. I need more.

I reach down to undo Alec's pants, but he stops me. "Not here," he murmurs against my lips. "Not where anyone can watch. You're mine," he growls. "Only mine."

Alec kneads my ass cheeks, digging his fingers into my flesh, as he lifts me off the wall. With me in his arms, he dips down, grabs my backpack, and carries me to the jeep. He sets me in the passenger seat then rounds the front of the vehicle. The entire drive home, I can't keep my hands off him. I run my fingers through his hair, palming his denim-covered crotch. I pepper kisses along his neck and stubbled jaw. More than once, I beg him to pull over so I can climb on top of him and fuck him, but he refuses, telling me he's going to take his time worshipping me.

When we finally get home, we rush through the condo and head straight to Alec's room. Georgia's door is closed, and since I saw Robert's car in the guest parking, I know he's in there with her.

The second Alec's door is closed, he's on me. He lifts and drops me onto the center of his king-sized bed. I part my thighs and smirk knowingly when his eyes land on my exposed panties.

"They're drenched," he growls, lifting his shirt over his head and dropping it to the floor. "I can see the wet spot where you came. Take your skirt off," he demands, unbuttoning and unzipping his jeans. With his pants like that, I can see his happy trail leading to his black briefs, and my first thought is how badly I want to lick down it, until I get to the top of his hard shaft and—

"Now," Alec says, shaking me from my own little fantasy.

I undo the buttons on my skirt and shimmy it down my thighs. My eyes stay trained on Alec, who's pushing his jeans and briefs down his muscular thighs. His hard length springs from its confines and bobs once against his stomach before it points straight out at me.

I lick my lips and squeeze my thighs together at the sight in front of me. I can't believe Alec is actually mine. Mine to kiss, mine to touch, mine to love.

All. Fucking. Mine.

He steps out of his clothes and saunters over to the bed. He crawls over to me and pushes my thighs back apart. I watch, unsure what he's going to do first. Will he kiss me? Fuck me? Touch me? The possibilities are endless, and the best part is, whatever we don't do right now, we can do later. Tomorrow, the next day, next week. We have our entire lives ahead of us to do whatever we want with each other.

He dips his face between my legs, and even though I can't see him, I can feel him run his nose along my damp center. And then, he inhales. Actually breathes in my scent, and I damn near orgasm on the spot.

"Fuck, Lex," he murmurs. I've never had a guy this up close and personal before. I should probably feel a little self-conscious, but with Alec, I feel nothing but comfortable.

He finally hooks my panties and pushes them down my legs. He places kisses along the insides of my thighs until he gets back to my center, and then he devours me—licking, sucking, nipping at my clit. He works me over until the most intense orgasm hits me like a tidal wave, wave after wave washing through me.

When I can't take it anymore, I pull him up and crash my mouth against his. He tastes like *me*, and hot damn, if that isn't a turn-on.

"I need you inside me, now," I whisper against his lips.

Alec leans over me and lifts my shirt over my head. Then reaching behind me, he unsnaps my bra and peels it off me, leaving me completely naked and under him. As he backs up, he trails kisses along my collarbone and down my chest, giving each of my breasts a kiss. He quickly licks my nipples before he sits back up. With him positioned between my thighs, he lifts my legs and hooks them over the crook of his arms. His palms land on either side of my face, forcing my legs to almost hit my chest.

With his mouth seared to mine, he enters me in one fluid motion, so deep my back arches off the bed. With our bodies flush against one another, he fucks me with abandon while devouring my mouth. With every swipe of his tongue, thrust of his pelvis, explosions of chills race up my spine. Butterflies swarm in my belly, and all too soon I'm losing myself to another orgasm. Alec's pace picks up, and then he quickly pulls out. He drops my legs and grips his shaft, stroking it tightly. His chest is rising and falling in quick succession, and his skin is glistening with sweat. His brown eyes watch with lust and fascination as cream-colored beads of cum spurt out and onto my belly and chest.

When there's nothing left for him to release, he drops his now-soft dick and sighs. "If I could, I would keep you just like this. In my bed, covered in my cum." My thighs squeeze at his dirty talk. This is a side of Alec I've never seen, and holy hell, if it doesn't make me want him that much more. What's that saying? *A gentleman in the streets, and a freak in the sheets...*

His gaze lifts and meets mine. "I've waited so fucking long for this, Lex." His fingers swipe up the sticky cum and he trails it up my torso and onto my breast. He swirls it around my hard nipple. "Now that you're mine, I hope you realize I'm never fucking letting you go."

My insides knot at his words, and I pull at his shoulders to bring his mouth to mine. "That's good, Alec, because I never want you to let me go."

ALEC

I wake up to the sound of Lexi softly snoring. Her body is draped across mine, and her head is nestled against my chest, with my arm wrapped around her. Since she was covered in my cum—something I was completely okay with but at the same time understood why she wasn't keen on going to sleep in that condition—we jumped into the shower together. Since I have the master bedroom, I also have an en suite bathroom. We stayed in the shower, kissing and washing each other, until the water ran cold, and then, after she dressed in a shirt of mine—and nothing else—we climbed back into my bed, where we made out like teenagers until we eventually passed out.

Now it's morning, and I wish we could stay in bed all day—hell, if it were up to me, we would stay in bed all fucking year. When Lexi is in my arms, the ache I feel over losing my dad hurts a little less. I know she can't replace him—nobody can. But for years, he was rooting for Lexi and me to get together. It's actually bittersweet when you think about it. I finally got the girl, but I lost my dad. He's not here to congratulate me, to be by my side when we one day get married—which, if I have it my way, will be sooner rather than later. He won't be here to hold his first grandchild when we have kids.

"What's going through that head of yours?" Lexi asks, running her fingers up my bare chest.

I glance down at her, and her brows furrow. "Alec," she says, scooting closer, so she's lying on me, our faces close. "Why are you crying?"

I blink rapidly and can feel what she's referring to. Thinking about my dad brought tears to my eyes. Not wanting to ruin our time together, I shake my head, but Lexi immediately shakes hers back.

"Don't tell me nothing. You have tears in your eyes." She lifts her hand and swipes at a tear that escaped. "Talk to me."

"I was thinking about my dad," I admit. "Of everything he'll miss. Everything I won't be able to share with him because he's gone."

Lexi nods in understanding, then climbs on top of me, so we're face-to-face. Her thighs grip my torso, and I can feel her heat against my skin. "I won't even pretend to know what you're going through," she says. "I've never lost anyone, except my bio mom, but really, I never had her, so I know it's not the same. But, I knew your dad, and he loved you so much, and I'd like to think he's in heaven watching over you."

"I hope you're right," I tell her, and then to lighten the mood, I add, "but hopefully not *all* the time." I waggle my brows and flex my hips, making Lexi giggle.

"You're such a perv." She swats at my chest playfully.

"And I'm *your* perv."

She snorts a laugh. "What are we doing today?"

"Is staying in bed an option?" I half-joke.

"I need to go to the beach later to get some surfing in. And I was thinking we could ask our parents to go to dinner so we could tell them about us. I don't want them to find out from anyone else but us."

I love that she wants to tell our families. It means she's serious about us, which is good since I'm dead fucking serious about her.

"That sounds good. I want to go by Lacie's to check on her. Want to go with me? We can grab a late breakfast afterward." I told Lexi about Lacie being pregnant and her plan to move closer to her sister. I offered to help her pack up, but she insisted on hiring a service.

"Of course."

After calling our parents and texting Georgia, we head out. As we're walking past Lexi's jeep to my truck, she stops and gasps. "What the hell?" Keyed into the driver side of her jeep, reads, *slut,* the line from the t continuing across the entire side of her vehicle. "Who would do this?"

"If I had to guess... Jason." I pull my phone out to call the police so we can file a report. "He's pissed you didn't want to date him and now he's being fucking immature."

Lexi's head whips around to look at me. "That asshole... When I see him, I'm going to kick his ass."

"You're not going anywhere near him. If he has the balls to do this shit, who knows what else he's capable of."

She growls, and I chuckle at how feisty my woman is.

After filing a report with the police, and then calling Lexi's insurance company to file a claim, we finally take off as planned.

Our first stop is to visit Lacie, who, for the most part, is doing okay. She tells us she's not ready to sell the firm she and my dad own, but she's going to delegate from her sister's. I tell her whatever she wants to do is up to her. My dad left me a nice-sized nest egg with his life insurance policy he had, but everything else was left to Lacie, which I completely agreed with. She was his wife, his partner.

She also tells us how happy she is that Lexi and I are finally together. "Your dad would be so happy for you," she says, tears filling her eyes. "He would always say you two were meant to be together."

"I wish he were here," I tell her, missing him so fucking much and hating that I'll never see him again.

"Me too," she agrees, rubbing her belly.

After talking with her for a little while longer, we say our goodbyes and then go to breakfast at Jumpin' Java in Larchmont.

It's Lexi's favorite coffee shop. We've both known the owner since we were little, so when we walk in holding hands, her face lights up. She runs around the counter and gives us both a hug. "I knew it! I knew one day you two would end up together. I'm so happy for you both."

After placing our order, Lexi suggests we take it to go, so we can walk around Larchmont since it's a nice day out. While we walk down the sidewalk, we hold hands and talk. Since my dad passed away, I've felt like I'm always one step away from losing my shit, but when I'm with Lexi, it feels like I can breathe. She chats away about the upcoming surfing competition and how excited she is, and I listen to her, enjoying her company.

"Dinner with our parents isn't until later," she says when we return to my truck. "If you want to drop me off at my jeep, I can take it to the beach to get some surfing in and meet you back at home later."

"I only have a little more time until I go back to work. I want to go." I also want to make sure Lexi doesn't confront Jason. I would hope he wouldn't do anything to her in person, but you never know what someone scorned is capable of, and I'm not about to risk Lexi going to the beach alone right now.

After stopping at the house so Lexi can grab her beach stuff, we head back out. When we get there, we find an area where there aren't too many people and spread out a blanket.

"I'll try not to be too long," she says, peeling her shirt off her.

"Take as long as you want." I pull her by the wetsuit that's hanging at her waist and tug her toward me. She falls gently onto her knees between my legs, and I pull her up so she's lying across the top of me.

Our mouths connect, and my tongue slips past her parted lips. I find her tongue, sucking on it until she moans into my mouth. She tastes like the mocha coffee she was drinking—sweet and fucking addictive. I slide my hands to her ass and squeeze her ass cheeks, pulling her closer, until she's on top of me and rubbing her warmth against my dick.

"Get a room!" someone yells, making Lexi groan and attempt to move off me. Not wanting her to go anywhere—and yeah, maybe I'm staking my claim—I grip her hips and pull her into my lap.

She squeals in shock, then laughs, but doesn't move. "Alec, I need to hit the waves."

"I need your mouth," I argue, fisting her ponytail and pulling her face to me for another kiss.

"So, this is why my sister called a family meeting," Lexi's brother, Max, says, dropping next to us with his camera in his hands.

"What are you doing here?" Lexi asks.

"Summer break," Max smarts.

Lexi glances around, and when her eyes land on a couple guys walking over, she laughs. "You're hanging out with Ricco?"

Max blushes. "I ran into him at the pier and he asked if I wanted to hang out." He shrugs.

"He's older than you, Max," she points out.

"Lex, be my sister, not my mom, please."

"I am being your sister," she says softly so the guys can't hear. "He's more experienced than you... Just be careful, okay?"

"Got it," Max says quickly.

"Well, looky here," Ricco says to Lexi. "I heard the rumors, but I wasn't sure if there was any truth to them." His eyes are filled with humor, so I know he isn't hating on us, but I also know the only person he could've heard the rumor from is Jason, since he's the one who saw us last night.

My eyes go to the owner of the *rumor*, Jason, who's standing back with his board in his hand, glaring at Lexi and me. Our eyes lock and I make it a point to wrap my arms around her waist, nuzzling my face into her neck and kissing her flesh.

"I want to say something to him," she whispers into my ear.

"Not worth it," I tell her. "Let the police handle it." The cops mentioned if we say anything to Jason, he can try to cover up his tracks, so the best thing is to not say a word and let them investigate.

"So, the rumors are true?" Ricco asks. "You two an item?"

"Yeah," Lexi says, giving my cheek a kiss and then standing. "We're a couple."

"About damn time," Max says, leaning over and patting me on the shoulder. "Welcome to the family, man."

"We're just dating," Lexi points out. "He's not family until we're married." She winks flirtatiously, then, grabbing her board, jogs down the beach.

"Semantics!" I call after her.

Max laughs. "Marriage, huh? Just make sure you ask Dad's permission first. You know how he is about his little girls."

Shit... I didn't think about that. I'm dating Tristan Scott's daughter. I'm going to be having dinner with him, and he's going to take one look at us and know I'm sleeping with her. Fuck! Maybe we can get married today, before we meet them for dinner. Then I can say I've made an honest woman out of her...

"You okay?" Max asks with humor in his voice. "You're looking a little pale."

"Maybe I should go pick up a ring now," I suggest, freaking the hell out.

Max cracks up laughing. "I'm pretty sure Dad knows Lexi isn't a virgin."

I swing my head around and glare at him. No guy wants to be reminded his woman has been with anyone before him. Of course, this only makes Max laugh even louder.

"Okay, my bad." He puts his hands up. "But seriously, we've all been waiting for you two to come to your senses for years. He's not going to be shocked that you're together. Just treat her right and you won't have any problems... with any of us."

"Got it."

I look out at the ocean just in time to see Lexi riding a rather large wave, and Jason sidling up to her. I don't know shit about surfing, but I do know from listening and watching Lexi, encroaching on someone's wave is a huge fucking no.

He comes so close, their boards almost touch, and Lexi ends up wiping out.

"What the hell," Max says, removing the camera from his face.

"He has a thing for your sister," I explain, "and he's pissed he didn't get her." I don't mention he's also most likely the guy who keyed her car, since she hasn't told her parents yet. She's planning to tell them about it tonight at dinner.

I stand, wanting to make sure Lexi is okay. She pops up and grabs her board. Even from up here, I can see the pissed off expression on her face. She is one sexy fucking feisty woman. She paddles to shore, following Jason, and once they're both out of the water, she's stomping toward him, yelling.

I can tell by the way Jason is smirking he got exactly what he wanted: Lexi's attention. The guy seriously rubs me the wrong fucking way.

"I apologized for things not working out between us," she says. "We went on one freaking date! One! For you to call me names and key my jeep is bullshit!" So much for not confronting him... "But fucking with me in the water is taking this shit too far. You don't. Fuck. With someone. In the water!"

"What do you mean he keyed your car?" Max asks.

"Someone keyed slut into the side of my jeep... hours after Jason called me a tease because I chose to date Alec instead of him."

"You did what?" Max says, stepping up to Jason, who still has a shit-eating smirk plastered on his face. "What the fuck is wrong with you?"

"You have no proof of that," Jason says with a shrug. "Maybe I'm not the only guy your sister was leading on. Who knows how many guys she's letting dick her."

Max punches Jason square in the face. "Don't you ever talk about my sister like that."

Jason stumbles back slightly, and once he gets his footing, steps toward Max.

"You need to get the fuck out of here," I tell Jason, stepping between Jason and Max. "You didn't get the girl, deal with it like a man, not a little bitch."

"Whatever you say," he says through a laugh, already walking away.

"I can't believe him." Lexi huffs.

"Forget him," I tell her. "He's gone now. Go surf and show me how you're going to win this competition." I pull her toward me and kiss her. At first, she's wound up tight, but eventually she softens into the kiss.

"Okay," she murmurs against my lips. "Sorry I let it slip about him keying my jeep."

"Don't worry about it. Just promise me you'll stay away from him." My request isn't coming from a jealous boyfriend, but from someone worried about what that asshole is capable of. I could tell by the smug look on his face he didn't give a shit about being called out or caught.

"I will," she says. "I promise."

For the next few hours, I watch Lexi surf. She's amazing out there. Completely in her element. Eventually Max and Ricco decide to head out, saying they're going to grab a coffee.

While I wait for her, I look up jewelry stores on my phone. I wasn't kidding when I said I'm planning to make her my wife sooner rather than later. I know without a doubt she's the one for me.

While I'm scrolling through rings, my phone goes off with a text.

Chase: I crashed on the couch after my shift. Woke up and realized all my shit was gone. Luckily Georgia was here to tell me you moved it all into Lexi's room. Thanks, man. And please tell Lexi thanks.

Me: It's hardly a hardship having Lexi in my room.

Chase: I figured as much. But still... thanks.

Me: We're going to dinner at the Scotts' tonight. Wanna join?

Chase: Thanks, but I'm going to crash. Shift tomorrow. You know, the job you haven't been to in weeks...

His text reminds me that I go back to work soon. I needed the time off to deal with my father's death. I knew in the state of mind I was in, I wouldn't be of any use to anyone at the fire station, especially if there was an emergency. But now, I'm looking forward to going back to work. I enjoy my job.

Me: Yeah, yeah... I know you miss me, sweetie pie. Don't worry, I'll be back next week.

Chase: Oh, thank God, pookie bear.

Me: If you change your mind, just let me know.

Chase: Thanks.

"You ready to go?" Lexi asks, standing in front of me. She's already unzipped her wetsuit and is pulling it down her toned body, exposing her tiny yellow string bikini she's wearing underneath. Her hair is up in a messy bun, and droplets of water are dripping down her neck and disappearing into the swell of her breasts. Her belly button is sporting a tiny navel ring, and on the curve of her hip is her moniker—a multi-colored silhouette of a woman holding a surfboard.

"What?" She glances down at herself.

"Come here." I grab her hand and pull her down to me. My mouth closes over hers for a hard kiss. "I can't keep my eyes and mouth and hands off you." I drag my hands down to the globes of her perfect ass. "You smell like the ocean," I murmur, kissing her again. Lexi laughs—it's light and carefree and it does crazy shit to my insides.

"We're really doing this, aren't we?" she asks, her ocean-blue eyes sparkling with happiness. I love that I'm the reason for her happiness—that *we're* the reason for her happiness.

"If I have it my way, for the rest of our lives."

After we're packed up, we head up the beach toward her jeep. We're about halfway there when Lexi stops and says, "Do we have any waters left in the cooler?"

"Yeah," I say, confused. It's not that long of a walk to her vehicle. Does she really need to stop and take a drink break?

She grabs a couple waters out of the cooler, then grabs the bowl of fruit we didn't finish. She drops her board where it is and runs toward the pier, yelling that she'll be right back.

Unsure where the hell she's going, I leave the cooler and her beach bag next to her board and follow after her. When she arrives under the pier, there are several tents popped up in the shade. This is common in LA, especially in the parks and on the beaches. Homeless folks sleep in tents anywhere they can pitch one up.

Lexi stops at a particular blue one and says, "Aiden, it's Lexi."

A second later, a tall man steps out of his tent. He looks to be in his late teens, maybe early twenties, dressed in a pair of raggedy jeans and a holey shirt. His long hair is on the greasy side and his face is covered in facial hair. He's wearing a pair of bright green glasses that look like something a child would wear. With a bright smile on his face, he removes the glasses, that is until his eyes land on me, then he immediately puts them back on.

"Lexi, someone is here," he says. "I don't know him, Lexi."

Lexi glances back at me, before turning her attention back to Aiden. "It's okay. That's Alec. He's my boyfriend."

Aiden's fists clench at his sides. "Boyfriends are bad, Lexi. My mom's boyfriend was bad." He grabs Lexi and pulls her behind him. "You go away, Lexi's boyfriend. You are bad."

"No, Aiden. Alec isn't bad. I promise," Lexi says.

"Boyfriends are bad," he repeats. It's clear there's something going on with this guy, but Lexi isn't fazed, which tells me she knows this guy on a deeper level.

"Aiden," she says calmly. "Why was your mom's boyfriend bad?"

"He hurt us," he tells her matter-of-factly. "He yelled at us and he hit us."

"Oh, Aiden, I'm so sorry," she says. "You're right. Your mom's boyfriend was bad, but not all boyfriends are bad. Alec doesn't yell or hurt me, and he's a firefighter. He saves people. He's a good guy."

"Like Fireman Sam?" Aiden asks.

"I don't know who Fireman Sam is," Lexi says honestly, but I know who he is.

"He was a cartoon fireman on YouTube," I tell her.

"He's my favorite hero," Aiden tells her. "But he isn't wearing his fire suit."

"No, he only wears it when he goes to work. I brought you some stuff," Lexi tells him, holding up the bag she placed the food and drinks into.

Aiden looks into the bag and smiles softly at Lexi. Then he pulls her into a tight hug. "Thank you, Lexi," he says. "I like water and fruit. But I like tacos more."

"I know," she replies with a laugh. "But you have to eat food that's good for you too. Not just tacos."

"But I like tacos," he argues.

"I know you do," she says. "I have to get going, but I'll see you soon, okay?"

"Okay! Bye, Lexi, and bye, Lexi's fireman boyfriend."

When we get back to the jeep, Lexi says, "Aiden is autistic... Well, I think he is. I searched his mannerisms on Google and that's what popped up. I don't know much about him except that he loves drawing and he's homeless. He's been living in that tent for the last several months. I always give him food and drinks when I come to the beach."

"Have you thought about telling someone?"

"Who? The police? No way." She shakes her head. "They'll cite him, or worse, arrest him. You saw how he reacted to you. It took months before he warmed up to me. What do you think would happen if the police approached him? No. He's better off where he is. At least he's left alone."

On the ride home, we're both silent, and I can't stop thinking about Aiden. There has to be something we can do to help him. He's not just homeless... There's clearly something more to him, like Lexi said. I make a mental note to ask the guys at work if there's anything in LA that helps or supports homeless people who have special needs.

"Want to shower with me?" Lexi asks once we're home.

I watch as she makes a show of untying the strings that hold her bikini top together and dropping it to the ground, exposing her perfect tits. Next, she pulls the strings on her bottoms and they fall to the floor, leaving her completely naked. I take a moment to take her in: her milky skin that doesn't match how often she's at the beach. Since her dad is naturally tanned, I would bet she gets her creamy complexion from her biological mom, but she never talks about her.

Her blond hair is down in waves. I can remember the day she dyed it. She said she needed a change, and after Georgia talked her out of getting a tattoo—which was a damn good thing since she wasn't eighteen yet—she showed up with her hair dyed blond. I loved Lexi as a brunette, but something about the blond fit her personality better. It was wilder, like her.

My eyes cut to her toned abs and thighs. She doesn't work out at the gym, but she surfs daily, which keeps her in shape. She's tiny, maybe five-foot-four, compared to my six-foot-three self, but for such a little thing, she's all badass. And I love how low-maintenance she is. She prefers to be in a bathing suit and flip-flops. And when she's not at the beach, you can find her in cutoff jean shorts, a tank top, and Vans. What you see is what you get, and I love that about her.

"Alec," she says, taking me out of my thoughts. "Shower?"

Not needing to be asked again, I cut across the room, shedding my shirt along the way, and lift her into my arms. When we get inside the bathroom, I slam the door closed, unsure if my bedroom door is shut, and set her on the counter next to the sink. I part her legs and step between them. She wraps her arms around my neck and her fingers thread through the strands of my hair.

"Fuck, Lex. You're so damn perfect." I take her breast into my hand and wrap my lips around the rosy pink nipple. As I suck on the hardened peak, her back arches and she pushes her chest forward, silently demanding more.

I feel like the luckiest guy in the world that I get to be with Lexi. I hate that we wasted so much time trying to ignore what was right in front of us, but there's nothing we can do about the past. All I can do is try like hell to make up for the lost time, and right now my plan to do that is by making love to her.

Spreading her thighs farther apart, I push a finger inside her. She's already wet, so I don't waste any time pushing another inside. I fingerfuck her until I know she's more than ready, kissing her all over—her neck, her breasts, her lips—and then I pull her to the edge of the vanity.

With my dick as hard as a steel rod, I guide myself into her warmth. Our eyes lock briefly before hers roll back in pleasure. I will never get tired of being the one who brings her pleasure.

Her legs wrap around my waist, and I fuck her slow and deep, enjoying how hot and tight she is. My thumb finds her clit, and I massage circles, working her up until she's screaming out her release.

"Fuck me harder," she demands. "Faster."

Grabbing her thighs, I tug her closer and pick up my pace, doing exactly what she wants. Her cunt clenches around me and she comes again all over my dick. Remembering I'm not wearing a condom, I pull out at the last second and am about to stroke myself, when Lexi drops to the ground and grabs my dick, taking over. Her warm mouth covers the swollen head, and, knowing she's tasting not only me but her own juices, I lose my shit, coming straight down her throat.

"Jesus Christ," I breathe through heavy pants. She looks up at me through her lashes and grins around my dick. Then, the little minx licks the excess cum off my flesh before she stands and runs her tongue along her lips.

"Shower?" she asks, quirking a single brow.

"Shower," I agree.

LEXI

"You ready to go?" Georgia asks, stepping into our room. I had assumed Alec and I would be driving together to my parents' place for dinner, but instead he told me he needed to meet me there because he had a couple errands to run.

"Yeah." I lean over the dresser and apply a thin coat of lip gloss. "Is Robert coming?" I ask, locking eyes with her in the mirror.

"Maybe, he's still at work." Georgia plasters a smile on her face, which has me turning around, concerned.

"Everything good with you two?"

"Yeah..."

"Don't do that." I walk over to her. "We don't lie to each other, ever."

Georgia nods. "I know. I'm sorry. This is all just new to me. I think everything is good, but I don't have anything to compare it to."

"What has you questioning it?"

Georgia's cheeks turn a light pink. "He, umm... He wants to have sex, and I told him I'm a virgin, and..."

"And he's respecting that, right?" I straighten my spine. I'll be damned if that guy thinks he can bully my sister into doing anything she's not ready to do. "He's not pressuring you?"

"Yeah, no." She shakes her head. "But when I told him I wasn't ready, he kind of looked... disappointed."

"Oh well." My voice rises in annoyance. "You've only been together for a short minute. He can wait as long as you make him, or he can skip rocks."

"You and Alec have had sex," she points out. Then, quickly, she adds, "I'm not judging."

"I know you're not." I take her hand in mine. "You're right. Alec and I made the decision to be together and went from zero to eighty. If he has it his way we'll be married by the end of the week," I joke—kind of. The truth is, I actually believe if I agreed, he would marry me tomorrow. Between the years we wasted not giving into our feelings and him losing his dad, Alec has no desire to waste a second of precious time.

Georgia laughs. "I'm glad you guys are finally together. I just don't know if or when the right time to have sex is. I feel like I've waited this long... Do I just do it and get it over with? Or do I wait for a sign? And if so, what sign am I waiting for? Is there ever a perfect moment to lose your virginity, except for on your wedding night?"

This time it's my turn to laugh. "I love you so much." I pull her into a hug. "As you know I lost mine our senior year. I wish I had waited for Alec, but I never thought we would actually get a chance to be together. I obviously can't change anything, so there's no point in dwelling over it. I don't think there's ever a perfect time, but I can tell you that if I could do it over again, I would've at least made sure I loved the guy I was giving my virginity to. Not because the act is so sacred or whatever, but because once I was with Alec, a man I love, it made it so much better. Every kiss and touch is so much more meaningful. Sex with Alec isn't just sex. We make love. He worships me, makes sure I'm taken care of. So, I guess to answer your question, make sure you love Robert."

Georgia nods. "Thank you, Lex." She hugs me. "He's not going to be thrilled, but I'm going to wait."

"And if he doesn't respect that," I say, pulling back and looking into my sister's bright green eyes. "Then dump his ass." She laughs softly. "I mean it. A man who cares about you will wait until you're ready. You're fucking beautiful, Georgia. Robert might be your first real boyfriend, but that's only because you chose not to date until now. Trust me when I tell you, you can get any damn guy you want."

Georgia rolls her eyes. "Whatever, Lex, let's go."

When we walk outside, Georgia sees the damage to my vehicle. "I can't believe Jason did that," she says.

"I know, we have no proof, but I would bet it was him." I tell her what happened at the beach earlier, everything Jason said to me, and how Max punched him.

"Good," she says, her nose scrunching up. "What a loser."

We take Georgia's truck to our parents' place, and when we arrive, I see Alec's truck already in the driveway, along with Mason's BMW.

We walk into the house and the first person I see is Alec. He's wearing a Station 115 shirt that's taut across his chest and a matching hat. He's talking and laughing with my dad, but when he hears the front door close, he stops and turns. Our gazes collide and my stomach does a small flip-flop. We're actually doing this. Alec and I are together.

Without thinking about anyone else who might be watching us, I cut across the room, straight to Alec. It's only been a few hours since I've last seen him, kissed him, but I already miss him. Our mouths crash against each other, as he takes me into his arms.

"I think we were supposed to tell everyone first," he murmurs against my lips when we break our kiss.

It takes me a second, but once I process what he's just said, I glance around the room and find everyone is watching us. My mom and Alec's mom, Mila, both have huge grins on their faces. My dad's face is a mixture of a smile and a glower. My brother and Georgia are both laughing, and Mason is sporting a knowing smirk.

"Well, I guess you all know now." I shrug, feeling a slight blush upon my cheeks.

"We do," Mom says matter-of-factly. "And we're very happy for you both."

She wraps her arms around me, and I sigh into her warm embrace. I might come across like I do whatever I want, but I still care about what my family thinks. Their opinion matters to me because they matter to me.

"Dad, you too?" I ask, just to make sure.

"As much as I hate the idea of my little girls growing up, I know it's inevitable, and it makes me feel a little better to know you're with a man who loves you and will support and take care of you." Dad kisses my cheek. "I love you, Lex."

"Thank you. I love you too, Dad."

"THEY TOOK IT WELL," I TELL ALEC, RUNNING MY HAND up his naked chest. We're lying in bed and have just finished making love for the second time. After we got home from dinner with our parents, we beelined straight to his room and to bed, where we've spent the last couple hours.

"Of course they did." He places a kiss to my temple. "We were apparently the only people who weren't on board with us."

"Hey, I was on board with us." I poke him in the chest and then roll over onto my elbows. "I just didn't think you were, and then once I knew you were, I was afraid you would change your mind, or if we did this and it didn't work out, I would lose you...

I'm still worried about that last one."

Alec pulls me on top of him. "I love you, Lex, and I can't say what the future holds because anything can happen." He swallows thickly, and I know he's thinking about his dad. "But as long as I'm alive and you're willing to let me love you, I'm going to spend every day loving you."

Since we're both still naked, I reach behind me and take his hard length into my hand, guiding it inside me. I sigh once I'm completely seated and our bodies are connected in the most intimate way. Leaning forward, I take Alec's face into my hands and whisper against his lips, "And I'm going to spend every day loving you back."

Fifteen

LEXI

"That was the perfect fucking air wave," Shane says, dropping onto the sand next to me. "If you hit the waves at the comp like you've been doing, I wouldn't be surprised if you take the entire thing. Your life will be changed. Tours, endorsements..."

"That would be awesome," I admit, grabbing a bottled water, twisting the top off, and taking a large gulp. I let Shane's words bump around in my head for a few minutes. For as far as I can remember my world has revolved around art and surfing, but up until now, they felt like hobbies. My parents always tell me how creative I am, and my friends comment on how good of a surfer I am, but none of that means anything if I can't create a future with them. But Shane is right, if I win this competition, I can make a career out of it.

My phone pings from somewhere, and I grab my bag to find

it. It's Alec asking where I am. I left him sleeping in bed to get some surfing in. He goes back to work in a few days and can use the sleep. Even though he seems happier with us being together, I know he's still having trouble sleeping at night. He misses his dad and his heart is still broken. I imagine it will be for a long time.

Just as I'm about to text him back, droplets of water hit the phone, making me shove it back in my bag. "Hey!" I exclaim, glancing up. With the sun shining, it takes a second for my eyes to adjust, but once they do, I find Jason standing above me.

"You're soaking my stuff," I tell him, pushing his thighs so he stumbles back.

"Where's your boyfriend?" He runs his fingers through his shaggy blond hair, flinging water all over me like a wet dog.

"Go away, Jason," I say, ignoring his question and pulling my phone back out so I can return Alec's text. I let him know I'm at the beach and will be home soon.

"I was hoping we can talk," he says as I stand, ready to leave.

"There's nothing to talk about."

"Look, I was being a dick." He shrugs a shoulder and scrubs his hand along his scruff. "I shouldn't have gotten that worked up over you and that pretty boy. Everyone knows you don't do serious. Pretty Boy will come and go, and I don't want to lose you in my life." Oh my God! Did he just admit to keying my car, and is acting like it's not a big deal? What the hell is wrong with this guy?

My phone goes off with another text from Alec: **I have the day planned. Meet me at home when you're done.**

I grab my towel from my bag and then throw my phone into it. "His name is Alec, and he isn't going anywhere," I tell Jason, looking him dead in the eyes so he knows I'm serious. "I love him, and it's serious. As for you and me... our friendship is over. Friends don't do the shit you did to me."

"Are you fucking serious?" he spits, stepping closer to me.

"You heard her," Shane says, popping up and stepping in front of me. "What you did wasn't cool, man. Now you gotta deal with the fallout. Walk away."

Jason's nostrils flare, and his fists tighten at his sides, but he does as Shane says and walks away.

"I can't believe him," I say once Jason is gone. "Thank you."

"It's all good," Shane says. "I heard about what happened, and he's way fucking wrong."

"Yeah, just sucks I have to see him here all the time now." Maybe I need to consider finding another surfing spot... "I'm going to head out," I tell him, giving him a hug. "I'll see you later."

On the way to my jeep, I spot Aiden sitting in the sand next to his tent. Remembering I have some extra bottles of water, I head over to give them to him. It's hot out and I bet he can use the fresh, cold water.

"Hi, Aiden. How are you?"

"Hi, Lexi," he says with a smile, his bright green glasses on his face. "I'm okay. I found some crabs. Look." He points to a small bucket with two crabs in it.

"Wow, how cool. Are you going to keep them?"

"No." He shakes his head. "I'm drawing them. See?" In his sketchpad is a drawing of the bucket and two crabs. "I won't hurt them, Lexi. I will let them go."

"That's really good," I say, pointing to the sketchpad.

"Thank you. Wanna see more pictures?"

"Sure." I sit next to him and take the pad from him.

"Be careful. Are your hands clean?" he asks, his head turning toward me.

"They're clean," I promise.

"Okay, good." He sighs, then removes his glasses and clasps them onto the front of his shirt. I noticed a while ago he only removes them when it's just us. A few times that I've been with my friends, he would say hello, but he wouldn't remove his glasses. My guess is he uses them as protection, only removing them when he feels comfortable.

I flip through the pages of his book, in awe of how talented Aiden is. I've seen his drawings before, but every time I see new ones, I'm amazed by just how good he is. It's also obvious he sees everything around him. There are several new drawings of people surfing and swimming. A family having a picnic. There are a few of people kissing and one that looks like two people having sex. I wonder if Aiden knows what he's drawing. If he knows what sex is.

"Aiden, what's this?" I ask, pointing to the drawing of the couple on top of each other.

"That's a man and a woman loving each other," he states matter-of-factly.

"Do you see this a lot on the beach?"

"Yes. I thought the man was hurting the woman, but when I tried to save the woman, they yelled at me and said they love each other."

I stifle my laugh, imagining poor Aiden hearing some woman getting fucked and screaming and him thinking she was being hurt. He's too innocent and sweet for his own good.

"These are really good," I tell him, handing him back his book. I wish there were something I could do to help him, but I have no clue where to even start, and I'm scared if I speak to the wrong people, I could do more harm than good.

"Thank you, Lexi," he responds, beaming with pride.

"I have some water for you." I grab the bottles of water from my bag and hand them to him. "Are you hungry?"

"I had breakfast," he says honestly. "Brian gave me extra bagels."

Brian is the owner of the breakfast restaurant on the pier. Instead of throwing out the food from the day before, he puts it out for the homeless to take.

"Okay, good. Then I'll see you soon." I always say soon instead of later or tomorrow. I made that mistake once and Aiden accused me of lying because I didn't return later that day or the next.

Fifteen minutes later, I'm stepping through the door as Georgia is walking down the hall with her backpack slung over her shoulder. It's crazy to think in a couple months she'll be graduating from college. I wish I had the motivation for school she does, but if all goes well, I'll win the Vans Surf Classic and be on my way to a career in surfing, which will hopefully open other doors of opportunity. I still plan to finish school, especially since it's so important to my parents, but at least I'll be able to say I've created a future for myself.

She doesn't see me walking up, since she's staring down at her cell phone with a frown marring her face. "Hey," I say to get her attention. Her head pops up and she gives me a strained smile. "What's wrong?"

"I don't know. Hilda sent another email requesting a meeting with me." Hilda is Georgia's biological father's mother—her biological grandmother. Her bio dad died when she was little and she's never had any contact with his family. Our mom is a lot like our dad, tightlipped about their past. I know they're that way to protect us, but we're not babies anymore and deserve to know the truth, even if it's hurt us.

"Have you told Mom?"

Georgia scoffs. "Yeah, right. She'll freak out, probably beg me to delete my email address."

"Maybe, or maybe she'll support you and be there for you. I think she would want to know, and if she finds out from someone other than you, she's going to be hurt. What if Hilda contacts her because you won't respond?"

"Since when did you get so wise?" Georgia jokes. "You're right, I'm going to set up a meeting with her."

"And you're going to tell Mom?"

"Not until I know what's going on. I don't want to upset her.

Every time her past gets brought up I can see the pain in her face. I'm not putting her through that if I don't have to. If I feel like I need to tell her, then I will."

"Okay, if you need me, I'm here."

"I know. Thank you. I better get going to class before I'm late. I'll see you later."

I head back to Alec's room and find him in the bathroom brushing his teeth. He's dressed in a pair of jeans that hug his perfect ass and is shirtless, his back glistening with tiny droplets of water from his shower. He glances up at me and smiles, and my insides turn to mush.

"I'm going to take a quick shower," I tell him, stripping out of my clothes and sliding into the shower. When I get out, I towel dry my hair, brush my teeth, and put on deodorant. Unsure of where we're going, I wrap my towel around my body and go in search of Alec to find out how I should dress. When I don't find him in the room, I venture out to the living room, only to find him standing next to Chase and some woman.

Shit, I didn't think about him being home. And who's that woman?

At the sight of my towel-clad body, Alec's eyes burn with lust, while Chase glances at me with laughter in his own. The woman next to Chase glares.

"Sorry," I say, quickly backing up. "I wasn't sure where we're going, how I should dress."

"I can show you," Alec says, walking toward me like a lion stalking his prey.

"Oh no!" I exclaim. "You showing me will lead to us never leaving." I turn and race down the hall with Alec following after. I swing open my bedroom door and am about to shut it on Alec, when he slips inside at the last second, slamming it closed behind him.

Gripping my hips, he pushes me against the wall and pulls the knot holding my towel, so it falls to the ground, pooling around my feet. "Fuck, Lex," he growls, capturing my mouth with his own. Heat floods through my veins, warming my entire body. Our kiss deepens, as Alec lifts me up. My legs wrap around his waist and my back hits the wall with a thud. Before my brain can even compute what's happening, his pants are undone and he's entering me. With his mouth devouring mine, he fucks me against the wall.

Every time we're intimate, it's as if the world around us disappears. I hope it's always like this. This hot, this intense, this emotion and lust filled. I rag on my parents for them being all over each other all the time, but now I get it. When you feel the way my parents feel about each other, the way I feel about Alec, all you want to do is show them. It's as if words aren't enough. You can try to explain it, but the depth of your feelings is lost in translation and the only way to completely make it clear is through your actions. Every kiss, every touch, every time we make love, I hope it conveys every emotion I'm feeling.

My body trembles as a mind-blowing orgasm slams into me, taking Alec right along with me. We continue to kiss through our orgasms, until he goes soft inside me, until I can feel his cum leaking out of me and dripping down my leg, and then it hits me...

"You came in me."

Alec's eyes widen and he pulls out, dropping me to the ground. "Shit, sorry, Lex." He winces. "We probably should've had a talk about protection. I've been so consumed with you..."

"Same," I agree. "I'm on the pill, but I'm a slacker about it. I haven't had sex in a while, so..."

Alec grins, liking the fact my sex life has been lacking.

I roll my eyes. "I'll make it a point to be more consistent."

He shrugs a single shoulder. "Worst-case scenario you end up pregnant."

"And my dad kills you," I half-joke, bending and grabbing my towel to wipe myself.

"We'll be married soon," he volleys. "And life is short. If we start a family sooner rather than later, would it be the worst thing?" His lips curve down into a frown. "I meant it when I said I don't want to waste a single day I have with you."

My heart cracks at his words, knowing they're stemming from his dad passing away. "And I want that too," I tell him, dropping the towel and framing his face, "but we're also young and I don't want to rush into anything. I'm hoping to pick up a surfing contract, and..."

"And getting pregnant and surfing don't exactly go hand-in-hand," he finishes.

"No, they don't. But surfing contracts are usually short-term." Which makes me realize the hole in my plan. After the few years of traveling and surfing, what then? I'll be right back to where I started.

"Lex, you okay?" Alec lifts my chin so I'm looking at him. "We don't have to get—"

"It's not that," I say, cutting him off. "I just feel like every time I think I've got my future planned out, something I'm missing pops out and blocks my path."

Alec shakes his head. "That's the beautiful thing about life, Lex. You don't have to pick a path and follow it. You don't have to know your future. Anything can happen at any time, so all you have to do is live and love. Enjoy the beauty in the moment. That's what I'm doing." He kisses the corner of my mouth. "I'm enjoying the beauty in us and finally finding our way to each other. And if you want to talk paths, I think that's a pretty fucking awesome path."

"It's easy for you to say that when you have a career. You're this amazing firefighter who keeps getting promotion after promotion. And if you hadn't chosen to be a firefighter, you could've easily had a career in the UFC. I'm a half-ass college student who surfs and graffitis walls."

"No, Lexi, you're a talented artist and a badass surfer who is only twenty-one and still finding her place in the world, and there's nothing wrong with that. Life isn't a race and in the end we all end up in the same place," Alec says, his jaw clenching. "Dead."

"Alec," I breathe, hating that our hot love-making has turned to this.

"It's the truth. My dad busted his ass to build up his business. He threw his marriage away and didn't find love until years later. Now he's gone and all that's left of him is his pregnant widowed wife and his son who misses the hell out of him." Tears glisten in his eyes. "Don't worry about what you think you should be doing. Focus on what you want to be doing, okay? Live your life and live it for you."

"Okay," I agree. "But what happens if I do win and get a contract? It would mean traveling..."

Alec smiles softly. "Then you travel. You see the world. When I can, I'll join you, and when I can't, I'll be right here waiting for you." He presses his lips to mine, and I sigh into the kiss.

"Nothing is going to keep us apart," he promises once we separate. "Let's get going. I had a plan for today and you're putting us behind schedule."

"Me?" I laugh. "You're the one who attacked me!"

"Because you walked out in a towel."

"I didn't know what to wear."

Alec chuckles. "How about something that covers your body, so I can control myself long enough to get us to our destination."

"Fine, I'll get dressed." I saunter around him, purposely brushing against his body.

"I'll wait for you outside," he groans.

I bark out a laugh as he darts out of the room, leaving me alone to get dressed.

ALEC

"Where are we going?" Lexi asks once we're in my truck.

I glance over at her and take in how beautiful she looks. Today, in the place of her usual cutoffs and tank, she's sporting a T-shirt and skinny jeans that of course make her look sexy as hell. Her gray shirt, which has Billabong written in big letters across the front, hangs off her shoulder, revealing her bright pink bra strap, and her ripped jeans show more of her flesh than they actually cover, and what is covered is plastered to her like a second skin. Instead of her signature flip-flops, she's sporting a pair of white Vans. And to top her look off, because all of that isn't sexy enough—insert eye-roll—her blond hair is down in messy waves and she's wearing my Station 115 hat that she stole.

Lexi in my hat is enough to make me want to pull the truck over, drag her into my lap, and fuck her while she's wearing nothing but my hat.

"Earth to Alec," she says, knocking me from my fantasies.

"Sorry." I clear my throat. "I was picturing you riding me in nothing but that hat."

She snort-laughs then her lips curl into a gorgeous grin. "In nothing but your hat, huh? We can *definitely* make that fantasy come true," she says, leaning over like she's about to make it *literally* come true right now.

When she reaches for her seat belt, I cover her hand with mine. "Not now."

Her brows hit her forehead. "Wow, already turning me down for sex. Does this mean the honeymoon period of our relationship is over?" She quirks her head to the side and pouts.

"No," I tell her, laughing at how adorable she is. "But I want to take you out, and if you're going to ride me in nothing but my hat, I would rather it be in our bed where I can enjoy it completely."

"Our bed?"

Huh? *Oh...* "Yeah, *our* bed... You can keep pretending you're sharing a room with your sister, but you've yet to actually sleep in there. My bed is now ours."

Lexi surprisingly doesn't argue, instead sitting back and bringing her knees to her chest.

"So, where are you taking me?"

"On a date."

She whips her head around and smiles. "A date?"

"Are you a parrot today?" I joke.

"A parrot?"

I laugh. "You keep repeating everything I say in the form of a question."

She rolls her eyes. "Whatever. Tell me more about this date."

"It's a surprise." I put my truck in drive and pull out.

"If I guess correctly, will you tell me if I'm right?"

"Sure." There's no way she's guessing.

"Lunch and a movie."

I give her a quick side-eye before focusing back on the road. "Give me some credit. It's our first official date. I'm not that cliché."

"Well, I've never been on a date before," she says, shocking the hell out of me.

"You've never been out with a guy?"

"Nope. I've only had a few boyfriends. They were either too young to drive, or once we were old enough, we just hung out." She shrugs. "Most guys don't want to actually date... They just want to hook up."

I want to argue, but she isn't lying. I can't even remember the last time I took a woman out on a date. We live in a world where people text more than talk, and hook up more than hang out. And when they do hang out, they spend more time taking pictures and going on social media than actually getting to know the person they're with.

That isn't happening with Lexi. She's my forever, which means we have to establish a solid foundation. Something Mason said when I went over to Tristan's to talk to him about wanting to ask

Lexi to marry me.

My thoughts go back to that awkward conversation...

I knock on the Scotts' door and Tristan answers. "Alec, how are you? Come in."

He opens the door wider and I step inside. "I'm good. I was wondering if we could talk."

"Sure," he says.

I follow him back to his home office-gym-man cave Charlie had made for him. It consists of a desk in one corner and a treadmill and workout bench in another. On the wall between two windows hangs a ridiculously huge flat screen television, and facing the television are two comfy-looking leather couches—one of which is currently occupied by Mason, who is lounging on it with his feet on the wood coffee table and his phone in his hand.

When he hears us enter, he looks up and smiles.

"Son." He drops his feet to the ground and stands. "How are you?" he asks, enveloping me in a hug.

"Alec is here to talk to me," Tristan says, trying and failing to contain his laughter.

"Oh yeah?" Mason quirks a brow at Tristan.

They both sit next to each other, crossing their arms over their chests and bringing their ankles up to their knees at the same time.

Fuck, can these two have any more of a bromance?

"So, what's up?" Tristan asks. "First." He raises his hand. "How are you holding up?"

So, we're going to do small talk first... well, okay then. *"I'm hanging* in there," I tell them honestly. "I miss my dad like crazy. We used to talk in the morning when I would get off my shift, while I was driving home. Sometimes I go to dial his number and it hits me all over again that he's gone."

Mason nods and leans forward, dropping his elbows onto the tops of his thighs. "I can't replace your dad, nor would I ever try to, but if you ever need to dial a number to talk, I'm here."

"I know," I tell him. "And it means everything to me."

"You have a lot of people who love you," Mason says. "You'll get through this."

And cue my perfect transition... "That's actually what I wanted to talk to Tristan about."

Mason and Tristan both laugh. Of course these assholes aren't going to make this easy for me.

"Go on," Tristan prompts.

Fuck it, I might as well just come out and say it... "I'm in love with your daughter."

"Which one?" Tristan asks. Fucker knows damn well which one.

"Lexi."

"Yes!" Mason fist pumps. "You owe me a hundred bucks."

Huh?

"Damn it!" Tristan says, grabbing his wallet from his back pocket and pulling a bill out, smacking it on the table. "I thought for sure you would wait until after Lexi graduated."

"I knew you wouldn't wait that long. At the rate Lexi's going, she could be in school forever," Mason says, swiping the bill up and stuffing it into his front pocket. "I do have to give you credit, though. You waited longer than your mom thought. She predicted you would give in once Lexi graduated from high school."

"What the hell... Did you all seriously bet on when Lexi and I would get together?"

"I didn't," a feminine voice says. I glance back and see Charlie standing in the doorway. When the hell did she get here?

"Oh, don't play innocent," Mason says. "The only reason you didn't bet was because you didn't think he would get the guts to admit his feelings."

"Really?" I ask, slightly offended, but also, not, because it did take me a long ass time to finally speak up and tell her how I feel.

She laughs and sits next to her husband. "Well, in my defense, I kind of figured Lexi would hightail it out of here after graduation."

Like she's planning to do if she wins her comp and gets a surfing contract...

I push the thought of Lexi leaving from my brain. I just want to be part of her life, even if it means she needs to travel and surf. I want to be there to watch her spread her wings and fly, not be the reason she feels like they've been clipped.

"So, I take it you finally reeled her in?" Mason asks.

"Do not refer to my daughter as a goddamn fish," Tristan says, pointing his finger at Mason in warning.

Mason raises his hands in surrender and laughs. "You know what this means, right?" he says to Tristan. When Tristan just glares, Mason continues, "We're about to be related." He waggles his eyebrows and

Tristan's gaze swings over to me.

"Is that why you're here?" Tristan demands. "To drop the bomb you're dating my daughter and to ask my permission to marry her?"

"Eeek!" Charlie squeals. "I get to plan a wedding!" She stands and does some weird dance, which has Tristan wrapping his arm around her and pushing her back down.

"Alec," Tristan prompts, his brows furrowing in... anger? Fuck, this isn't going as planned.

"Yes," I croak out.

"Yes, what?" Tristan says.

"I'm in love with Lexi and I'm dating her and I want to marry her," I rush out.

Mason slaps his hand on his leg, and I glare at him. "You're seriously not helping."

"What did I do? This is great. I wish your mom were here to see you sweating bullets." He pulls out his phone. "Can you start over, so I can record it?"

I shoot him the finger, which only makes him laugh.

"Of course you have our blessing to marry Lexi," Charlie says, ignoring Mason. "And I think it's so sweet you came to ask her father for permission."

"Oh, yeah," Tristan adds sardonically. "Really fucking sweet."

"Oh, stop," Charlie says, slapping his chest. "Alec is a good man, with his life together."

"Thanks," I tell her, still waiting for Tristan to give his approval.

"When are you planning to ask her?" Tristan asks.

"Soon," I admit truthfully. "I don't want to wait. Life is too uncertain."

"Are you doing this because of your dad's death?" Tristan asks. "Because I get how something like that can rock your entire world, but if you're wanting to marry Lexi because you think life is short and you want to seize the day and all that shit, you need to consider there's a chance she'll live to be a hundred. Are you sure you can handle her for the next eighty years?"

"Umm..." I begin, unsure how the hell to answer him. I think there might be a joke mixed in there somewhere, but I can't say for sure. "I'm okay with handling Lexi for the next eighty years."

Mason snorts out a laugh, which has me replaying the words I just said in my head. "That came out wrong," I say, trying to backtrack. "Nobody can handle Lexi."

Mason laughs again, and this time Charlie joins in.

Fuck, this is all coming out wrong. "What I mean is, I love Lexi and I just want to spend the rest of my life with her, however long that is."

Tristan finally smiles. "You're right, nobody can handle Lexi, and the fact that you know that and still want to marry her speaks volumes. You have my blessing." He extends his hand and I meet him halfway shaking it. "Besides, you marrying her means she's no longer my problem." He shrugs. "It's the husband's job to take care of his wife... emotionally, financially..."

"Oh, whatever," Charlie scoffs. "Stop acting like you're so tough. Lexi and Georgia will always be your little girls, and you will forever give them everything and anything they want and need." She leans in and kisses Tristan's cheek. "It's one of the reasons why I love you. You're the best damn dad."

"I know you're only joking," I say, "but I do have a good job, and with my recent promotion I make a decent living. I'm prepared to take on the role of being Lex's husband in every way. I know we're young, but I love her and know she's the one. Whether it's her dream to travel the world surfing, or to paint, I plan to fully support her. I just want to spend my life with her."

"Good man," Tristan says.

"When are you planning to ask?" Charlie adds. "Can we throw you guys an engagement party?"

"I'm thinking this week, before I go back to work. I know it's soon but..."

"Hey," Mason says. "When it's right, it's right. I married your mom in a chapel in Las Vegas on a whim. Almost twenty years later and we're still going strong."

"You mean I'm still putting up with you?" my mom says, walking into the room.

"Semantics," Mason says with a laugh, standing and walking over to my mom to give her a kiss.

"What's with the powwow?" Mom asks, sitting on Mason's lap. I should be disgusted, but I'm used to it. They've always been all over each other since as far back as I can remember.

"Alec came over to ask Tristan's permission to marry Lexi," Mason says.

"What?" Mom shrieks. "You're marrying Lexi? I didn't even know you two were dating! About freaking time. I thought the two of you would've—"

"Gotten together when she graduated high school?" I finish dryly. "Yeah, I heard all about your bet."

Mom at least attempts to look a little sorry.

"I won," Mason says, pulling out his hundred-dollar bill. "How about I take you out to dinner tonight?" He lifts his brows up and down playfully, and my mom laughs.

"It's a date," she says. "Oh, can we go to The Melting Pot?"

Mason groans. "Woman, you know I hate that place."

"But I love it," Mom quips.

"See this?" Mason says to me. "This is marriage. Making sacrifices like eating at an overpriced cheese place that makes you cook your own damn food."

Mom smirks. "It's hardly a sacrifice when afterward, when we get home, you always get to—"

"Whoa now," I say. "Nobody wants to hear what happens once you get home."

Mason laughs. "The beauty of marriage. You give and then you receive." His brows bounce up and down and I swear I throw up a little in my mouth.

"Any real advice?" I ask. The truth is, no matter how disgustingly sweet they are together, I'm sitting in a room with two couples who have been married for almost twenty years. Something that doesn't happen often these days.

"That is real advice," Mason says. "You give and receive. I give by going to that restaurant your mom loves, and I get by..." He grins and winks.

"What Mason is trying to say is," Mom adds, "in order for a marriage to be successful, you have to be willing to give and take."

"And keep it fresh," Charlie adds. "Surprise her with flowers just because. Don't wait for a holiday." She beams at her husband. "I love when Tristan comes home with dinner or my favorite candy on a random night."

"Start your relationship with a firm foundation," Mason says. "What you do now will set the tone for your entire relationship. Make sure she knows she comes first. Take her out, order in, cook her dinner, find time to spend alone time together. It doesn't have to mean spending money, just being there is what creates that foundation."

Mom smiles softly at Mason, as I soak in every word he says. He might be one of the biggest smartasses I know, but he makes my mom happy, and I want nothing more than to make Lexi happy.

"Always communicate," Mom says when he's done speaking. "No matter how hard the truth is, always give it."

"Don't run," Charlie adds softly. "There will be ups and down along the way, but never run, unless it's to each other. Face whatever comes your way together."

Tristan kisses her cheek then says, "If you ever need anything, we're here. Always."

"Thank you," I tell them. "Lexi is planning to tell everyone we're dating at dinner tonight, so try to act surprised."

"Oh, that's why she texted me she wants to do dinner with all of us," Charlie says with a laugh. "I thought for sure she was going to announce she's dropping out of school and wanted an audience so her father wouldn't kill her."

"Have you bought a ring?" Mom asks.

"Yeah." I pull it out of my pocket and show them. The guys congratulate me, and the women ooh and aah over it.

"Once I figure out when I'm going to ask her, I'll let you know, so you can plan the celebration," I tell Charlie.

"Sounds perfect," she says. "We better head out before Lexi gets here and finds us all together." She and Tristan both hug me then leave.

Once it's just Mason, my mom, and me, they both stand and walk over to me.

"I wish your father were here," Mom says, getting choked up.

"I know," I tell her. "Me too."

"He would be so proud of you," she says into my shirt.

When we separate, Mason says, "I've told you this before. I can't and won't attempt to replace your dad, but I'm here if you need anything."

I choke out a laugh. "You've said that to me so many times over the years, but what you don't get is, you're just as much of a dad to me as mine was."

With tears in his eyes, Mason nods and pulls me into a hug. "Thank you, Son, that means the world to me."

"Alec, are you okay?" Lexi asks, pulling me out of my thoughts. "You have tears in your eyes."

"Yeah." I clear my throat. "I was just thinking about my dad." Not a complete lie... But I can't tell her the entire truth without admitting I met with her dad before the barbeque.

I pull into the parking garage and Lexi looks around. "I wasn't paying attention to where we were going. Where are we?"

"You'll see."

We get out of the vehicle and walk through the garage, ending up on Seaton Street. Immediately, Lexi's face lights up. "We're in the Arts District!"

"Yep, I figured you could show me around since it's your favorite place. We can go by a couple of the galleries, and then get lunch."

Lexi stares at me for a long second, then nods. "That sounds like the perfect first date."

She takes my hand and, since she knows this area like the back of her hand, proceeds to show me around. We walk up one street then down another, while Lexi and I discuss each graffitied piece.

"This is the Colette Miller Angel Wings Project," Lexi says when we step onto Colyton Street.

"What's that?" I ask, as we walk over to the life-size angel-looking wings that are painted on the wall.

"She created this project to remind people that we are the angels of this Earth. It's our job to be the good." She steps between the multicolored wings and turns around. "Take a picture of me."

I pull my phone out and snap the picture. "You are without a doubt the most beautiful angel," I tell her, putting my phone away and pulling her into my arms.

"This is what I want to do," she says, pointing to the wings.

"Draw on the walls? You already do that, Lex, and your pieces are amazing."

"No, not that. I want to make a difference with my art. I want it to be something people recognize, and not because it's graffitied on a wall or because it's good, but because it means something."

"Then make it mean something."

Her eyes lock with mine and she nods. "Yeah, maybe one day." She shrugs. "Let's go look at some more art."

She tries to pull away from me, but I hold on to her. "Hey, don't do that."

"Do what?"

"Brush off your passion. You love art and want to make a difference. You just have to think about how you can do that. What's important to you and how you can use art to accomplish whatever it is you want to accomplish."

"You make it sound so easy."

"I didn't say it would be, but that doesn't mean you can't do it. You're one of the most passionate people I know. You feel lost right now, and you keep talking about finding your path... Maybe combining your passion of art and your want to make a difference is where your path leads. You just have to figure out how to make them work together."

Lexi's lips curve into a beautiful smile. "You're right. I just need to take some time to think about it."

"And you have plenty of time."

After we check out more art on the buildings, we stop at a

German restaurant neither of us has been to and eat lunch.

"I had a really good time today," Lexi says on our walk back to my truck. "You know this date set the bar high, right? Every date following will be compared to this one."

I laugh, remembering what Mason said about setting the tone of our relationship, and pull her into my side. "I'm okay with that. I have every intention of raising that bar higher and higher."

Seventeen

LEXI

"Lex, your alarm," Alec groans into my ear, tightening his hold on me.

I pry my eyes open and grab my phone, pressing end so the noise will stop. It's 5:00 a.m. and I need to head to the beach to get some surfing in, but the only thing I want to do is stay in bed with Alec. He returns to work in a few days and all I want to do is soak up as much time with him as I can. I know him going back to work isn't life-changing. He actually has a pretty cool schedule that gives him four days off in a row. I'm just not looking forward to sleeping without him the two days he's gone for his twenty-four-hour shifts. I've gotten used to sharing a bed with him, and it will suck to be in it by myself.

With a deep breath, I pry myself from Alec and sit up. With one more inhale and exhale, I stand and head into the bathroom to get my bathing suit and wetsuit on. When I come out, Alec is up.

"What are you doing?" I ask, grabbing my beach bag. "Go back to bed. I'll pick up breakfast on my way home."

He shakes his head. "I want to go."

"You don't have to do that. Surfing is my thing, and I don't expect you to come and watch every day."

"I know, but I hate you going out in the dark alone, so if I can go, I want to." He grabs the fabric of my wetsuit and tugs me toward him. "I know you like to surf early, but when I'm at work and you're going alone, can you consider going when the sun is up since you don't have classes to get to?"

"Alec..."

"I know," he says. "You're a strong, independent woman, and I love that about you. But LA is a scary place and Jason giving you shit doesn't help any." To say Alec was pissed when I told him Jason approached me would be an understatement. He flat out said the next time Jason comes near me, he would make him regret it.

"Fine," I say, giving in.

"Thank you." He gives me a kiss that makes me want to go back to bed with him instead of going to the beach.

I spend the morning surfing while Alec hangs out and watches. I run into Shane and Ricco, and luckily Jason isn't around. Maybe he finally got the hint...

After I'm done, we stop for breakfast and I grab an extra meal for Aiden. When he sees me, he removes his glasses and gives me a hug. Alec stays back but waves and Aiden waves back.

When we get to my jeep, I immediately notice two of my tires are flat. "What the hell," Alec says, bending down to check out one of the tires. "This tire isn't just flat, it's been slashed."

"What?" I look around, as if the person who did this would've been stupid enough to hang around afterward. "I only have one spare."

"Yeah, and you need two new tires," Alec says, fuming. "We'll have to get your jeep towed to a garage nearby."

While we wait for the tow truck, Alec finds an officer who's patrolling the area and tells him what happened. The officer takes down my information so we can make a formal report. We also tell him about my jeep being keyed and how Jason all but admitted to doing it. He says they'll look into it, but doesn't sound very hopeful.

We're just finishing up with the police officer when the tow truck arrives. The guy quickly loads up my jeep and gives us a ride.

Luckily the garage has my size tire and I pay for two new ones. While we're there, Alec has them change my oil and rotate my tires. Once my car is ready, we head home.

"I have somewhere I want to take you," Alec says once we're home. "Shower and dress in something nice."

"Nice? Like a dress or just something without holes?"

Alec laughs. "A dress would be good."

"WHAT ARE WE DOING HERE?" I ASK WHEN WE PULL UP IN front of my mom's paint studio and my dad's gym—they're located directly next to each other—and Alec kills the engine.

Ignoring my question, Alec says, "Wait here," before he gets out and runs around the front of the hood and over to my side to open my door. He extends his hand to help me climb out—even though it has a sidestep he had installed so I could get in and out without breaking my neck—and kisses the top of my hand once I'm down.

I assume we're going to visit one of my parents, so I'm confused when we bypass both of their places.

"I've known since I was nineteen years old that I was in love with you," Alec says, stopping once we get around to the side of the building. He grants me a soft smile that has my insides twisting into knots. "You had snuck out of your mom's paint studio and run over here. I followed you and watched while you painted the entire wall." He nods toward the wall I graffitied years ago. Since my parents own the building, it's never been painted over.

I laugh, recalling that day. It was the first time I graffitied a public wall and signed it using my moniker. "It was because you followed me, I got caught." I roll my eyes, remembering how Uncle Mason went looking for Alec because he was supposed to be sparring with him but had disappeared.

"You painted the Starry Night by Vincent Van Gogh," Alec

says, glancing up at the wall. "Do you remember why?" His eyes move back to meet mine.

The memory comes back to me like it was just yesterday. "A woman was visiting the paint studio and talked to my mom. When my mom asked how she was liking LA, she said she was disappointed because there were no stars in the sky. She said it's supposed to be a city where people go to make their dreams come true, yet there wasn't a single star to wish upon." I smile sadly, remembering Zoe tell my mom that her mom had passed away years ago from cancer.

"Her name was Zoe, and she was looking for local businesses to participate in the charity gala to support cancer awareness. The Delilah Cross Wish Upon a Star Charity. Charlie donated several paintings to the gala to be auctioned off." We were given tickets in exchange for her donation and attended the gala. It was the most beautiful event I'd ever been to. The entire theme was about wishing upon a star.

A wayward strand of hair falls in front of my eye, and Alec smiles softly, tucking it behind my ear. "When your dad came out and saw that you had recreated the Starry Night, he said you could've done that on a canvas for it to be auctioned off for the cause. That your graffiti on the wall couldn't be sold. It was of no value. You stood right here with your hands on your hips and said, 'My painting is worth more than a charity can raise. The city lacks all the beautiful stars, and now everyone who walks by will have a star to wish upon, so they can all make their dreams come true.'"

"I was like fifteen." I laugh, remembering how inspired I was by her story. I knew I needed to paint it on something bigger than a two-by-two canvas.

"Your age didn't matter," Alec says, shaking his head. "It wasn't even what you painted. It was your heart. It was how passionate you were about the meaning behind the painting. In that moment, I stopped seeing the messy, clumsy little girl with paint permanently in her hair and saw your beautiful soul. You're like this ray of sunshine in a dark, cloudy world. It's why Georgia gravitates toward you. You light up everyone's life around you without even meaning to."

Tears prick my eyes at his kind words because I definitely don't see myself the way he sees me.

"And now you're twenty-one and still drawing hope all over the walls of LA, and one day you're going to figure out how to change the world, and I can't wait to be there when you do."

Alec takes a step back and pulls something—a ring box—out of his pocket. "I knew back then what a big heart you had, and it's only grown over the years. I want that heart, Lex. I want it to be mine. I want your heart, baby."

He drops to one knee, and my hands cover my mouth, realizing what's happening.

"Alexandria Scott," he continues, opening the box and revealing the beautiful heart-shaped diamond engagement ring. "Will you marry me?"

I don't even have to think about it. I may not have any idea what my future holds, but I do know one thing. I want Alec by my side while I figure it out. "Yes!" I tell him. "Yes, I will marry you."

Alec rises to his feet and swoops me up into his arms, twirling us around in a circle. His lips connect with mine and he kisses me hard, showing me how happy he is with my answer.

When he sets me back onto my feet, he takes my hand in his and slides the ring onto my third finger. "I don't want to wait," he says, bringing my hand up to his mouth and kissing the finger that now holds my engagement ring. "I want to get married as soon as possible."

I'm not shocked by his admission, since he's made his intentions clear every step along the way. But what I am shocked about is the fact I'm completely okay with marrying him as soon as possible.

"How about in August or September?" I offer. "It will give us enough time to plan the wedding after the competition is over."

"Okay," he agrees. "We can discuss it with our parents and set a date."

Oh shit... our parents. "Alec, we just told everyone we're dating not too long ago. Don't you think they might freak when they learn we just went from dating to engaged in less than a couple weeks?"

"Nope," Alec says confidently. "Everyone already knows."

"What?" I sputter.

"You don't really think I would ask you to marry me without asking for your dad's permission first, do you?"

"You asked for his permission?" I choke out. "When? Where?"

"When I told you I had some errands to run the day we all got together for the barbeque, I went to pick up your ring and speak to your dad."

"And how did that go? I mean, you're still alive, so at least we know he didn't kill you..." I half-joke.

"It went well. I'll tell you about it later, but right now, we have people waiting to help us celebrate our engagement."

Alec takes my hand in his and walks us around to the front of the building. Before we get to his truck, he pulls his phone out. I glance at it and see he's texting someone.

"Everything okay?"

"Yeah." Instead of steering us toward his truck, he turns at the last second and steps in front of my mom's paint studio. Before I can ask what he's doing, he opens the door and pulls me through.

The second we enter, everyone yells, "Congratulations," and my parents are on me, hugging me.

Next, Georgia envelops me in a hug. "I'm so happy for you," she says, holding me tight.

"Thank you," I tell her, my heart so full. "You'll be my maid of honor, right?"

"Oh, so what am I, chopped liver?" a feminine voice says.

Georgia and I separate, and I find Micaela standing there with her hand on her hip and a playful smirk on her face. "Micaela!" I shriek, running into her arms. "I can't believe you're here."

"And miss your engagement party?" She scoffs. "Not on your

life."

"Are Ryan and RJ here?" I ask, looking around for her husband and son.

"Yes," she says, a smile gracing her lips. "They're around here somewhere. Probably at the dessert table. RJ is obsessed with the cupcakes."

I give her another hug because I've missed her. The last time I saw her was at Alec's dad's funeral, and that wasn't exactly a social visit. "I'm so glad you're here."

"I was just kidding about the whole maid of honor thing," she says with a laugh. "But I better at least be invited to the wedding."

"Oh my God, stop! You will be in my damn wedding and you know it."

We both separate and laugh.

"Go on and make your rounds," she says. "We're in town for the weekend at the beach house."

"Oh, yay! We're totally hanging out. We should have a barbeque."

"Sounds good," she says.

My eyes lock with Alec's mom and she pulls me in for a hug. "I'm so happy love found you and Alec," she says. "Welcome to the family... officially."

"Congratulations," Mason adds. "About damn time that boy hooked you." He winks, and Mila smacks his chest.

"How many times do I have to tell you?" my dad says, coming up next to me. "My daughter is not a damn fish."

Mason throws his arm around his wife's shoulders and shrugs. "There's nothing wrong with being a fish. I hooked Mila and it was the best damn catch of my life." He bends slightly and kisses her cheek.

"You mean I caught you," she says playfully.

"Damn right, you did, and there was no throwing me back in."

"You guys are so damn cheesy," Anna says, rolling her eyes. "Please promise me you and my brother will never be as gross as they are." She gives me a hug.

"Too late," Chase says, walking over. "You should hear the noises coming from their room." He fake gags, and my dad chokes on the drink he's holding.

"Chase!" Georgia scolds. "Like you're one to talk. All those women you've been sneaking into our place." She makes a gagging sound.

"What women?" I ask, confused.

"The women you wouldn't have noticed because you've been too busy in your little bubble with Alec," Georgia says with a laugh. "But I know, because I can hear them through my wall. 'Oh, Chase, right there, no, not there... right there!'" She mocks in a fake nasally voice.

Everyone cracks up laughing at her interpretation of Chase's women. Well, everyone but Chase.

With a straight face, he leans in close to Georgia, so nobody but her can hear him—and the only reason I can hear him is because I'm standing so close to her—and whispers, "At least my women make noises. I don't hear shit coming from your room, which tells me one thing..." He moves closer, so I can't hear what he says, but based on the look on Georgia's face, whatever he's said upset her, because as soon as he's done speaking, she's running away from him toward the back of the studio, where the bathroom is.

"Nice going," I tell him before I run after her.

When I get to the bathroom, I open the door and find Georgia sitting on the toilet seat, sniffling back tears.

"I forgot to lock it," she mutters.

I sit on the decorative chair across from her. "What did he say?"

"The truth." She smiles sadly. "That nothing is going on with Robert and me in the bedroom... Well, that, and if something is going on, he must not be satisfying me."

"Which is it?"

"Nothing's going on."

"So, you told him you weren't ready?"

"Yeah." She nods. "He wasn't thrilled, but he said he would wait until I am."

"Good," I tell her. "And fuck Chase. What you're doing or not doing in the bedroom isn't any of his business."

"No, it's not," Chase says from the doorway. "But maybe Georgia shouldn't play with the big dogs if she's gonna pee like a puppy."

"What?" I laugh.

"It's an old saying," Chase says. "You know... if you can't take what's being thrown at you, you shouldn't be throwing it yourself."

"Look here, mister." I stand, about to rip him a new one, when Georgia stands as well and steps between us.

"He's right. I shouldn't have made fun of... your women's sounds."

I snort a laugh. "Are they using our bathroom? If so, you're going to need to pitch in more. We shouldn't have to clean up after your one-night stands."

Chase rolls his eyes. "You don't clean at all. You have a cleaning lady." True... That was a great housewarming gift our parents got us when we moved in.

"We should go on a double date," I tell Georgia. "Since our last one got ruined." I glare at Chase, remembering how Alec and Chase crashed it.

"Damn right, we ruined that shit," Alec says, joining the mini bathroom party. "Because you belong with me." Alec pulls me into his side and kisses my temple. "Everything okay in here?"

"Yeah," Georgia says. "Again, I'm sorry," she says to Chase, who at least has the decency to look ashamed at the way he upset Georgia.

"Sorry for what?" Alec asks, looking at each of us confused.

"Nothing," I tell him. "Let's go celebrate our engagement."

We exit the bathroom, and I notice Georgia and Chase stay back. I make it a point to glare at him, silently warning him that he better apologize to her.

We spend the rest of the evening celebrating with our friends and family. Once it's late and people start making their exit, we thank everyone for coming and, after thanking our family for throwing us this party, go home.

"I LOOKED UP THE WOMEN'S INTERNATIONAL SURFING tour dates," Alec says. "If you win the competition and snag a spot on the tour, the next tour date is in September."

"That's a big if," I point out. There will easily be a couple hundred women competing for a slot.

"You will."

We're lying in bed, with my body wrapped around his, his fingers drawing circles along my back. After we got home, we hung out with Georgia and Robert for a little while and then retreated to our room. After participating in our own little engagement celebration—which involved both of us naked with Alec inside of me—we showered and then fell into bed, exhausted.

"I think we should get married in August," he says, rolling onto his side so we're facing each other. "Whether you're going on tour or going back to school, August comes before either one and after the competition."

"Micaela got married in August. We would have to make sure it's on a different weekend."

"Done."

Eighteen

ALEC

"Welcome back!" the guys holler as Chase and I walk into the station. They all surround me, giving me a hug. Some congratulate me on my engagement and others express how sorry they are for my loss. It's crazy how quickly time flies by. In the last several weeks, I've lost my father, found out I'll be a brother again, finally admitted my feelings to Lexi and got engaged, Chase officially moved in, and my stepmom moved away. Life is fucking crazy and if you blink too slowly it will all change before your eyes.

"Thanks, guys." I want to say it's good to be back, but the truth is, I've only been away from Lexi for twenty minutes and I'm already missing being in bed with her. "So, what did I miss?"

The guys get me caught up with everything that's been going on here, then Chase and I head to the workout room to get a workout in. The day flies by, with only one text from Lexi wishing me a good morning and letting me know she's going surfing. I hate the thought of her heading to the beach on her own, but I can't act like an overbearing fiancé. Surfing is Lexi's passion and I can't stop her from doing it while I'm at work.

The afternoon flies by with a couple calls involving an oven grease fire and a vehicle that caught on fire. In the evening, I text Lexi and she tells me she's home from surfing and hanging out with her sister and they're planning a double date for us tomorrow night. I tell her that sounds good and I'll see her in the morning.

When nighttime rolls around, she sends me an image of her sleeping in our bed, and in place of where I should be, she's drawn in a stick figure guy.

An accompanying text comes in right after: **Pretending you're here with me.**

Finally, eight o'clock comes and Chase and I head home. We both go straight to our bedrooms, and when I open the door to mine, the sight in front of me has my dick hardening.

Lexi, lying in our bed with her legs wrapped up in my blankets. Her back is completely bare, telling me she's not wearing a shirt, and her ass cheeks are on display, only a thin black scrap of material running down the center of her ass.

Not wasting any time, I strip out of my clothes and slide in behind her. She stirs but doesn't wake up, and her ass juts out, rubbing against my hard-on.

I encircle my arms around her, my hand massaging her breast while I trail kisses along her smooth shoulder blades and up to her neck. I brush her hair to the side and kiss the spot she loves just below her ear, which makes her moan softly and squirm.

"Lex, baby," I murmur into her ear. She stiffens against me, and I know she's now awake. I tweak her nipple between my thumb and finger, turning it into a hard peak, and she groans softly, the sound vibrating straight to my dick. Fuck, I've missed her so damn much and it was only twenty-four hours without her. I don't know what will happen if she wins that sponsorship with Vans, but if I have to use personal time to chase her ass around the globe that's what I might have to do because there's no way I'm going too long without having her in my arms.

Moving my hand down her stomach, I dip it inside her underwear and find her center. I work my fingers between her warm hole and sensitive clit. Stroking and massaging her. She wriggles her body, clenches her thighs together, and moans, spurring me on. I suckle on her neck, working her over until she's dripping wet.

"Alec," she breathes, on the same page as me.

Shoving her underwear down, I part her legs and guide my dick into her. The feeling of her pussy sucking me in is the equivalent of coming home after a long as fuck shift. Right here, with Lexi, in Lexi, is the only place I want to be.

While I thrust into her from behind, I work her clit over. She's so fucking close, I can feel her cunt squeezing my dick. And then she releases a loud moan as she comes completely undone. Her legs shake and her pussy spasms. She screams out my name so loud I'm positive anyone home can hear her. She clenches tightly around my shaft, and I bury my face into the crook of her neck, coming right along with her, draining every drop of my seed into her.

"Is this how you're going to wake me up every morning when you get home from work?" she asks, her breathing labored. "Because if it is, you going to work won't be half bad after all." She giggles, and if I hadn't just drained myself into her thirty seconds ago, the sound would have me hard and ready to go.

I pull out of her and flip her onto her back, climbing over her. "Oh yeah?" I drop my hands onto the bed on either side of her. "So, you're willing to go twenty-four hours without seeing me, if it means I fuck you?" I part her legs and she wraps them around my waist, pulling my hips toward her. My dick is already hardening, and I enter her again.

"Jesus, Lex," I groan, my hard length pushing into her cum-filled pussy. "I missed you so fucking much." I give her a chaste kiss then pull back slightly. "I could live right here, in you, for the rest of my life."

"I'm completely okay with that," she says, grabbing ahold of my neck and pulling my face to hers. "How about you show me *exactly* how much you missed me?" Her mouth crashes against mine, and her tongue delves between my parted lips. She holds me close to her, kissing me, while I make love to her again, showing her exactly how much I missed her.

"What do you mean Robert doesn't want to go on a double date?" Lexi slowly asks her sister. "Like he can't because he has to work?"

"No." Georgia shakes her head, the expression on her face filled with embarrassment. "He didn't like the way Alec and Chase crashed our double date before." She rolls her eyes then glances my way. "I'm sorry. He's been stressed about some case at work and I don't want to add to that."

I can tell Lexi is fuming, but she's holding back, not wanting to get into an argument with her sister. I figure it's best to say something before Lexi does. "It's okay, Georgia. Give it some time. Maybe we can all get together at your parents' place for a barbeque and he can get to know me in a neutral setting." He was supposed to come to the barbecue the night Lexi and I told our family we were together, and then again, the day I proposed, but he bailed both times, saying he had to work. I'm definitely seeing a pattern here, and if it continues, Robert and I will need to have a chat.

Georgia exhales a deep breath. "That would be good. I'm going to study for my exams. First half of summer classes are almost over."

"But what about going out?" Lexi's bottom lip juts out in disappointment.

"I really need to study," Georgia says.

"Seriously, Georgia?" Lexi asks, her tone now annoyed.

"I have to study," Georgia argues.

"If Robert had said yes to going out you wouldn't be using

that excuse."

"Maybe not, but that doesn't mean it's not true. I really do need to study. Just go out with Alec and have a good time. I promise we'll go out soon."

Before Lexi can argue further, Georgia retreats to her room.

"She's going back into her shell," she says once Georgia is in her room with the door closed. "Robert was supposed to help her break out of it. Now, because of his stuck-up ass, she's sinking back in."

"Just give it some time," I tell her, trying to remain neutral. One thing I've learned over the years is not to get in the middle of Lexi and Georgia's shit. They'll argue and make up quick enough to give you whiplash.

Lexi glares. "She's my sister. I'm not giving it time. If her boyfriend doesn't want to be around her best friend and sister, then we have a problem."

She stomps to Georgia's room. I stay where I am, unsure of what I'm supposed to do. Thank God I'm a man. Men don't have these issues.

"Alec," she hisses. "C'mon." Okay then... Guess I'm part of this.

She swings the door open and Georgia looks up from her books that are spread across her bed. I stay back, trying to camouflage myself against the wall, still not wanting to get in the middle of this.

"I'm your sister," Lexi says. "And he"—she points to me—"is your best friend." So much for camouflaging myself. "If Robert doesn't want to double date with us, then fuck him!"

Georgia's eyes go wide in shock. As much of a spitfire as Lexi is, she always handles her sister with kid gloves. No matter how many times I've seen them disagree, Lexi has never yelled at her sister.

"I'm serious, Georgia," Lexi says. "So far, I've seen him talk shit about what you choose to eat, not show up to any of our family functions, give you shit about you not wanting to sleep with him, and—"

Whoa, now that has my attention. "What the hell does she mean giving you shit about not wanting to sleep with him?" I ask, cutting Lexi off. "Don't tell me that asshole is giving you a hard time because you're not jumping into bed with him as quick as he wants."

Georgia's cheeks turn a light shade of pink and she opens her mouth to say something, but before she can get a word out, Lexi speaks first. "Yes, that's exactly what's happening, and now, he's refusing to hang out with the two most important people in her life."

Georgia opens her mouth again, but Lexi continues. "This is not happening, Georgia, I mean—"

"Stop!" Georgia yells, and Lexi's mouth closes quickly in shock. "If you would let me speak, then you would know I agree, which is why I just ended things with him."

"You did?" Lexi asks, sitting on the bed next to her sister.

"Yes, through a text." Georgia shrugs. "Then I blocked him

because you know I hate confrontation."

Lexi laughs and hugs her sister. "I'm so proud of you. The right guy for you is out there, I just know it."

"Yeah, maybe." Georgia's voice cracks, telling me even though she's trying to appear nonchalant she's upset. "For now, I think I'll just focus on school."

Lexi's lips twist into a grimace. "Don't let one dumbass ruin all men for you."

"I won't," Georgia argues, but we can all hear the lie in her words. She put herself out there for the first time and the guy was a dick. For most women, that wouldn't be a big deal, but Georgia isn't most women, and it will take time for her to put herself back out there.

"Okay," Lexi says. "I know you're studying, but how about taking a little break and coming out to dinner with us? We can skip the movie."

Georgia is already shaking her head before Lexi can even finish her sentence. "I really do need to study. I promise another time."

"Okay," Lexi repeats, clearly at a loss as to what to do.

We exit Georgia's room and Lexi says, "I don't want to leave her."

"Of course not," I agree. "We can order in and get her favorite and then drag her out here to watch a movie with us."

Lexi wraps her arms around my neck. "Thank you, Alec. That asswipe Robert needs to take some lessons on how to be a boyfriend from you."

"But I'm not a boyfriend," I say, holding up her hand. "I'm a fiancé."

"And the best one ever."

LEXI

"Yay!" Mom shrieks. "So, we have a date? You're sure?"

"Yes," I tell her, taking a sip of my coffee. "That's the date. It's before fall semester starts, after Micaela and Ryan's anniversary, and the surfing comp will be over. Alec already put in for that weekend and the following week. He's insisting we go on a honeymoon, but he won't tell me where. He says it's a surprise."

"We have less than two months," Mila says, scrolling through the calendar on her phone. "It's not a whole lot of time, but we can do this. We're going to need a venue—"

"We're thinking Micaela's parents' beach house in Venice," I tell them. "I love the beach and they have a private one. It's free and simple..."

"Sweetie," Mom says, putting her hand on mine. "You only get married once." She flinches at her own words, but quickly recovers, smiling extra hard. "You want to make sure your wedding is what you want. Your dad and I are paying for it, so please don't go with what's free and simple."

As if I didn't think I could love my parents any more... "I know that, and I appreciate it, but you know me, and I like simple. If you have this dire need to spend money, make a donation to a cause for the arts. All I need is Alec and me standing in front of someone who can legally marry us. I love him and just want to become his wife."

Mom and Mila both sigh.

"Okay, fine," Mom agrees. "But how about a hotel on the beach instead, so we can have a reception there? The beach house won't fit everyone."

Knowing this is important to her, I agree. "All right, just promise me you'll keep it simple," I say, standing.

"Where are you going?" she asks.

"Surfing."

"Don't you usually go at the crack of dawn?"

"Yeah, but since Jason keyed my car and my tires were slashed, Alec made me promise to only go when it's daylight out. When he's off, he gets up early with me and watches me surf."

When we told our parents about Jason, my dad and Mason were damn close to going after him, but since nobody seems to know his last name—which is kind of weird—and he's been MIA from the beach, they wouldn't even know how to find him. So, my dad called the station to ask about my jeep and was told there are no cameras in our complex or in the parking lot at the beach, and with no eyewitnesses, there isn't much they can do.

"You raised a wonderful young man," Mom says to Mila, who smiles at the compliment.

"It's so crazy to think that in less than two months we'll officially be family," Mila gushes.

"I know! Go ahead, Lexi," Mom says. "Have fun surfing. We'll put together a list of things we need to do, and we'll get together soon to go over it all."

"Thanks, Mom." I give her a kiss on her cheek. "Thanks, Mila." I kiss her cheek as well.

When I get to the beach, I text Alec I'm here, so he knows that if he texts or calls why I might not answer him right away. He's on shift, and I've noticed when he's at the station and there are no fires, he gets bored and will text me. As much as I hate being away from him, I enjoy our nightly conversations. Sometimes they even get heated and end with us having phone sex.

After I get a good practice in, I head home. As I'm walking toward the door, my phone goes off. I check it and see it's Alec: **Happy Anniversary.**

Anniversary? I text back. We've only been together for a few weeks.

Alec: It's been one month since you agreed to be my girlfriend.

I laugh at how cheesy he is.

Me: Is this your way of ensuring you'll get laid when you get home? Because

I can assure you, I'm a sure thing.

I pull up my calendar and set a reminder to notify me every month so I can be as cheesy as he is. When I type in the event, I notice there are only a few weeks until the surfing comp. It's kind of crazy how quickly a month has passed and how much has changed during that time. In August, Alec and I will be getting married, and then shortly after, I'll either be heading off to tour the world surfing or signing up for my fall classes. My stomach sinks at the thought. I know Alec said we would make it work, but when I signed up to do this competition, I never imagined leaving to follow my dream would mean leaving him. It's definitely something I need to think about.

Alec: Getting to be inside you is always a positive, but all I need is you in my arms when I get home.

I smile at how sweet he is, and then an idea hits...

"ALEXANDRIA SCOTT!" GEORGIA YELLS, COVERING HER ears. "What are you doing?"

"I was baking brownies for Alec's and my anniversary," I yell back, trying to stab the smoke alarm with the end of the broom.

"Your what?"

"It's our one-month anniversary," I explain, bashing the alarm. "Go tell Ms. Holden not to call nine-one-one!" I grab a chair and stand on it, reaching up to press the button. I keep hitting it, but it doesn't stop alerting everyone in the vicinity that I once again fucked up something I was trying to bake.

"Oh my God!" Georgia yells. "Did you turn the oven off?"

"Oh, shit! I forgot." I was too busy trying to shut the damn alarm off. I jab my finger into the alarm and it finally silences it.

Jumping down, I run over to the oven Georgia just turned off and open it to take the brownies out, so they'll stop cooking even more.

"No, wait!" Georgia says, but it's too late. The smoke fills the air, and the alarm starts blaring again.

"Go tell Ms. Holden not to call nine-one-one," I tell her again, dropping the burnt to a crisp brownies on top of the stove.

"Too late," a deep voice says. "If you wanted to see me, all you had to do was ask."

I remove the oven mitts and run into Alec's arms. Since he was gone before I woke up this morning, I haven't seen him since last night.

The blaring comes to a halt, and I find Chase and a couple of the other guys Alec works with standing there, dressed in matching uniforms, wearing matching smirks. I back up slightly and run my eyes down Alec, who's wearing the same thing they all are. There's just something about a man in a uniform...

"Lex," Alec groans, shaking his head. "What happened?"

"I was making you brownies for our anniversary. I was going to bring them to the station."

Alec's face lights up before he quickly schools his features.

"I'm telling you there's something wrong with that oven." I point to the offending object that keeps burning my shit. "It said to bake for fifty-five minutes. I set the timer and it hasn't even gone off yet. I don't understand how it could even be burnt."

"One," Georgia says. "Fifty-five minutes is for an eight-by-eight pan. This is eight-by-thirteen, so it should've only been twenty-five minutes." Oops... "And two, the timer isn't on." She presses the blinking numbers and the timer starts. "You never hit start."

"You know they're going to charge you," Alec says with laughter in his voice.

I swivel around and step close to him. "Maybe tomorrow when you get home I can work on paying off some of it..."

Chase snorts. "Alec isn't the one who charges you. It's the city."

"Shut up," I quip, making Alec grin.

I take another step toward Alec, until we're so close our bodies are flush against each other. "While you're here," I whisper, "you think we can go to our room and—"

"No," Chase says, cutting me off. "And FYI: you suck at whispering almost as badly as you suck at baking. Stop trying to do both."

The guys chuckle, and I glare. "Careful," I warn him. "You might come home and find out you're homeless."

Georgia snorts out a laugh, and Alec encloses his arms around me. "I have to get going," he says. "Thank you for the brownies." He kisses me, and the guys all groan.

"Do you realize you just thanked your fiancée for brownies she burned?" Chase asks. "You are so fucking pussy-whipped."

"Hey," Alec says, pulling away from our kiss. "Don't be talking about my woman's pussy."

Chase raises his hands in surrender, then heads out the door with the other guys.

Once they're gone, Alec says, "I'll see you in the morning. No more baking. I appreciate the thought, but next time, maybe buy them..."

"Yeah, yeah." I roll my eyes. "Ricco texted me he's heading to the beach. I might meet him there to get some more waves in."

"All right, baby," he says, kissing my cheek. "Have fun and be safe."

ALEC

Hey baby

Lex?

You still at the beach? Text me when you get this.

Lex, I'm getting worried. I haven't heard from you in a while.

I stare at my phone, confused and worried. I'm probably overreacting, but any time I text Lexi, she texts me back. If she's surfing, it may take a little while, but not hours.

I pull up Georgia's name and hit call.

"Don't worry, she hasn't attempted to bake anything else," she says with a laugh.

"She's at home?" I ask, getting straight to the point.

"No, she went surfing. I haven't seen her all afternoon."

"It's dark out."

"It won't be the first or last time she's surfed after the sun went down."

"She agreed she wouldn't," I say, feeling like an overprotective crazy asshole. "With her jeep being vandalized and Jason starting shit…" My heart pumps harder. Maybe it's nothing, maybe I am overacting, but something feels wrong…

"I'm sure she's fine," Georgia responds, her tone no longer light and carefree. "She's probably hanging out with her friends. You know she spends more time at the beach than home. She probably has her phone on silent and lost track of the time."

"Can you call your brother and get Ricco's number? She said she was meeting him at the beach."

"Yeah, don't worry, though. I'm sure she just got caught up in the waves."

We hang up and I try calling Lexi several more times, each time getting no answer.

I'm grabbing my keys to drive over to the beach to look for her when Georgia calls back. "He was there with her and then left with Max. Last time he saw her was hours ago."

"Fuck. I'm heading to the beach to look for her. Call your parents and anyone she might be with."

"Okay, will do."

"Where're you going?" Chase asks, walking up next to me.

"I'm going to the beach to see if Lexi is there. She's not answering or returning my calls. I'm worried something's happened to her."

Chase opens his mouth, I'm sure to make a smartass comment, but when his eyes meet mine, he nods in understanding. "I'll come with you."

The drive to the beach is filled with silence. Georgia calls me and lets me know nobody has seen or heard from Lexi, and she hasn't posted anything on any social media platform.

"It shows she's at the beach," Tristan says when I answer his call. "I have a tracker for all my kids. It shows she's been at the beach for the last eight hours." I'm assuming Georgia or Max told their dad I'm looking for her.

"Thank you."

"Keep me updated."

"Will do."

We hang up as I'm pulling into the parking lot for the beach. I immediately spot her jeep and drive over to it. I glance inside, but it's empty.

"She must still be surfing."

"Yeah, but it's not like her to go this long without texting or calling me."

We head down the sidewalk and onto the beach. I go straight for the area where she usually surfs, but she isn't there. It's late now and the beach is dark and empty.

"Maybe she's eating on the pier," Chase suggests.

"Maybe... Can you go check? I'm going to walk down the beach, see if she's somewhere else." My eyes land on the dark area under the pier. It's a long shot even getting Aiden to talk, but maybe he's seen her and can at least tell me that much.

I run toward his tent, slowing down the closer I get so I don't spook the guy. As I step up to his tent, I notice Lexi's board and beach bag are lying next to it. My heart goes erratic. I've seen her stop here and talk to him, but I've never seen her actually go in his tent. And the thing is small, would barely hold the two of them.

"Aiden," I call out.

There's some shuffling and then the material is being unzipped. Aiden pops his head out and puts his glasses on. "Lexi's boyfriend," he says. "Lexi is hurt. She's bleeding and won't wake up."

That's all I need to hear to sprint into action. Quickly unzipping the tent the rest of the way down, I gently push Aiden out of the way so I can get to Lexi, but stop when I see my fiancée laid out in front of me. Because of the lantern that's lighting up the area, I am able to see every feature of her, and the sight in front of me almost brings me to my knees.

She's lying on her back and her eyes are closed. Her hair is soaking wet and all tangled. And on her head is a giant gash with blood pouring down the side of her face.

"Lexi is hurt. She's bleeding and won't wake up," Aiden repeats.

"What—"

"Alec!" Chase screams before I can finish my sentence. "What the fuck is going on?" he yells, his eyes bouncing between Aiden and me.

Aiden falls backward. "I don't know him. This is my home. You can't be here." He shakes his head and backs into a corner of his tent. "Lexi's boyfriend, I don't know him," he repeats.

"What happened to Lexi?" Chase asks.

"I don't know," I tell him honestly. "It looks like she hit her head. We need to get her to the hospital." My shock from seeing her like this is wearing off and my EMT training is kicking in. "Call the ambulance. I don't want to move her in case she's injured anywhere else." Chase pulls out his phone and steps away to make the call.

"Aiden, can you tell me what happened?" I ask, dropping down next to Lexi and checking for a pulse. It's there, and she's breathing. Since she's not awake and has a huge gash on her head, this can be brain related.

"The man hurt her," Aiden says. "He wasn't loving her."

"Who?" If it was Jason, so help me God, I'll fucking kill him.

"The mean sur—"

"They're on their way," Chase says, cutting off Aiden. "I don't know what the fuck you did to Lexi, but I'm calling the police."

"I didn't do that," Aiden says, shaking his head. "I didn't do that."

"Then who did?" Chase yells.

"I didn't do that," Aiden repeats. "I didn't do that."

"Chase, stop," I bark. "He's autistic."

As I check out the gash on Lexi's forehead, Aiden rocks in the corner repeating the same thing over and over again. Any chance I had of him telling me what happened has been thrown out the door, but right now all that matters is getting Lexi to the hospital.

The fact she hasn't woken up yet isn't a good sign. I lift her lids and her pupils are dilated, concurrent with a head injury.

I run my hands down her body, checking to see if she's injured anywhere else. Her knees are torn up, both of them covered with fragments of rock and blood, but aside from that she looks okay.

"EMTs are here," Chase calls inside. He had run up to meet them so he could show them where we are.

"Aiden, I need you to step out so they can get in here to help Lexi. Can you do that?"

"Lexi is hurt," he says. "They'll help her?"

"Yes, they'll help her."

"I didn't do it," he repeats.

"I believe you." And I do, but I still don't know what happened. Right now, though, I just have to focus on getting Lexi help.

Aiden steps outside and I explain to the EMTs what I know, which isn't much. After they carefully move her onto a gurney, they bring her up the beach and roll her into the ambulance. Aiden asks if she's going to be okay and I tell him I'll let him know before jogging to my truck so I can follow them to the hospital.

"Let me drive," Chase says. "You need to call her family."

"Thanks."

I call Tristan first, since he's her dad, and tell him I found Lexi passed out and we don't know anything else. He says he and Charlie are on their way to the hospital now and he'll call Georgia, Max, and my parents, so I don't have to.

"Who the fuck was that guy?" Chase asks when I end the call.

"Aiden. He's a friend of Lexi's. He's homeless and lives in that tent."

"We need to call the police. He could be the one who did that to her."

"No," I argue. "He said someone hurt her. My guess is he saved her. No police until she tells us what happened."

"If he didn't do anything wrong, he has nothing to worry about."

"No," I repeat. "She's protective of him and if he's arrested and didn't do anything wrong, she'll be upset."

We get to the hospital and head straight for the Emergency Room since that's where they'll bring her through. Since I'm also an EMT, I have a card that lets me through. Chase offers to stay back and wait for our families.

They wheel her into a room, and my heart sinks when her eyes are still closed. Her not waking up can't be good. I stay out of the way while the EMTs explain their findings to the doctor, who immediately orders tests and asks that I wait in the waiting room.

The next few hours are long. We all sit together, waiting for information. It's late and everyone is exhausted. Our nerves are frayed. Nobody bothers to say a word or make fake conversation. The nurse comes out once to let us know the doctor is still running tests, and once he has answers, he'll let us know.

"Family of Alexandria Scott," the doctor says.

We all jump to our feet.

"Yes," Tristan says. "I'm her father."

"Alexandria was brought in with a head injury. After running tests, we've found that she has a traumatic brain injury. There doesn't appear to be any permanent damage to the brain itself, but from speaking with Miss Scott—"

"She's awake?" I blurt out.

"Yes, she woke up a little while ago. We asked her a few questions, and it's clear she's disoriented. She knows who she is and where she is, but she can't recall the last several hours leading up to the incident, which is very common amongst brain injury patients. She suffered a severe concussion, but luckily the swelling has gone down. We'll need to monitor her for the next forty-eight hours and run another MRI to make sure everything's okay."

"Can we see her?" I ask, trying like hell to be patient, but freaking the fuck out. She has a concussion, swelling in her head... She can't remember the last few hours. This could've been worse, way worse, but it's still bad. And whoever the fuck did this to her is going to pay.

"Yes," the doctor says. "Let's start with one at a time, and once she's moved to her private room, she can have more visitors."

Twenty One

LEXI

My head is pounding—a mixture of the hit I took to the head and the obsessive need to know how I hit my head. The constant *thump, thump, thump* feels like my skull is being drop-kicked over and over again like in the MMA fights the guys my dad trains participate in. I'm down, tapping the hell out, only the ref isn't stopping the fight. The harder I try to remember what happened, the worse the thumping gets.

With my eyes closed, I try to rest and calm down. The doctor said he was going to let my family know how I'm doing and allow them to come back. Hopefully someone will have some answers for me. Did I hit my head while surfing? And if so, who saved me? All the doctor could tell me was that I took a hit to my head, which caused me to get a bad concussion. It's the reason I feel nauseous and lightheaded. Apparently there was even swelling to my brain, which thankfully went down. And now they're just monitoring me to make sure I'm in the clear.

The door opens and in walks Alec. His face is pale and he has purplish-black bags under his eyes. He looks like he's aged several years. The second he lays his eyes on me, they well up with tears. He rushes over and gently cups my face in his hands. Taking a deep breath, he kisses my forehead.

"Seeing your beautiful blue eyes open is the best fucking thing," he murmurs, his lips lingering on my skin.

"Why wouldn't you see them?" I ask, confused.

Releasing my face, he pulls back and snags a chair, quickly dragging it over so he can sit close to me. He takes the hand closest to him and threads our fingers together, bringing it up to his lips to kiss. He closes his eyes again and inhales, like he's taking in my scent.

"Alec, what happened?"

He opens his eyes. "What do you remember?"

"Nothing... Well, nothing that would lead to me being here. The last thing I remember is going to the beach." I try to conjure up a single memory past that, but all that happens is the thumping worsens, making me flinch in pain.

"What's wrong?" he asks, his eyes widening in fear.

"My head hurts, and when I try to remember what happened, it gets worse, like I'm straining my brain or something."

"Don't do that."

"How did this happen?"

Alec sighs. "I don't know. When you didn't return my calls or texts, I went looking for you. It was dark out, and I was worried..."

"The last thing I remember was surfing and it was day time. Ricco and my brother were there."

"Anyone else?"

"Sean had stopped by but left with some friends."

"What about Jason?"

"No, not that I remember."

"Aiden found you. Based on the little he said, you were attacked by someone. By the bump on your head and your knees being torn up, I think you hit a rock. Aiden brought you to his tent but didn't know what to do. You were knocked out."

I hear everything he's saying, but none of it makes any sense. I don't remember any of this. Surely, if all this had happened, I would remember something, anything.

"When I got to the beach, I went to Aiden's tent and found you. Chase called an ambulance and you were brought here."

"None of that sounds familiar," I tell him honestly. "Where's Aiden? I want to talk to him."

"He's at the beach. Chase yelled at him, not knowing his condition, and he kind of freaked out."

"He must be so worried." I glance around as if I can somehow get up and leave. Alec must sense what's going through my head because he shakes his.

"You're not going anywhere. You took a damn blow to the head, Lex. I could've lost you. Your fucking brain was hit."

"I know, but I'm okay, and I need you to go to Aiden and let him know that I'm okay. He's got to be freaking out. Please."

Alec exhales a deep breath. "Okay. I'll go in the morning."

"No, now. And bring him some food and water," I plead. "I once saw some surfers upset Aiden and he retreated into his shell. Refused to leave for days. I had to bring him food and water and coax him to come out."

"All right," he reluctantly agrees. "But before I go, I think we should report this to the police."

"Report what? That I hit my head and scraped my knees, but we don't know how it happened?"

"Okay." He stands and kisses the top of my head. "I'm going to go talk to Aiden and hopefully he'll be able to tell me who did this to you, and then we're filing a report."

"Alec, don't upset him," I argue as he steps back. "If you get there and he's upset, do not make it worse."

"Lex," he barks, then closes his eyes for a brief moment to calm himself down. He opens his eyes and his gaze sears into mine. "You could've died tonight. Chase thinks Aiden—"

"Nope, do not fucking go there," I yell, making my head explode. "Aiden would never do this to me. Chase doesn't know him like I do. If someone did this, it wasn't him. You can ask him, but if he gets worked up, leave him alone. I'm alive and safe in the hospital and that's all that matters."

He stares at me for a long minute like he wants to argue, but he must think better of it because he lets out a loud sigh. "Fine,

I'll be back."

He exits the room, and a few minutes later the nurse comes in and says they're moving me to a private room since I'll be here for the next couple days. Once I'm situated, my family comes to visit.

Georgia cries that she was worried and feels bad she didn't worry sooner. Of course, I tell her that's ridiculous. My parents coddle me, asking if I'm okay and if I need anything. Max stands in the corner, feeling guilty because apparently he left me at the beach alone, which I tell him is an absurd reason to feel guilty since I've been going to the beach by myself since I was sixteen and have stayed after dark too many damn times to count. Mason and Mila visit with Anna but leave shortly after so I can get some rest. Micaela calls Georgia, who tells me she's thinking about me and loves me.

Once everyone has seen I'm okay and alive, I tell them all they can go home. It's late—or rather early—and they all look like zombies.

A couple hours later, while my family is still hanging out and refusing to leave, Alec walks through the door. He says hello to my family and then says, "I spoke to Aiden."

"Aiden?" Georgia asks. "You think he did this?" I can hear it in her voice, she doesn't believe he's capable of doing something like this. I don't know who did this or why they would want to hurt me, but my gut tells me it wasn't Aiden.

"Who's Aiden?" Dad asks.

"He's the homeless boy, right?" Mom says, remembering the

times I've talked about him.

"You think a homeless guy did this?" Dad rises to his feet.

"No, calm down," I tell him. "Aiden is homeless and I believe also autistic. Alec went to talk to him because he's the one who found me."

Everyone looks at Alec. "I didn't mention it because I knew Lexi wouldn't want him brought in until we knew all the details," he explains. "And Lexi would've been pissed if they'd brought him in for questioning and upset him." My heart warms at his words.

"Thank you." I take his hand and squeeze it. "What did he say?"

"He was worried about you and on a one-track mission to make sure you were okay. I told him you're okay and once he calmed down, he said the same thing he told me when I found you. That a man hurt you."

"He doesn't know who?" Dad asks.

"If he does, he couldn't say. He was worked up and that's all I could get out of him."

"We need to file a police report," Dad says. "We need a record of what happened."

"We don't know what happened," I spit out, frustrated that I can't remember. "For all we know a guy hurting me means I was walking past someone and tripped over them and hit my head."

Alec glares. "My guess is Jason did this. Can you remember getting into a fight with him?"

"He wasn't there," Max says. "Hasn't been around since he tried to get Lexi to talk to him and Shane told him to go away... But that doesn't mean he wasn't around where we couldn't see him."

"Exactly," Alec agrees.

"We can't jump to conclusions," I insist. "This could've been an accident." But even as I speak the words, my gut is telling me this was anything but an accident. Jason was pissed at me the last time I saw him. I could see it written all over his features.

"I think we should let the police know," Dad adds. "We can be honest with what we know."

"Which will have them harassing Aiden. No." I shake my head. "At this point it would be his word versus whoever's and they would destroy him."

"Fine." Dad sighs. "But no more going to the beach alone."

"Then he's won," I argue. "I'm not going to let some asshole steal the most important thing to me." The throbbing in my head intensifies and I close my eyes.

Alec must notice because he says, "How about we let Lexi rest. She's been through a lot and needs to sleep."

"I agree," Mom says.

Lips brush my forehead. "We'll be back tomorrow to see you. I love you, sweetheart." When I open my eyes, Mom's are filled with tears.

"Mom, don't cry. I'm okay."

"I know," she says. "But any time something bad happens to your children it's scary. We don't know what happened, but we do know that we could've lost you."

"We love you," Dad says. "I know you're strong, but whoever

did this could've hurt you and I'm going to find out who it was."

"I love you too, Dad."

One by one everyone files out. Everyone except Alec, who's adamant about staying since he has the next few days off anyway. He gets as comfortable in his chair as he can and insists I get some sleep.

I close my eyes, when a weird flash of something—a memory?—hits me.

"Ow! That's hurts. Please don't do this."

My eyes pop open and I glance around, chills running up my arms. Alec's eyes are already closed, and I can hear soft snores, telling me he's asleep.

Where did that come from? Was I attacked? Did I fight back? The voice is muffled in my head, so I can't make out who it is. I try to close my eyes to remember more, but nothing else comes, and soon, I'm lost in a fitful sleep.

Twenty Two

LEXI

"You're a fucking tease! And teases like you deserve what they get."

"Ow! That's hurts. Please don't do this."

"Lexi, Lexi, wake up, baby."

I snap my eyes open and the light from outside attacks me, forcing my eyes to close. It's been almost a week since I was released from the hospital and my headaches have only lessened slightly. The only time I can escape them seems to be when I'm asleep, but the problem is every time I fall asleep I'm hit with nightmares that wake me up. It's a never-ending cycle that has me exhausted and irritated.

"Hey," Alec says softly, concern etched into his features. Every time I'm trapped in a nightmare, he wakes me up. I know he wants to ask what's going on, but he hasn't, which is good since I wouldn't know how to explain it.

With every nightmare that plagues my sleep, I question if they're just that—a nightmare—a story my conscience is conjuring up out of fear of not knowing what happened that night—or if, subconsciously, I'm remembering pieces of the attack. I'm not sure if I'd rather it be the former or the latter. On one hand, if it's not real then I still don't know what happened, but on the other hand, if it *is* real, then I'd almost rather not know what happened. Because if my nightmares are any indications as to what went down that night... well, I don't even want to consider that.

"Lex, I need you to talk to me," Alec pleads, picking me up and settling me into his lap. His arms encircle my body, making me feel safe. I close my eyes and rest my head against his chest. Whether it's his incessant texting—both me and Georgia, who is on babysitting Lexi duty while he's at work—to make sure I'm okay, or waiting on me hand and foot when he's home, he's been here in some shape or form since the second I was brought to the hospital.

Up until now, he's made sure not to do or say anything that might upset me, but based on his tone, I think he's getting frustrated. And I don't blame him. Every time I go to sleep, I wake a few hours later screaming and crying, dripping in sweat.

At first, he thought it was because I was in pain, but then I apparently spoke in my sleep, begging someone to stop, and he knew then something else is going on.

"I don't know what you want me to say," I murmur into his chest, inhaling the clean scent of his bodywash. He must've showered when he got home from work, because even though he's wearing a T-shirt, I can smell his body wash through it. "I'm having nightmares, but I don't know what's real and what's made up."

Alec tightens his hold on me. "Can you tell me about them?"

No, because if I do, I'm afraid that will make them real.

When I'm silent for too long, he says, "What about seeing someone? Like a therapist... someone you can talk to who isn't close to the situation." His suggestion tells me he's thinking the same thing I am. The only reason I would need or want to speak to someone on the outside is if I didn't feel comfortable talking to him, and there's really only one reason I wouldn't feel comfortable talking to him...

"Lex, please." He kisses my forehead. "I'm worried about you. You're barely talking when you're awake, you haven't gotten out of bed except to use the bathroom, you're screaming in your sleep... There's this wall that you're building between us and it's scaring the fuck out of me."

I close my eyes and swallow thickly, silently willing the tears burning behind my eyelids not to fall. He's not wrong, but I don't know what to do, what to say. I need answers, but I don't know how to get them. Unless...

"I want to go talk to Aiden."

Alec nods. "When?"

"Now..." While I'm having a moment of fearlessness.

"All right."

After throwing on a pair of cutoff jean shorts and a tank, and throwing my hair up into a bun, we head to the beach in Alec's truck. The closer we get, the more my heart rate accelerates, and that makes me sad as hell because the beach has always been the place I go to relax. It's almost an extension of myself and now I'm scared to be here.

After I insist on grabbing Aiden something to eat and drink from the pier, we walk toward where Aiden's tent is located. As I glance around for anyone who might be watching us, I realize just how scared I actually am, and that pisses me off.

Alec holds my hand, and I know he can feel me squeezing with every step we take.

When we get near Aiden's tent, I let go. "I need to talk to him alone."

"Lex..."

"He trusts me and is comfortable around me, and if we're alone he might give me details he didn't give you."

Alec scrubs his hands over his face in frustration. "Okay, I'll be right here." He grabs me by my hips and pulls me close, his mouth fusing with mine. Before I can kiss him back, several flashbacks hit me, one after another.

A mouth attacking mine.

Hands gripping my hips.

A pelvis grinding into my front.

The onslaught of horrific images has me pushing Alec away.

"Lex?" The hurt in his voice has me opening my eyes and remembering that I'm here safe with Alec.

"I need to talk to Aiden," is all I say before I turn my back on Alec and head over to the tent.

When I get there, he's sitting in the sand, sketching in his sketchbook with his neon green glasses on. He must hear or sense me because he glances up and then drops his book.

"Lexi!" He pops up onto his feet and meets me halfway, engulfing me in a hug. It's in this moment, I know with certainty Aiden would never hurt me and if anyone tries to accuse him of such, I'll fucking destroy them.

"I was worried about you," he says. "That man wasn't loving you."

Our conversation from not too long ago pops into my head.

"That's a man and a woman loving each other," he states matter-of-factly.

"Do you see this a lot on the beach?"

"Yes. I thought the man was hurting the woman, but when I tried to save the woman, they yelled at me and said they love each other."

Bile rises up in my throat. "What man?" I ask him slowly.

"The mean surfer man."

I swallow thickly at his words. "Can we sit and talk? I brought you tacos."

Aiden releases me and nods, taking the bag from me. "Thank you. Tacos are my favorite."

We sit in the sand where he was sitting a moment ago.

"Thank you for saving me," I tell him after a few seconds of silence.

He removes his glasses and looks into my eyes, something he doesn't do often. "The man yelled at me. He said I hurt you. I wouldn't hurt my friend, Lexi."

"I know you wouldn't. They were just really scared and didn't know what happened."

"The man hurt you." He takes his book and opens it, then thrusts it at me. "See? The man wasn't loving you."

I take the book from him and stare at the page for several long seconds. It's of a man and a woman. She's wearing a bathing suit top but no bottoms and is bent over a cluster of rocks. He's pulling her hair, his front flush against her back. It looks like they're lost in a moment of passion, and the thought makes my stomach roil. Before I can stop myself, I'm running toward the edge of the water and throwing up.

"Lex, what's wrong?" Alec comes running over. "What happened?"

"I'm okay," I insist, hating that I'm lying to Alec.

Aiden stands. "I didn't hurt her. I didn't hurt her," he repeats, pushing his glasses back on to protect himself.

"I know, buddy," Alec says slowly.

"I'm not buddy. I'm Aiden, and I didn't hurt my friend Lexi."

"He knows," I tell him. "It's okay." Not wanting to upset him any further, or risk him showing Alec the picture he drew, I change the subject. "Eat your tacos before they get cold."

"Tacos are my favorite," Aiden says, sitting back down with his bag of food.

"Here." I pull a few bills from my back pocket and hand them to him. "For tacos."

Aiden eyes the money. "I didn't work. I only get money when I work."

He shoves my hand away, refusing the money, and I sigh.

The first time I tried to give Aiden money to eat, he told me this, so instead of giving him money, I always make it a point to give him food. But since I'm not sure when I'll be back to the beach, I won't be able to buy him food, and I need to make sure he's taken care of.

"Okay," I tell him, not wanting to argue. I'll have to think of another way to get the food to him. "I'll see you soon, okay?"

"Okay, Lexi," he says, devouring his tacos. "See you soon."

When we get home, I head straight for the shower. It's too late, it's been days since I was attacked, but seeing that picture makes me feel dirty and gross. I can't remember it, but the picture is clear as to what happened, and based on his mean surfer comment, there's only one guy I can think of who would be mad at me enough to do this to me.

I let the hot water rain over me as I use my loofah to scrub every inch of my body, until my skin is red and sensitive and the water has turned cold.

When I finally get out, Alec is waiting for me, a frown marring his face. I need to tell him what I think happened. This isn't something I can keep from him, but first I need to find out if it was Jason who attacked me. Because the second I tell Alec, I know without a doubt he's going to go after him.

"You were trying to give him money because you're not planning to return to the beach," he says, calling me out.

"Yeah," I croak.

"Why? What did he tell you?"

"He said what we already know," I half lie. "I was attacked."

"And..." Alec prompts.

"And I'm scared," I admit, giving him some of the honesty he deserves.

"So, you're going to let whoever attacked you win?" He steps toward me and tucks a wayward hair behind my ear. The soft contact of his flesh touching mine sends sparks through my body. "You said in the hospital you weren't going to let whoever did this to you win. You have your surfing comp in a couple weeks..."

"I'm not doing it."

"Bullshit," he hisses. "You've been busting your ass for this. Georgia, Max, me... we'll go with you while you practice, but you're not giving up. This is what you want more than anything, and you're not letting some asshole take that from you."

He's right, and I love him even more for saying it. He could easily tell me to forget it. I suffered a concussion and he's been worried sick about me, but he's putting my wants over his fears, and I need to do the same thing.

"Thank you," I tell him, pressing my mouth to his. Our lips curl around each other, and Alec's hands find my face, deepening the kiss. I can tell he's treating me like glass, worried I'll break, and

I hate that I'm scared that he might not be wrong.

I focus on staying in the now, refusing to let any of those horrible flashes ruin the moment. But the second his hand glides to the back of my head and his fingers thread through the strands of my hair, tugging gently on my bun, the picture Aiden drew flashes behind my lids.

Me being thrust onto the rock.

My knees screaming in pain

A man behind me, fisting my hair.

My scalp is burning.

My neck is straining.

He's squeezing my breast.

Pain is radiating through my body.

And then.... Everything goes black.

"Lexi!" Alec screams, snapping me back to the present.

My eyes dart around and I realize I'm huddled in a corner, in a fetal position.

"Baby, you've got to talk to me," Alec begs. "Why are you crying? Did I hurt you?"

He's so confused and worried and I owe him an explanation. I hate what this is doing to him, to us.

But the moment the words leave my mouth will make them real, and I don't think I can handle that. It's hard enough thinking them, I can't actually speak them.

"You didn't hurt me. I—" I take a deep breath. "I'm having flashes from the night I was attacked."

Alec drops to the floor and sits Indian style, giving me space and his full attention.

"I think it was Jason who attacked me."

Alec's eyes widen slightly.

"Aiden said it was a mean surfer," I add. "So it would make sense." I swallow thickly. "In my flashbacks, the guy calls me a tease." Just like Jason did the night he saw me with Alec.

I can tell he's trying really hard to remain calm for my sake, but his hands are fisted and turning white, and his jaw is ticking like it's about to crack, giving away he's anything but calm.

I consider telling him what else I think, but before I can, he stands and says, "I'm going to kill him."

"Alec, you can't." I stand as well. "You would go to jail, lose your job. I can't lose you." I wrap my arms around his waist.

"You have to report him. The cops need to know."

"It will be my word versus his, and all I have are some flashes, which may or may not be real. They've yet to get him for keying my jeep or slashing my tires."

Alec sighs. "What about Aiden?"

"I don't want to put him through that." I place my hands on his chest, hoping it'll calm him. "I know this is a lot to ask, but whatever he did, he did to me, and as of right now I don't even know what that is. I've seen all the shows. A woman goes into the station and accuses a man of something she isn't sure he did. Nobody takes her seriously."

"This isn't a show, Lexi. This is your life."

"I know, and if I was sure of what happened, I would go. But I'm not, and I don't want to throw shit out there that won't stick."

He nods. "Okay, I don't like it, but I'll do whatever you want. But I'm telling you right now, if I see him somewhere with no one around, all bets are off."

Twenty Three

ALEC

It's four in morning and I need to wake Lexi up soon so she can get ready to head to Huntington Beach for the surf competition. It's a day she's been working toward for months. But as I watch her whimper in her sleep, something that's become the norm since she was attacked on the beach, I don't have the heart to wake her yet. On one hand, her whimpering means she's probably having a nightmare, and if I wake her it would stop, but on the other hand, since she rarely sleeps anymore, I hate to wake her up when she's actually sleeping.

Her lips form a soft pout and I run my thumb across them, trying to straighten them out. I hate to see her like this: lost in herself. I can't confirm what's been going through her head, and I know she isn't giving me all the pieces, but I've put enough of the puzzle together to take a guess as to why she's struggling. Why she jumps when I kiss and hold her. Why we haven't had sex since that night. I want to be there for her, but I'm trying to give her space. I'm afraid if I push too hard, Lexi will break.

Her hand reaches out, and when it finds me, she snuggles into my chest. I love that even in her sleep she's drawn to me. I've spent the last few weeks asking around for Jason. He's apparently gone MIA and nobody knows anything about him. Not his last name, where he lives. It's almost as if the guy doesn't even exist. I'm hoping for Lexi's sake he isn't at the comp today, but a small part of me would love to finally be able to get my hands on him.

"You look like you're in deep concentration," Lexi says, her voice gravelly.

"Just watching my beautiful fiancée sleep."

"I don't know if I can do this," she says softly, making my entire body go rigid.

"Do what?"

"Surf today."

I release a sigh of relief. I finally have Lexi in my life, there's no way I'm letting her go now. I don't know what the hell I would do if she said she meant she couldn't be with me.

"I'm not going to tell you that you have to." I pull her on top of me, then pull us up the bed, so I'm sitting against the headboard and she's straddling my middle. "But if your reason for not wanting to surf today is because of that asshole, I'll say what I said before, don't let him win."

"I'm scared," she admits, so unlike the Lexi I've known most

244

of my life. I hate this for her and would do anything to make sure she's never scared again.

"Of what?"

She averts her gaze—something both she and Georgia do when they're lying—telling me that whatever she says won't be the entire truth. "Of choking out there... I haven't practiced in the last couple weeks."

"The Lexi I know wouldn't let fear stand in her way." I kiss the tip of her nose. "Everyone will be there, watching you, supporting you. My family, your parents, brother and sister, Micaela and Ryan will even be there. If at any time you don't feel up to it, then we leave."

"Okay." She leans forward and kisses me. "I'll go get ready."

We get to Huntington Beach, and I remain by Lexi's side the entire time she's setting up and getting checked in. The beach is packed with hundreds of people since this is a pretty big competition.

We find our families, who have a spot on the beach with a blanket and beach chairs. Lexi hugs them all and thanks them for coming, then heads off to practice. There's a short window of time allotted to surfers practicing before the competition begins. I watch as she grabs her board and drops it into the water, then paddles out.

"How's she doing?" Tristan asks.

"She's having flashes she thinks might be memories, some nightmares," I tell him. "She won't really talk about it, though. I told her she should see a therapist."

"I'll find a couple who take her insurance," he says. "She'll get through this. We just need—"

"What's wrong with Lexi?" Max asks, cutting his dad off.

My eyes quickly find her. She's standing along the edge of the water, her fists at her sides. Her board is in the water floating away, and she isn't moving, isn't attempting to grab it. I follow her line of sight, and that's when I see him: Motherfucking Jason.

"Grab Lexi!" I yell to her dad, as I jump to my feet and run toward Jason. I'll be damned if he's going anywhere without me finding out who the fuck this guy is.

I try to keep eyes on him, as I run up the beach, but there are too many people, the beach is too packed, and I lose him. I scour the area, the parking lot, combing the beach, but I can't find him.

When I get back to the area where everyone is, Lexi has a large towel wrapped around her and her sister is hugging her tightly, her mom and dad both hovering over them with pained expressions on their faces.

"What did he do?" I ask her, taking her from Georgia.

"He didn't do anything," she says, her voice cracking with emotion. "It was just... the way he looked at me." She visibly shivers. "I don't want to be here. Please take me home."

My eyes meet with her dad's, and his jaw ticks, but he nods once, silently asking me to do as she wants. I fucking hate this asshole for getting to Lexi, for fucking with her, and I'm not going to stop until I find him and uncover what he did to her. Lexi needs answers, and if I have to beat them out of him, I will.

After saying our goodbyes to everyone, we head home, where Lexi excuses herself, saying she's tired. Unsure if I should lie with her or give her some space, I pace the hallway, until finally I've had enough and I go in.

She's curled up in our blankets, her eyes closed. I know she's not sleeping because she isn't softly snoring, but she must want me to think she is. So I edge onto the bed next to her and wrap my arms around her carefully, holding her close but not too hard. She sighs in contentment and a few minutes later the snoring comes.

Twenty Four

LEXI

"Oh, Lexi," Mom breathes. "You look absolutely gorgeous."

"I agree," Mila says. "Stunning."

Georgia nods. "Most beautiful bride ever."

"It's perfect." Micaela sniffles. "Sorry, I'm just kind of emotional right now." She wipes a tear, and everyone laughs. She recently found out that she and Ryan are expecting their second baby and she's been crying over everything.

I glance at the three-part mirror that shows off every angle of me and try like hell to smile. They're all right. The dress is beautiful. It's classy, not too girly. Ivory instead of white like I wanted. It's a floor-length, sleeveless, A-line design, which will keep me cool during our summer wedding.

It's the perfect wedding dress, and I should be happy that after only trying on a couple I found the perfect one. But it's hard to be here, in the moment, and be happy, when I can't get Jason out of my head. The way he evilly smirked at me when our eyes met at Huntington Beach, I could feel it in my bones. He was the man who attacked me on the beach that night, and by the smarmy look on his face, he didn't give a shit that I knew. He knew he got away with it, and the thought equally has me fuming and makes me sick to my stomach.

"Lexi," my mom prompts. "What do you think?" Her sympathetic eyes meet mine in the mirror and I hate that I'm ruining this. Today should be a happy day. I should be laughing and smiling and so excited. We've had this day booked for weeks, and when she offered to cancel, I insisted we go. There are only so many weeks left until our wedding and so much still to do.

"It's perfect," I tell her. "And it doesn't even have to be altered."

She comes up behind me and smiles warmly. "You're going to make a beautiful bride."

"Thank you, Mom." I turn around and wrap my arms around her, needing to feel her warm motherly touch. "I love you so much."

"Oh, sweetheart, I love you too."

Since we're keeping the wedding small, we're not doing bridesmaids or groomsmen. Alec has asked Chase to be his best man and Georgia is my maid of honor. They'll be the only people up at the altar with us and will sign as our witnesses. So, after I confirm with the saleswoman I would like this dress, she helps me out of it and bags it up, and then we're on our way.

"Lunch?" Mila suggests.

"Sure," we all agree.

We stop at a deli we all enjoy and order soups and sandwiches to eat out on the patio. While we eat, Mom and Mila go over the details for the wedding, and Georgia and I look at the latest pictures Micaela took of her son RJ. He's so adorable and seems to be a little terror. He definitely gets that from Micaela and not his daddy.

I'm taking a bite of my sandwich when my phone dings with an incoming text.

Alec: Have a bag packed when I get home. We're going away for a few days.

My heart and stomach both flutter at the thought of some time away with Alec. The last couple weeks, even though we've slept in the same bed whenever Alec isn't working, has felt like we're floating in the water, and each of us is being pulled in separate directions. Alec has been trying so hard to get to me, but I've been so lost in myself, I haven't even attempted to meet him halfway. Maybe this is what we need. Some time away from here to find our way back to each other.

Me: I'll be ready!

"Everything okay?" Georgia asks carefully, turning her attention to me. She's been practically walking on eggshells when she talks to me lately, scared the wrong thing will send me over the edge. Me going away will also give her a little break.

"Yeah, Alec and I are going to go away for a few days."

Georgia's brows dip together. "For how long? My graduation

is next Friday."

"You think I would miss your graduation?" I scoff. "Only a few days."

Georgia releases a sigh of relief, then frowns. "Oh, great. You're leaving me alone with Chase." She scrunches her nose up in disgust.

"What's wrong with Chase?" I know they've gotten into it a few times in the past, but I didn't realize things between them were bad enough she doesn't want to be alone with him.

"Nothing," she says quickly, shaking her head.

"Don't do that." I lock eyes with her. "I know I've been... a little lost lately. But don't walk on eggshells around me, please. I already feel like things between Alec and me are rocky. I can't handle you and me not being us."

Georgia sighs. "I'm sorry. I just don't want to upset you."

"I'm not going to break," I promise her. If I haven't broken yet, I think I'm in the clear...

"Okay, well, you're right about being a little lost," she says. "Because if you were paying attention then you would've noticed Chase and his overactive dick." She rolls her eyes, and I crack up.

"His overactive dick?" She's mentioned he's hooked up with a few women since his divorce was finalized, but it's to be expected. He's young and was married for years, and his ex-wife hurt him.

"Yeah. Every day he's off, he has a different woman in his room, sometimes two." She gags. "I think Alec asked him to tone it down a bit since the day at the beach, because he's actually been quiet.

But the second he finds out you and Alec are leaving he's probably going to throw an orgy." She fake shivers. "He's definitely proven a dick can't fall off from overuse."

Micaela and I both laugh, and Georgia glares. "You wouldn't be laughing if you had to hear him and the bimbos he's with every night."

"Hear who?" Mom asks.

"Chase," I tell her.

"The women are ridiculous," Georgia complains. "Oh, Chase, your dick is so big." She huffs. "If I have to hear one more woman stroke his ego, I'm going to kill myself."

"Sounds like that's not the only thing they're stroking." Mom snorts.

"Oh my God, Mom!" Georgia shrieks. "No, just no."

"Good one," Mila says to my mom, giving her a high five as Micaela and I crack up laughing.

After lunch, we head to the bakery and pick out the cake, then go shopping for my shoes and Georgia's and Micaela's dresses. When we're all completely shopped out, we say goodbye to Micaela, who only came up for the day, and then head home.

Since I'm not sure where Alec and I are going, I pack a couple casual outfits, a bathing suit, and something nice to wear out. Then I find Georgia so we can hang out.

"Up for some *O.C.*?" I ask from her doorway.

She glances up at me from her laptop, more than likely studying for her last final, and smiles brightly. "Always." She shuts the lid and sets it on her nightstand, then pats the mattress next to her.

I hop onto the bed and cuddle up next to her, as she clicks the remote, turning on the television. She finds the show she left off on and it starts: Marissa and Ryan are arguing and Seth is begging Summer to give him attention.

We watch in silence for a few minutes, before Georgia lays her head on mine. "I've missed you," she whispers. My throat fills with emotion, and I close my eyes, so tears don't escape.

"I've missed you too."

We watch one episode after another, until neither of us can keep our eyes open and the program asks us if we want to continue to watch. I should probably go back to my bed, but I'm comfortable in here, with my sister, so instead, when she clicks off the show, I snuggle up next to her and wrap my arms around her.

"Night, Georgia."

"Night, Lex."

***

STRONG ARMS WRAP AROUND ME FROM BEHIND, jolting me awake.

"Ow! That's hurts. Please don't do this."

He tears at my bathing suit bottoms and then his fingers—

"Lex," Alec prompts, shaking me slightly and knocking me back to the present.

I take a deep breath and roll over, away from Georgia who's still asleep, and into my fiancé's safe arms. I bury my face into his chest, inhaling his scent, reminding myself over and over again, he's who I'm here with. I'm in my sister's bed, in Alec's arms. I'm safe.

Alec doesn't say anything, just holds me tightly, until I lift my face up and make eye contact with him. "I'm ready to get out of here."

The pained look on his face tells me he wants to ask me what just happened, but he doesn't. Instead, he nods once. "Okay, let's go."

When I climb off the bed and stand upright, a sudden bout of dizziness hits me, making me wobble slightly. Alec notices and clasps onto my forearms. "Hey, you okay?"

"Yeah, I just felt a little lightheaded. I must've gotten up too fast."

He stares at me for several heartbeats and then says, "All right, let's get you something to eat. You haven't been eating much lately."

He's not wrong. I think I've lost an entire clothing size the last few weeks. Between the nightmares and the thoughts while I'm awake, I haven't had much of an appetite.

Alec grabs my overnight bag and his and throws them into the back of my jeep and then we're off. He hasn't mentioned where we're going, and I haven't asked. I like that he's surprising me. Something sweet and fun is just what I need right now.

The drive is done in awkward silence and I pray this isn't how the next couple days will be. Neither of us knowing what to do or say. Alec not wanting to say the wrong thing, and me having no damn clue what to even say.

We arrive in Santa Barbara and pull up to a beautiful hotel that's right on the beach. We get out and Alec tells the valet his name.

"Your luggage will be in your room, Mrs. Sterling," the gentleman says to me. Being called Alec's last name has me smiling, like a real smile, for the first time in a long time.

"Did you hear that?" I say to him as I hook my arm in his. "Mrs. Sterling. Has a nice ring to it."

"It sounds fucking perfect." He leans over and kisses my temple.

We get situated in our room and once the bags arrive, we change into our swimsuits. As I step out of the bathroom, I notice Alec is standing on the balcony staring out over the water.

I take a moment to admire him from behind. My best friend, my fiancé, and my soon-to-be husband. He's wearing a pair of board shorts and is shirtless, his arms resting against the top of the railing. From here, I can see his roped neck and back muscles, and his corded muscular forearms that don various tattoos he's gotten over the years. Alec is without a doubt the strongest man I know—and not just on the outside. He lost his father not too long ago, and instead of drowning in his grief, he turned it around, taking control of his life and living not only for himself but for his dad as well.

It makes me realize how much I want to be like Alec, be strong like he is. I can't change what happened to me... hell, I don't even know what happened to me. But I can change how I react to what happened. Every day I dwell on what happened is another day Jason wins. And I'm done letting him win.

I step up behind Alec and circle my arms around his torso, resting the side of my face against his back. He stiffens slightly, and I close my eyes, hating that he's shocked his fiancée is actually trying to touch him. He doesn't know what to do, what to say. And it's my fault because I've pushed him away.

"Alec," I say, sliding around and under his arm, so we're face-to-face. My back is against the railing and I'm standing between his arms. He glances down at me, assessing me, wondering what's wrong.

"I've missed you," I tell him, running my hands up his six-pack abs and over his taut chest. I encircle my arms around his neck and bring his face down to mine. My lips softly caress his. Tasting him for what feels like the first time. He doesn't move, letting me lead. But when my tongue pushes against his lips, he grants me access. I've missed how he tastes, how he feels.

The kiss deepens, and I pull him closer to me. "I need you," I murmur against his lips. His eyes pop open, searching my face to make sure I mean what I say. "Please, I need us."

My words must be what he needed to hear, because the next thing I know, I'm being lifted and brought back into our suite. He carries me over to the big bed and gently lays me down, climbing over me. Our mouths reconnect, this time with more passion. It's been weeks since we've been intimate, and it shows in our moves. The way Alec possessively nips at my bottom lip, then trails kisses down my neck. The way I thread my fingers through his hair, pulling him toward me, needing him closer.

He kisses his way across my collarbone and stops at my breasts. Pulling the triangle material to the side, he sucks on one nipple and then the other. Electric currents zap through my body, going straight to my core. I need Alec, to feel close to him. To replace any possible flashback with memories of him.

I watch as he kisses along the center of my belly, stopping to tug gently on my belly button ring. He continues his descent, placing a small kiss to my hip where my tattoo is. Then he works his way down to the apex of my legs. He spreads my legs open, then pulls on the strings on my hips to remove my bikini bottoms, leaving me completely bare to him.

He places an open-mouthed kiss to the hood of my pussy, before he opens me and licks up my center. I want to close my eyes and get lost in the sensations of what he's doing to me, but I keep my eyes open, memorizing every lick, every suck. Replacing every flashback, every nightmare with Alec. His kisses, his touches...

He pushes a finger, and then two, inside me, and our eyes lock. "You're mine," he growls, as if he knows exactly what I'm doing, what I'm thinking.

"Yours," I breathe in agreement.

He goes back to fucking me with his tongue and fingers and

I make sure to stay right here in the moment with him. When my orgasm rips through me like a tidal wave, I scream out his name.

"Fuck me," I beg, needing him inside of me. Not wanting this moment to end.

He pushes his shorts down and hovers above me, his strong arms caging me in. "Lex, when I'm with you, I don't fuck you," he murmurs against my mouth. "I make love to you. Understand me?"

Tears prick my eyes. "Yes," I choke out. "Make love to me, please."

"My pleasure," he says as he pushes into me, filling me completely. His mouth crashes against mine. My hips rock against his. I tug on the ends of his hair as he makes love to me. And for the first time in weeks, my body relaxes. My heart slows. My brain feels free. This is exactly what I needed. Alec.

I allow myself to close my eyes, to enjoy the moment, to get lost in the feeling, but before I can stop it from happening, flashes from that night surface.

The beach.

The sand.

The rocks.

Hands, not Alec's, hurting me.

"Lexi," Alec says, "stay with me, baby."

I wrench my lids open and my eyes meet his. I focus on Alec, on his warm, chocolate brown eyes that look at me with love and adoration. On his perfect lips that say the sweetest words to me. On the way he feels inside of me, as if I was made just for him.

With Alec's eyes locked with mine, we both find our release, and I know without a shadow of a doubt, this man is everything I need. He's my path. My forever. And it's time I get the help I need, so I can be everything he needs.

ALEC

"I'm going to see a therapist," Lexi says to me when she steps out of the shower from rinsing off. I'm pulling my board shorts up, and I stop, meeting her eyes in the mirror.

"Yeah?"

"Yeah. There's a chance I'm never going to know what happened that night, but I need to speak to someone about it. Get my thoughts out and find a way to move past it."

I finish putting on my shorts and turn around to face her. "I think that sounds like a good idea."

"Thank you for being patient with me these last few weeks."

"You never have to thank me for that," I tell her, drawing her naked body into my arms. "I love you, and we're in this together."

She smiles, a soft, genuine smile. One I haven't seen in a while. "I love you too, and I can't wait to become your wife."

"And I can't wait to become your husband." I bring her hand up to my mouth and kiss her engagement ring. "Have you thought about where you want to go from here?" Lexi had been hoping to get picked up by Vans, but because she left the competition without even competing, that's no longer an option. She hasn't mentioned it, but I'm worried she's been dwelling on it.

Lexi chews on her bottom lip. "Honestly, I don't know." She shrugs as her eyes turn glossy. "Would it be okay if maybe we just focused on us while we're here?"

I open my mouth to argue, but she adds, "I know I have to deal with it, and I will. But right now I just want to be with you."

"Okay," I agree, hating that she's pushing shit aside, but hopefully when we get home and she meets with a therapist, she'll start dealing with everything. "What do you say we head out to the beach? Catch some sun, some waves. We can have dinner downtown..."

"Sounds perfect."

And the next three days are spent just like that. On the beach, in the water, in Lexi. Little by little, day by day, we find our way back to each other. We make love all over the hotel room: in the bed, in the shower, on the balcony. We check out the art galleries and do some shopping downtown. By the time check-out comes around, I consider quitting my job and extending our stay.

But since I kind of need my job, and we can't actually stay here indefinitely, after we have one last lunch downtown, we head home.

When we walk through the door, there's yelling and screaming, and Lexi rushes in, worried. I drop our luggage by the door, and we both go in search of where the voices are coming from.

"We have to share a bathroom," Georgia yells. "Is it too much to ask that you make sure your conquests don't touch my stuff?"

"I said I was sorry," Chase says. "I'll replace your shaver."

"I could've used it!" Georgia shrieks, sounding like she's ready to cry. "What if she had an STD?"

"I'm sorry," Chase repeats.

"Hey, what's going on?" Lexi asks, stepping up next to her sister and glaring at Chase.

"He had some girl over last night and she used my stuff," Georgia says. "My shampoo and conditioner and my shaver!"

"Ewww…" Lexi thumps Chase on the top of his arm. "Keep your hoochies out of my sister's stuff."

"I'll just… bring my stuff into my room," Georgia says, stepping out of Chase's room. "It's fine," she mumbles.

"No, it's not," Lexi says, shooting me a glare that says *this is your friend, you better handle this.*

Before I can say a word, though, Chase speaks up. "Look, I'm going to look for my own place, but until I find something, I won't bring any more women here."

"You don't have to find your own place," I tell him. "But yeah, maybe you could hang out at their place instead…" We talked about this before, but it was because I didn't want to upset Lexi. I'm assuming since Lexi and I were gone, he thought it would be okay.

"Done," he says. "I'm going to head out." He walks over to Georgia's room. "It won't happen again. I promise."

"Okay," she says softly. "Thanks."

He steps back out, and with a shake of his head, he grabs his keys and disappears out the door.

The rest of the afternoon is spent watching reruns of the girls' favorite shows and eating pizza that we have delivered. We all fall asleep in the same bed, just like old times, and in the morning, when I get up to go to work, leaving them both asleep, I feel like shit is finally getting back to the way it was before that asshole Jason fucked everything up.

When I get to the station, Chase is already there, talking with the other guys. "You never came home last night?" I ask.

"I did, after you guys were asleep, and I left before you. Figured I would give them some time to calm down. I also replaced Georgia's stuff. Left it in the bathroom for her."

"Thanks, man," I tell him. "They'll get over it. You don't have to find a new place to live." After he left, and Georgia calmed down, she felt bad for making Chase feel like he needed to move out.

"Eh, I'm newly single, and you're about to be married... I never planned to stay with you forever." He shrugs. "Are you and Lexi planning to get your own place after you get married?"

"We haven't really discussed it." I can't imagine her living anywhere without her sister. Those two have been inseparable for as far back as I can remember.

My phone dings with a text from Charlie, Lexi and Georgia's mom, letting everyone know they'll be hosting a dinner Friday night after Georgia's graduation and to please RSVP, so she knows how many people to order for.

"You going to the dinner?" I ask Chase, who laughs.

"Ah, no. That girl can't stand the sight of me. I think me breathing personally offends her. I'm not about to ruin her graduation by being there."

"I don't think *you* offend her," I say with a laugh. "Just you fucking all those women so loudly that Georgia feels like she's forced to listen to a porno." I clasp him on his back. "I'm going to get a workout in, you coming?"

"Always."

LEXI

"Lexi, you ready to go to the meeting?" Georgia asks through the door.

"Yeah, just give me a minute." I climb onto my feet and flush the toilet, then wash my mouth out and brush my teeth for the third time this morning. The last several days I haven't been feeling so hot. It started when Alec and I were away, but I ignored it. It wasn't too bad, and I figured I probably just ate something that didn't agree with me, or I was stressed and exhausted from everything that's happened the last few weeks.

But then, the morning Alec left to work after returning from our trip, I went over to my parents' house to visit with them and get my insurance information so I could make an appointment with a therapist. As I walked through their door, the smell of bacon cooking hit my nostrils and I ran to the bathroom to throw up. I knew right then something was wrong. Very wrong.

I step out of the bathroom and Georgia is standing there, assessing me with her knowing, sisterly eyes. I release a harsh breath and she envelops me in a hug. She doesn't ask and I don't say anything. We don't need to.

Twenty minutes later, we walk into Klein's, an upscale bistro downtown. Our gazes both search for the woman we're meeting. "I think that's her," Georgia says, nodding toward a gray-haired older woman sitting in the corner. She's dressed in an expensive looking pant suit and her hair is pulled up into a tight chignon.

"You can do this," I tell her, squeezing her arm. "And I'll be with you the entire time."

"Are you Hilda Reynolds?" she asks when we approach.

The woman glances up and smiles stiffly. She has brown eyes, as opposed to Georgia's green and nothing about her reminds me of Georgia. They might be related, but they don't look it. "I am." She stands and extends her hand, which Georgia takes. Kind of weird that a woman meets her granddaughter for the first time in years and she shakes her hand instead of hugging her. Our grandma from our dad's side can't hug us enough when she comes home from traveling.

"Thank you for finally meeting with me." Her words are polite, but her tone is strained, like she's forcing herself to be civil. It's a good thing I'm here with Georgia, because if this woman says anything to hurt my sister, I'll have no problem throat punching her.

"And who is this?" She juts her chin toward me.

"I'm Lexi," I tell her. "Georgia's sister."

"You look to be the same age," Hilda says. "Impossible."

"Not biologically," Georgia says softly, clearly intimidated by this bitch.

"But we might as well be," I add.

The waitress comes over and we order drinks. Once she walks away, Hilda cuts straight to the chase. "I've asked you here today because you're about to graduate. Your father, Justin Reynolds, left in his will that until you're twenty-two or graduate college, I was to oversee the company he left behind."

When Georgia squints in confusion, Hilda says, "Of course your mother didn't tell you." The way she spits out the word mother has my hackles rising. She doesn't know shit about our mother.

"If she didn't, it was with good reason," I tell her. "Please get to the point of this meeting." I've had about enough of this uptight stuck-up woman.

"My point is"—she keeps her eyes on Georgia—"he left you a multimillion-dollar empire, and now that you've graduated, I would like for you to sign it over to me." She pulls out a folder from her purse and opens it up like she didn't just drop a huge bombshell.

Georgia gasps, and I glare. "Why would he do that?" she asks as the waitress sets our drinks down. One whiff of my caramel macchiato and I almost upchuck right here at the table. Discreetly,

I push it away, so I don't have to smell it. Georgia eyes me curiously but doesn't question it.

The waitress takes our orders and I go with a parfait, hoping it will be easy on my stomach. Hilda orders one as well, and Georgia orders pancakes.

"Contrary to what your mother has probably told you," Hilda says, once the waiter has stepped away, "your father was a good man who loved you."

Georgia flinches. "She didn't tell me anything... and I barely even remember him." She quickly averts her gaze, and I immediately wonder what's going through her head.

Hilda huffs. "That's because your mother killed him when you were little." This time we both gasp. "Of course she didn't tell you any of this. I'm surprised she even let you meet with me."

When Georgia stays quiet, Hilda laughs evilly. "She doesn't know, does she?"

"Whatever she knows or doesn't know isn't your concern," I say. "So, her bio dad left her a company... and you want it... She's not going to just sign it over to you."

"I don't think—" Georgia begins, but I cut her off.

"You said it's worth millions. I'm not completely sure how it all works, but if she owns a company and you want it, I think you would have to *buy* it."

Hilda shoots daggers at me. "My husband and I have been running it for years."

"My grandfather?" Georgia asks. "I thought he was dead."

"He is. Thomas Faulding is my husband and the COO of Reynolds Oil. He's been running the company since your father was killed."

There she goes with that shit again... "You need to stop saying that," I warn. "Our mother wouldn't kill anyone. Now, if you want the company, you'll have to buy it from Georgia."

"Listen here, little girl," Hilda says, finally losing the little bit of restraint she had. "This is my damn company. Justin wrote that will before he knew Charlotte was a lying, cheating whore."

"We're done here." I stand, taking Georgia by the arm. "Georgia's attorney will be in contact." I pull her out of the bistro, all the way to my jeep, not stopping until we're inside.

"We have to tell Mom about her. That woman is fucking crazy."

"I can't." Georgia shakes her head. "It would break her heart that I went behind her back."

"She'll understand." Our mother is the most understanding person I know.

"Okay. Will you go with me?"

"Of course."

<hr />

"YOU DID WHAT?" MOM GASPS, GLANCING FROM US TO our dad. "Why would you meet with her?" Mom's bottom lips wobbles and tears prick her eyes. Dad envelops her in a side hug to comfort her.

"I thought I could go there, find out what she wanted, and you would never know," Georgia says. "I'm sorry."

"Oh no," Mom tells her, "you didn't do anything wrong. I just wish you had told me so I could've gone with you."

"Did you know my..." Georgia's words falter, unsure what to call the man who is her biological dad. "Umm... my... I don't know what to call him," Georgia finally says.

Dad moves from Mom to Georgia. "You can call him whatever you're comfortable with," he says. "Your dad, your father, Justin... I won't take offense."

"You're my dad," Georgia says. "This is just so confusing. She said he loved me..."

Mom sniffles. "I can't do this."

"You never can," Georgia snaps, shocking the hell out of me. "She said you killed him."

Mom gasps, and Dad curses.

"Why would she say that?" Georgia asks. "I need you to tell me, because all I've heard about him is from my grandmother, who said he loved me and that you killed him. And she said other stuff too..." She trails off. She might be upset and want answers, but she would never intentionally hurt Mom's feelings.

Just as I'm wrapping my arms around Georgia, so she knows I have her back, my stomach roils, and I'm jumping up. "Need to go pee!" I yell, as I sprint to the bathroom. I spend the next few minutes dry heaving, since I haven't eaten since last night. When I'm done, I attempt to wash my mouth out and then go back to join my family.

"Charlie," Dad says. "I think it's time we talk to the girls." I sit next to Georgia, taking her hand in mine in support.

Mom shakes her head, closing her eyes, but then nods. "Hilda was right," she says softly. "I did kill Justin."

"It was in self-defense," Dad adds. "Your mom left him and he came after her. He had a gun and they fought. Had she not shot him, he would've killed her."

Tears stream down Mom's face, as Georgia and I both fly off the couch and hug her tightly. "I should've told you," Mom says. "It was just a horrible time and I never wanted you to be tainted by it."

"She said I own his company," Georgia says. "Reynolds Oil, and she wants me to sign it over to her."

Mom's lips turn down into a frown.

"I think she should have to buy it," I add. "I've seen enough shows to know if it's worth millions, Georgia should be getting money. That woman tried to meet with Georgia to get her to sign it over so she wouldn't have to pay her. I told her we would have Georgia's lawyer contact her. There's no way Georgia is giving that dreadful woman anything for free."

Dad chuckles. "You sure you don't want to major in law?" His comment is meant as a joke, but it reminds me of how uncertain my future is. I have a year left of school in a major that will lead to nowhere, and a surfing career that, if I'm right about why I'm throwing up, won't be happening any time soon.

"So, what do I do?" Georgia asks, thankfully bringing the attention back to her.

"We'll hire an attorney, as Lexi said," Dad tells her. "Request to see the will Justin had drawn up and go from there."

"And don't worry," I tell her. "We'll all be here with you every step of the way. That evil woman might think she could get one over on you, but she doesn't know who she's messing with."

"Thank you," Georgia says, giving me a hug, then standing to give Dad and then Mom one.

When we get home, it's almost four o'clock. I place a call to my doctor, and the scheduling nurse tells me they can get me in this week.

"Do you know roughly how far along you are?" she asks.

"Umm... I'm not sure." I try to remember when my last period was, but I suck at keeping track. *Just like I suck at taking my pills...*

"No problem, the doctor can figure it out when you're here."

"Thanks."

I end the call and consider texting Alec, but figure I should wait to tell him tomorrow when he's home from work, in person.

What the nurse asked about my period has me curious, so I pull up my calendar and try to remember when I got my last period. I think about since Alec and I got together... We haven't used protection, and I haven't gotten my period once. I swipe back to the previous months, unable to recall when I got it last. My period has always been all over the place, and since I suck at taking my birth control pills, that doesn't help any.

I should probably be more anxious about possibly being pregnant, but the thought of having Alec's baby kind of excites me. We're getting married next week... He has a good job... He mentioned before that if I did get pregnant, it wouldn't be the worst thing in the world, since he's all about seizing the day.

I lie back in my bed and close my eyes, imagining our life. Him coming home from work and us spending the day with our baby. Going to the parks and the beach, teaching him how to swim and one day surf. Teaching him art. I bet Alec will love to teach him MMA, just like Mason taught him.

As the imaginary reel of images scrolls through my head, my heart picks up speed at the idea of becoming a mom. I would make sure I'm a good mom like Charlie. I would be there for our baby, love him with my entire being. Maybe this is what my future looks like... being a mom. Maybe this is what I was meant to do, the path I'm meant to take. Charlie runs her paint studio, but aside from that, growing up, she was always around, hands-on. I'm not saying I don't want to figure out what else I want to do with my life, but maybe being a mom and wife is what I'm meant to do. And over time, I can figure everything else out.

Suddenly excited, I pull out my phone to text Alec that we need to talk when he gets home, but before I can get the words out, a text from him comes in.

Alec: Luke and Finn are both out with flu. Chase asked me to fill in with him. I won't be home until Friday morning.

Damn, not only will he not be home for me to tell him our news, but he won't be able to go to the doctor with me. As I'm texting him back, telling him to stay safe and that I'll see him Friday morning for Georgia's graduation, the need to throw up hits me again. I probably shouldn't have eaten so much at my parents' place. But I was starving and my dad's burgers smelled and tasted so good.

I run to the bathroom and throw up my entire lunch, and then it hits me. What if I'm not pregnant? What if I'm sick? I feel like if I were, I would have other symptoms, but just to be sure, I should get confirmation from the doctor, and then once I know for sure, I can tell Alec, and hopefully he'll be as excited as I am, and we can celebrate.

Me: Sucks. Miss you and I'll see you Friday.

Alec: I'll be off through Sunday. We should do something fun.

Me: Sounds good!

ALEC

Ninety-six-hour shifts suck. Sure, it means overtime, which is great, but it also means four days without seeing Lexi, four days of sleeping at the station without her.

"Thanks again for staying," Chase says as we walk up to the condo. "The last thing we needed was one of them giving everyone else the flu."

"No worries," I tell him. "You know I got your back."

"I'm going to sleep for the next twenty-four hours," Chase half-jokes before he slips into his room.

Since there were three pretty big fires yesterday—a dryer that was left on and caught fire and a building with faulty wiring—and another one last night—a candle that caught a curtain on fire while a family with little kids were sleeping—we're both exhausted as fuck. But today is the day of Georgia's graduation, so the last thing

I'll be doing is sleeping. It's later this afternoon, but she said we have to head to the university auditorium early to get good seats. I'm hoping Lexi will at least be in bed, so we can cuddle for a few minutes before we both need to get ready.

When I enter our room, the bed is empty. She's probably sleeping in Georgia's bed. But when I walk in there, Georgia is up and typing away furiously on her laptop.

"Have you seen Lexi?" I ask.

"No." She stops typing and turns toward me. "Actually..." Her brows furrow in thought. "I haven't seen her since yesterday." She glances at her phone. "Shoot! It's already eight fifteen. I need to get ready for my graduation."

"What do you mean you haven't seen her since yesterday?"

Flashbacks of the last time Lexi disappeared flash before my eyes, and I'm running to the bathroom to make sure she isn't there. "Lexi!" I call out. No answer. "Lex!" Still nothing.

I grab my phone and pull up our conversation. Our last text was yesterday afternoon. I got so busy with putting out fires, I lost track of time.

"When's the last time you saw her?" I ask Georgia.

"Umm... Yesterday afternoon," she says.

"Not last night?"

"No." She shakes her head. "This company I work for... their site crashed and I've been working all night getting it back up. I lost track of time."

I call Lexi's phone, but it goes to voicemail. "I'm going to check the beach."

Georgia's eyes meet mine. "Alec, there's no way..."

"I have to make sure."

I run out the door and hop into my truck, noting that Lexi's jeep isn't in the parking lot. Fuck, where the hell is she? There's no way she would go to the beach, right? As far as I know, she hasn't been back there since she went to talk to Aiden. And to go without saying a word to anyone... No, no way. This doesn't make sense.

I dial her dad's number, hoping this is just some kind of shitty miscommunication. "Alec," he says.

"Have you seen Lexi?"

"No."

My heart squeezes in my chest. It's fucking hard to breathe. "Nobody has heard from her since yesterday afternoon."

"Fuck," he curses. "If that asshole..."

"I'm almost to the beach now. If he has anything to do with this, I'll kill him. Can you check her phone for the tracking?"

"Yeah, give me a second." A few seconds later, he says, "Her phone is off."

"Damn it." I slam my fist against the steering wheel.

"Keep me posted."

We hang up and I pull into the parking lot. I don't spot Lexi's jeep anywhere, but I still head down to where Aiden is to see if he's seen her.

"Hi, Lexi's boyfriend," he says when I walk up. I want to

correct him and tell him I'm Lexi's fiancé, but right now it really doesn't fucking matter. He's sitting in the sand, drawing in his sketchbook. He grabs his neon green glasses and puts them on.

"Hey, Aiden," I tell him, trying like hell to remain calm. If I upset him, he'll shrink up and I won't get any answers. "Have you seen Lexi?"

"Yes. She brought me dinner." He goes back to coloring in his sketchbook.

"Last night?" I ask to confirm.

"Yes, she brought me my favorite tacos," he says, not looking up.

Fuck, Lexi, what the hell were you doing here alone?

"Hey, Aiden, remember that bad man who hurt Lexi?"

Aiden's head pops up. "I didn't hurt her. It was that mean surfer."

Mean surfer... Jesus, if that doesn't prove it was Jason...

"I know. Did you see him here last night... with Lexi?"

"No. He isn't Lexi's friend. He's mean and he didn't love Lexi. He hurt her. She's not his friend."

"I know," I agree, trying to piece together what he's saying. "Did Lexi say where she was going last night?"

"She was sad. She was crying."

Fuck. Fuck. Fuck. This just keeps getting better.

"Did she say where she was going?" I repeat. "She never came home."

"No, she brought me tacos and cried. I gave her a picture to make her happy."

"When she left, was she alone?"

"Yes."

"And did she say where she was going?" I try again.

"No, but she said she'll see me soon. And my Lexi doesn't lie, so I'll see her soon. I'll tell her when I see her you want to see her."

I sigh in frustration. "Okay, thank you."

"Bye, Lexi's boyfriend."

I walk up to the pier and find the taco place where Lexi always buys Aiden his tacos. "Excuse me," I say to the gentleman who's wiping down the counter. "My fiancée, Lexi Scott, comes here a lot to buy tacos..."

"Yeah, I know her," he says before I can finish.

"Was she here last night buying tacos?"

"Yeah, she was. Real nice girl. She paid in advance for me to have tacos, every day, delivered to that homeless guy down under the pier."

Of course she did. Fuck, Lexi, where the hell are you? And why were you here?

"She showed up last night and gave me enough money for the next couple months, then bought some tacos and said she would bring it to the guy herself."

"Did you see her leave?"

"Nah, after she got the tacos and left, I didn't see her again."

"All right, thanks."

I'm heading to my truck, when I see that asshole walking

down the sidewalk with a board under his arm. He's talking to some woman, who is laughing at whatever he's saying.

Without thinking, I stalk over to him. He doesn't see me coming, until it's too late, and my fist is connecting with the side of his face. He stumbles back, his board hitting the ground. The girl screams. I punch him again and again, landing each blow, not giving him a chance to get a single punch in.

He's on the ground, his face covered in blood, and I'm about to yank him back up to hit him again, when someone comes up from behind and pulls me off him. His body falls to the ground.

I try to shove whoever it is off me, so I can finish this, but the guy is too strong. "Alec," Mason barks. "What the fuck are you doing?"

"Get off me," I yell, trying to go after Jason again. He's now crawling backward, spitting blood onto the concrete. The woman he was talking to is at his side. "He's the asshole who attacked Lexi."

Mason pauses for a second, and then Tristan steps up. "This is him?" Tristan asks, walking up to Jason.

"Yeah, and Lexi was seen here last night and now I can't find her."

"You see my daughter?" Tristan asks.

Jason laughs. Fucking laughs.

"Let me go!" I shout at Mason, who's still holding me back.

"No, you handle this shit right. The last thing you need is him charging you with assault." Too late for that shit.

"I asked you a question," Tristan says. "I suggest you answer me."

"I don't have to answer shit," Jason spits, rising shakily to his feet.

"Then I'll call the cops and you can answer to them." We already know the cops won't do shit. There's no proof Jason attacked Lexi that night and she couldn't confirm it. Except... Aiden. Holy shit, he witnessed it, and when I asked him about last night, he seemed like he knew who Jason was. Maybe he can identify him.

My phone goes off and I pull it out. It's Ryan. **Thought you should know Lexi is here. She asked us not to tell anyone, but if Micaela ran, I would want to know she's safe.**

What the fuck? She ran. Why?

"Tristan, I found her," I tell him.

He turns around. "She okay?"

"Yeah."

He glances back at Jason. "I know damn well it was you who attacked my daughter. And now that I know what you look like, you better watch your fucking back." He picks up Jason's board, and while holding it, he uses the weight of his foot and snaps it in half. Then he walks toward Mason and me. "Let's go."

We follow him over to my truck. "Ryan texted me that she's at their house."

"In San Diego?" Tristan asks, sounding as confused as I am. "Her sister's graduation is in a few hours. What the hell is she doing there?"

"I don't know. He said she ran and asked them not to tell anyone, but he knew I would be freaking the fuck out." Speaking of which...

Me: Thank you. Is she driving back down with you guys?"

Ryan: I don't think so. She's crying and Micaela is talking to her. She said she's not going. I just wanted you to know she's okay.

Me: Thanks.

"He said she's not planning to go to the graduation."

"What the hell happened?" Tristan asks. "She would never miss her sister's graduation."

"Did you two get into a fight?" Mason asks.

"No, I haven't even been home in four days. Had to pull a ninety-six-hour shift. Got home and she was already gone. She came by here last night and saw Aiden. Bought him tacos. He said she was crying and he drew her a picture to make her happy. Then she left."

"All right, well, she's safe," Tristan says. "I need to get to Georgia's graduation. Then, afterward, we can figure this out."

"What?" I give him a look I'm sure matches my frustration. "I'm going to San Diego."

"She doesn't want you to know where she is," Mason says.

"And going to her will throw Ryan under the bus," Tristan adds. "She's safe there. Nowhere near Jason. Whatever is going on can wait until after the graduation."

"And like you said," I argue. "Lexi would never miss her sister's graduation. Something is fucking wrong." I glance at the time on my phone. "It's a two-hour drive. If I leave now, I can get her back in time."

Tristan blows out a harsh breath. "I want to tell you not to, but..."

"But you know damn well if that was Charlie, you would do the same thing." I look at Mason. "And you would too."

Mason nods. "Yeah, I would."

I open my truck door and get in. "I'll keep you updated."

The drive to San Diego is filled with me questioning every conversation from the last few days, trying to figure out what happened from the time we got back from our trip to now. None of it makes any sense. I'm missing a piece, and until I find out what it is, I won't know what's going on. When I'm halfway there, Ryan texts me to let me know they left to the graduation and Lexi stayed behind.

When I arrive at Micaela and Ryan's house, I see Lexi's jeep in their driveway. Since I don't have a key, I knock on the door. When nobody answers, I walk around the house like a creepy stalker, peeking into every window. Finally, I find the one I'm looking for. Lexi is lying on the bed, curled up into a ball and crying. Fuck.

I bang on the window and she jumps. "Lex," I yell. "Let me in."

Her eyes go as wide as saucers. She walks to the window and raises the blinds, giving me a full frontal view of her. Her eyes are bloodshot and puffy from her crying. Black rings underneath from lack of sleep. She's paler than usual, almost ghostly looking. Her blond hair is up in a messy bun and she's wearing my Station 115 hoodie with a pair of tiny cotton shorts barely peeking out from under it.

"You scared me, baby," I tell her.

Instead of telling me she'll open the door, she unlocks the window and lifts it slightly. "I'm sorry I didn't tell you I left."

"It's okay. We need to get to Georgia's graduation, though. So, why don't we talk on the way back?" I'll deal with getting her car later.

She flinches then shakes her head. "I'm not going with you."

"Lex, whatever is going on, we can deal with it... together. But you can't miss Georgia's graduation. You will never forgive yourself. This is a big day for your sister."

She sniffles and fresh tears surface. "You're right."

I sigh in relief. "I'll meet you in the front." I walk around the house and a minute later, Lexi steps out. "We can come back and get your jeep."

"No, we can't," she says, stepping up to me. "Because..." She releases a sob that hits me in the chest. It's as if someone is gripping my heart with a vice grip. "We're not together anymore." She slides her ring off her finger and tries to hand it to me.

"What the fuck are you doing?" I step back as if the ring has the potential to burn me. "What's going on?"

"I'm calling off the wedding... our engagement," she says, tears streaming down her face. She grabs my hand and forces the ring into my hand, closing my fingers around it.

"Why?" None of this makes any damn sense.

"Because I'm pregnant," she sobs. My eyes go to her belly. She's pregnant... We're having a baby. Then why the fuck would she leave me? I'm about to ask, when her next words stun me into silence. "And I don't know if the baby is yours."

LEXI

The look of pain and confusion on Alec's face damn near makes me throw up. I didn't plan to tell him like this, not right now, which is why I ran, so I could take some time to figure out how to tell him. I should've known Ryan would tell him I was here. I'm not mad, though. I shouldn't have left without telling anyone where I was going, especially Alec. He must've been so worried. I was going to text him that I was okay, but my phone died last night, and I didn't bring a charger with me. By the time I thought about it, after Micaela and Ryan left, I couldn't find one. They must've taken the chargers with them.

"Lex," Alec croaks. "You're going to have to explain this to me, because I know damn well you would never cheat on me."

He's right, I wouldn't. Because he's my entire world. Which is why I had to break up with him, because he deserves more...

better... than what I can give him.

My head feels fuzzy, probably from all the crying and throwing up and lack of eating. "Let's sit down and I'll explain."

We have a seat on the porch swing, and it makes my heart hurt. Micaela and Ryan have the cutest little family home. They have a large backyard with a jungle gym for RJ, a wraparound porch with a swing that fits the three of them, and there's even a white picket fence. My hand goes to my belly, as I think about how badly I wanted this: the house, the family, the white picket fence. Only a few short days ago I was fantasizing about being a mom. Now, I...

"Lex, please," Alec pleads.

"Sorry." I take a deep breath. "As I said, I'm pregnant... and it might not be your baby." My thoughts go back to yesterday...

"Alexandria Scott," the nurse calls out with a smile on her face.

"That's me," I tell her, standing.

We go through the standard visit stuff: weight, blood pressure, temperature check.

"It says you're here to get your pregnancy confirmed," she says once she's done jotting it all down on her iPad.

"Yes."

"Go ahead and change into this gown and pee in a cup in the bathroom. Write your name on it and slip it through the metal door." She hands me a white gown. "I'll be back in a few minutes.

Once she's gone, I do as she says, then have a seat on the table. As she said, a few minutes later, she returns, bringing with her my doctor.

"Lexi," Dr. O'Neil says, shaking my hand. My mom, Georgia, and I have been seeing her for years. "How are you?"

"I'm okay."

"The urine test confirmed you're pregnant." I expect to suddenly feel nervous or worried. I mean, this is it. It's been confirmed. I'm pregnant. But I don't. I feel happy. Images of me telling Alec and him being as excited as me flit through my head.

"It said in your chart you weren't sure when your last period was," she adds. "So, we're going to do an ultrasound so we can give you an estimated date."

"Okay."

She rolls a condom onto the probe and explains she's doing an internal ultrasound because if I'm not too far along, she won't be able to pick up a heartbeat with the external one.

She turns the screen on and almost immediately a loud whooshing sound fills the room. "That's your baby's heartbeat," she explains. My eyes stay trained on the small fluttering heart as I tear up. A heartbeat. My baby has a heartbeat. There's a living being in my body and in several months I'll be able to hold him or her in my arms. I immediately regret not telling Alec. I didn't want to get his hopes up if I was wrong and wasn't pregnant, but now he's missing out on this amazing, magical moment.

"Based on the size of the fetus, I'm estimating your due date to be March twenty-first," she says. "It might change give or take a couple days." She clicks on her iPad, then turns to me. "That puts you at roughly seven weeks."

Jeez, has it been that long since I got a period? I'm almost two months along. I do the math in my head. That would've been around... And like a bucket of ice water has been poured over me, I sit up quickly, trying to take in oxygen. My heart is going erratic and I can't catch my breath. It feels as though all the blood has drained from my body. My trembling hands clutch my chest as I try to slow my heartrate.

"Lexi, are you okay?" Dr. O'Neil asks, concerned.

"Can you tell... based on your calculations... when the baby was conceived?"

The doctor's brows dip in confusion, but she doesn't question my question. Instead she clicks on her iPad, then says, "We can't pinpoint the exact date, since days of ovulation for everyone differs, but based on your due date, it would be around July first."

July first.

The day I was attacked.

That date remains engrained in my brain. And I'm pretty sure it always will.

One hand roughly grips my mane, tugging my head back.

My knees slam against the rocks.

"Stop!" I plead.

The other hand slides under my bikini bottoms.

"Please don't do this," I beg.

"You're a fucking tease! And teases like you deserve what they get."

"Ow! That's hurts. Please don't do this."

"Lexi... Lexi, baby. Come back to me." Alec. His soft voice.

I open my eyes, and I'm back on the porch swing with Alec.

"I think he raped me," I whisper, my eyes refusing to meet

his. It's the first time I've said the words aloud, and they feel like sandpaper as they leave my lips. "All the flashbacks in my head..." I choke out a sob. "They lead to him raping me. And the doctor... she said my estimated date of conception was July first."

When Alec doesn't say anything, I glance up at him. His jaw is hard and his eyes are closed. I can't imagine what's going through his head. This baby... it's supposed to be our baby. But there's a chance it's not. And it's not fair to put him through this.

"That's why I can't marry you," I explain. "I can't ask you to commit to spending your life with me when there's a chance I'm carrying another man's baby."

Alec opens his eyes and looks at me, and the pain radiating in them is enough to cripple my heart. "I should feel disgusted that I'm possibly carrying a baby by a man who raped me, but I can't find it in me to be. Because even though it's possibly half his, this baby is also half mine, and when I saw him on the monitor—"

"Him?"

"I don't know. It just felt wrong calling him or her an it. He had a heartbeat..."

Alec nods. "Why didn't you tell me about your appointment?"

"I wasn't completely sure if I was pregnant. When you mentioned the guys at work had the flu, I wondered if maybe I had it too. I wanted to confirm it and then tell you so we could celebrate. But then the doctor gave me the dates and I realized celebrating wouldn't be happening."

Alec turns his body toward me and takes my hands in his. His gaze locks with mine, and I feel sick to my stomach. He warned me to be careful. Not to stay on the beach too late. I didn't listen...

"I need you to listen to me very carefully," he says. "I love you with every part of my being. I knew years ago you were the one for me, but I was a coward, too scared to lose you to tell you how I felt. But then my dad died, and it gave me the courage to not waste a single moment. I realized from his death how precious life is. How short it is. You can do everything right and it can still end before you're ready for it to."

His words cause my throat to fill with emotion.

"You're mine, Lexi Scott," he continues. "You've been mine our entire lives in some way or another, and if you think this news is going to change that you don't understand how strong my love for you is."

"But—"

"No," he says. "No buts. This baby you're carrying is ours. End of story. We're going to go home and get ready and then go to Georgia's graduation. And then when it's over we'll go to your parents' house for the graduation party. Tonight, I'll hold you in my arms and we'll talk about our future..."

A fresh round of tears form and spill over. My body racking with sobs.

"Next week we'll get married in front of our friends and family, and when we're ready we'll announce that we're expecting a baby. And in seven months we'll welcome that baby into the world. We'll love him and protect him and he will be ours." His eyes and tone carry such conviction, goose bumps cover my arms.

"But what if he isn't—"

"He is," Alec says, speaking the two words slowly.

"I can't let you—"

"You can't let me do what? Love a baby that's part you? An innocent baby who will have your blood flowing through his veins. When I was eight years old, I met Mason, and from the moment he moved into my mom's house, he loved me as if I were his own. And you know why? Because I was my mom's son, and he loved her. He treated me like his flesh and blood, the same as my sister even though she really is his. The same way your dad treats Georgia, and your mom treats you."

Tears course down my cheeks. I'm crying so hard I can't speak. I'm hiccupping between sobs, and it's hard to breathe. "I know, but you deserve better than this."

"What I deserve is you," he says. "What I want is you... the good, the bad, and the ugly. I want it all with you. Life isn't always beautiful, Lex." He reaches out and tucks a hair behind my ear.

"Sometimes it's downright ugly. And it's during those times we want to give up, hide so we don't have to deal with it. Like when my dad died... I wanted nothing more than to wallow in my grief. But it's because of those ugly times, we're able to appreciate the beautiful. What might've happened to you, the possibility that that asshole might've raped you is really fucking ugly, but, baby, you have a healthy baby growing in you, and if that's not fucking beautiful then I don't know what is."

Alec edges closer and wraps his arms around me. I close my eyes and inhale his fresh scent, immediately calming down, my body relaxing. I don't know what I was thinking running from Alec. He's the other half of me. My path. My past. My present. My future. My forever.

Alec takes my hand in his and slides my ring back on. "Don't ever take this off again. This is where it belongs and where it needs to stay."

He kisses the top of my forehead and I sigh into his chest, feeling like I can breathe for the first time since finding out the date of conception. But then I remember what the doctor told me...

"Dr. O'Neil, my OB/GYN, said that in California, even if I can prove Jason raped me, if he's the father he can fight for rights to the baby." I couldn't believe what she said, so I looked it up when I left her office and she was right. In California, on several occasions, the men who were tried and found guilty, later went on to receive some sort of visitation.

"It's not going to happen," Alec says. He lifts my chin, so I'm looking at him. "That baby is ours and nobody will ever know anything different."

Twenty Nine

ALEC

Lexi is pregnant and she ran because she was scared I wouldn't be able to love her and the baby she's carrying if it turns out he's not mine. I hate that she didn't have enough faith in our love, in me, to know that I could never stop loving her, and I would die for that baby in her belly. But at the same time, I get it. She was scared. She still is. What she went through, is still going through, is traumatic as fuck. She still doesn't know what happened that night she was attacked, and she more than likely will never know. And now she's carrying a baby that was possibly conceived out of hate instead of love. But I meant what I said: nobody will ever know that. As far as everyone will ever know, that baby is ours, created out of love. And that asshole, Jason, will never know that Lexi is pregnant or that the baby might carry his DNA. I'll make damn sure of it.

I pull into our complex and Lexi parks next to me. I tried

to convince her to leave her vehicle there, but she wanted to get it over with and bring it home now, so I followed her home. We need to run inside and quickly change and then head to Georgia's graduation. We'll just barely make it there, but at least we'll be there, and Georgia will have her sister there when she walks across the stage.

As I step out of my truck, I take a look around at the complex with new eyes. This place isn't exactly family friendly. It's adjacent to a busy road. The majority of the tenants are college students and young couples. There's a park, but it's about a half-mile down the street. When my parents bought me the place as a gift for graduating from the fire academy it was perfect, but now...

"What are you looking at?" Lexi steps closer to me and glances around, trying to see what I'm seeing.

"We need to buy a house. This place isn't meant for a family." I take her hand in mine and bring it up to my lips to kiss the top of her knuckles. Her skin is warm and soft and smells like her vanilla body wash. I miss the scent of the ocean on her. It's been a while since she's been surfing, and I guess with the baby coming, she'll have to wait a while longer.

"I want to buy a house on the beach," I tell her. "So you can go surfing on a private beach. I don't want you going back to that beach." I don't want her anywhere near where Jason might be.

"What about Aiden?" she asks.

Of course that's her concern. Lexi has such a big heart, and she's going to make an amazing mom.

"We're going to figure out how to help him," I promise her. "Get him off that beach and somewhere safe."

"Thank you," she says, standing on her tiptoes to kiss me.

We make it to Georgia's graduation on time and cheer for her as she walks across the stage. While we're there, Lexi tells me she's not sure if she wants to go back to school. She's not sure what she wants to do, but she knows she's excited to be a mom. I tell her she has plenty of time to figure it out. I make more than enough to support us, and with the life insurance money my dad left me, I can buy us a house to start our family.

———

THE NEXT WEEK FLIES BY. WHEN I'M HOME, WE HANG out with everyone who's in town for the graduation and wedding. And at night, when we're alone, we lie in bed, wrapped up in each other, talking about our future, about the baby, about us. Lexi read that twelve weeks is when you're supposed to announce you're expecting, so we plan to tell everyone then. She hasn't even told her sister, which I'm surprised about. I think she's still grasping at the reality that she really is pregnant and in seven months she'll be giving birth to a baby.

When I'm at work, we text and video chat. I can see it in her eyes, she's scared. Of me changing my mind, of me regretting my words, my promise. She's waiting for me to tell her I can't do this. But it's never going to happen. I love Lexi and I'm going to marry her. The odds of this baby actually not being mine are slim. *If he raped her, it was once, compared to the dozens of times we had unprotected sex during that time.* Sure, it only takes once, and if he did rape her, the baby she's carrying could carry his DNA, but that baby, regardless of his blood type, is mine. He will carry my last name and will be loved by both of us. From the moment she told me, there was never a doubt in my mind.

But even though Lexi is one of the strongest women I know, I also know she's insecure when it comes to this topic. Her own mother, her flesh and blood, walked out of the hospital without her and never looked back. So, through my actions, I'll show her that I'm serious. That I'll love and protect her and this baby. That she and I are forever.

Starting with marrying her, which is what I'm about to do. With the wedding march playing in the background, I watch, mesmerized, as Lexi walks down the wooden walkway that is doubling as a makeshift aisle. On either side are white and pink flowers. She's dressed in a beautiful off-white dress that shows off all of her curves. In her hands is a bouquet of matching pink and white flowers. She's wearing a see-though veil that covers her face, and her hair is down in waves. When she steps down to where Chase, Georgia, and I are standing with the marriage officiant, she lifts her dress slightly, showing off her sparkly shoes. Of course my girl would wear Vans instead of heels.

She hands Georgia her flowers, and then, with tear-filled eyes, her dad leans over and kisses her cheek, murmuring something to her that makes her smile.

"I love you, Dad," she says.

"Love you too, Lex."

He extends his hand, and we shake. "I don't need to tell you to love her and take care of her. I know you will," he croaks.

I nod once. "Damn right I will."

He pulls me into a hug and then takes a seat next to Charlie and Max.

I take Lexi by the arm and walk her up to the altar then lift her veil. She smiles softly and her indigo eyes sparkle with happiness and love.

"You look breathtakingly beautiful," I tell her, not wanting to take my eyes off her.

"You look very handsome," she says. "But nothing beats your firefighter uniform."

She speaks loud enough that everyone hears, and they all chuckle, making her blush.

The officiant begins speaking, but I don't hear any of what he's saying. I'm too entranced by the woman in front of me. My soon-to-be wife, mother of my child, best friend. I never thought I would see the day when she would officially become mine.

"Do you, Aleczander Sterling, take Alexandria Scott to be your lawful wedded wife, to have and to hold, for richer or poorer, for better or worse, until death do you part?"

I laugh at the similarity of our names. Once upon a time, when Lexi was born, my mom was there and helped name her. It's like it was fate.

"I do." I slide the wedding band that matches her engagement ring onto her finger.

"Alexandria Scott, do you take Aleczander Sterling to be your lawful wedded husband, to have and to hold, for richer or poorer, for better or worse, until death do you part?"

"I do," she says with a watery smile, as she slides my fire-proof wedding band onto my finger. We decided to go with traditional vows, since everything we wanted to say was said between us when we were alone.

"I now pronounce you husband and wife," the gentleman says. "You may kiss the bride."

I step up to Lexi and, cradling the side of her face with my palm, press my lips to hers. The kiss is soft and sweet, unrushed. But then she wraps her arms around my neck and deepens the kiss, sliding her tongue past my parted lips. And the next thing I know, I'm lifting her into my arms as everyone around us claps and cheers.

Lexi pulls back, with the most gorgeous smile on her face. "Whoops," she says, not at all sorry.

I set her down and, with our fingers intertwined, we face our family and friends, ready to start our lives together as husband and wife.

We walk back down the aisle, and after taking pictures, we make our way onto the back deck of the resort. The reception is being held outside. There are tables set up all around, a bar in one corner, and on the other side is a buffet of food. In the center of the large area is the dance floor.

The deejay announces us, and everyone claps, welcoming us. Before we have time to speak to anyone, the deejay asks us to the dance floor for our first dance.

"I can't wait to hear the song you picked," Lexi says. She handled most of the details for the wedding, but she left the first dance song up to me, and I took the job seriously, making Chase and the other guys listen to dozens of songs before picking the one that was perfect.

"I wanted 'Love You Like I Used To'," I tell her. "But Chase said it would be too fast to dance to."

Lexi smiles. "I love that song."

"You and Me" by Lifehouse starts and I take Lexi into my arms. Her lips curl into the most beautiful smile and I kiss her softly. "It's just you and me, baby."

"Yeah, it is," she agrees.

As we sway to the music, neither of us can take our eyes off each other. Words don't need to be spoken, as the song is saying everything that needs to be said in the moment. When it ends, I kiss her one more time before we make our way off the dance floor, since the next song will be the father-daughter dance.

As we're walking over to her dad, Aiden approaches us. Lexi insisted he be at the wedding. Chase was nice enough to bring him and Georgia promised she would keep an eye on him for us.

"Congratulations, Lexi," he says with his bright green glasses on. "Congratulations, Lexi's husband."

I laugh. "Thank you, Aiden."

"Thank you," Lexi says, giving him a hug. "And thank you for coming."

"I drew you a picture," Aiden says, handing Lexi the paper. It's a picture of the two of us saying our wedding vows. He must've been drawing it while we were up at the altar.

"Oh, Aiden," she says, choking up. "It's beautiful." Tears slide down her cheeks and she tries to swipe them away.

"Lexi," Aiden says. "Lexi's husband loves you."

"He does," she agrees. "He loves me, and I love him too."

LEXI

The deejay announces that it's time for the father-daughter dance, so I thank Aiden for the beautiful picture and give the paper to Alec to hold for me.

My dad comes over and takes my hand, guiding us onto the dance floor. He's the strongest man I know, but today I've seen him shed tears no less than three times.

The music starts to play, and it's a song I've never heard before. For several seconds I listen to the lyrics, as my dad and I dance. It's about a father who loved his daughter first, before her husband. He prayed she would find a good man, but it's still hard to give her away. As the lyrics continue, the tears I was trying to hold back fall.

"Oh, Lex," Dad says, holding me closer. "I love you so damn much."

"This song is beautiful," I tell him, resting my head against his chest.

"It's called 'I Loved Her First' by Heartland." We dance for another minute, before he says, "I can't believe my little girl is all grown up."

I glance up at him and sniffle back the tears. Realistically nothing is changing. I'm still living in LA with Alec, only a few minutes from my parents, but it feels like everything is changing.

"I can still remember when you were little," he says. "Coloring everywhere, so damn carefree... I know I've been pushing you to find your place in this world, but, Lex, I need you to know how proud I am of you. Whether you go back to college, or surf again... or continue to paint the sides of those damn walls." He chokes out a laugh and I join in. "I know whatever you decide to do you're going to be amazing, because you already are."

"Thank you, Dad." He has no idea how much I needed to hear that right now.

The song ends and Mason comes over to dance with me. "First my goddaughter, and now my daughter-in-law," he says. "That boy better treat you right, or I'll throw his ass over the pier."

"You helped raise him," I tell him. "So you know how good of a man he is."

"Yeah, I do," he says, "and I'm so happy that you both found your way to each other."

"Thank you."

We dance as the song plays, and once it's over, Alec takes

me back into his arms as the deejay announces that everyone is welcome to join us on the dance floor.

After we finish our dance, we eat and spend time with our friends and family. We cut and feed each other cake and Chase and Georgia give emotional and funny speeches. The day couldn't be any more perfect.

When it gets late, Alec reminds me we have a plane to catch. We thank everyone for joining us, and then after hugging and kissing our family, we take off on our honeymoon.

"HEY, MRS. STERLING, YOU READY?" ALEC ASKS.

I glance over at him, a huge smile splayed across my face. I'll never get tired of him calling me that, and I know he says it because he loves hearing it just as much.

"Hell yes, I am, Mr. Sterling." I wink, and Alec laughs, pulling my face to his for a kiss.

We follow the crowd through the airport, then, after grabbing our bags, head outside to snag a cab. The honeymoon he planned is a week in London, visiting the art galleries and exploring the city, and I couldn't be more excited. I hated leaving Aiden, but Georgia promised she would check on him, and Greg has been paid for the tacos for the next few months.

The ride to our hotel doesn't take too long, and since Alec planned everything so well, check-in goes smoothly. When we step up to the door leading to our room, Alec scoops me up into his arms and walks us through the door. "Not our threshold," he says, "but it will do."

He sets me down and pulls me into his arms. "I need you," he murmurs against my lips.

"And you can have me."

"We're supposed to go sightseeing," he says.

"I'd rather see you."

Since our flight left right after the wedding, this will be our first time making love as husband and wife. Slowly, Alec removes my hoodie that has *Just Married* scrawled across the back and then my tank top.

He cups my breasts, which are sensitive thanks to being pregnant, and kisses the top of each one gently before he reaches around and unclasps my bra, exposing my hardened nipples.

"I can't believe you're mine," he says, wrapping his lips around a nipple and sucking. "These are mine." He takes my other breast into his hand and sucks on it the same way, sending zaps of pleasure through my body.

Stopping momentarily, he reaches behind him and removes his shirt, and I take a second to admire my husband. His tight abs and taut chest. I'll never tire of looking at him.

We both reach for each other's pants at the same time and laugh. After we're completely naked, he lifts me into his arms, carrying me to the bed. He lays me out in the center and climbs over me. He trails kisses down the center of my breasts and stops when he gets to my belly.

"I can't believe there's a baby growing in there," he says, awe in his tone. He kisses the spot just below my belly button. "I can't wait until your belly is big and I can feel the baby kicking."

Butterflies flood my belly and my thighs clench in want. I love when he talks about the baby and how excited he is. Since I told him, he's already started looking for houses and saving baby furniture websites. At night, he looks up information about pregnancy and babies and tells me all about it. He reminds me every day how blessed we are and that everything will turn out okay.

"Make love to me," I tell him, grabbing his shoulders and pulling him back up to me. "Make me yours."

"It would be my pleasure."

THE NEXT WEEK IS FILLED WITH SEEING THE SIGHTS. WE visit so many art galleries, and I take millions of pictures. When we aren't out sightseeing, we're holed up in our room, making love. I wish our honeymoon could last forever, but all too soon, it comes to an end and we're forced to return home... back to reality.

Thirty One

LEXI

Three Weeks Later

"How'd it go?" I ask Georgia as she walks through the door, her heels click-clacking against the wood floor. She looks so grown up and professional in her blazer, pencil skirt, and heels that she wore to court. Dad walks in behind her, also dressed smartly in a gray suit.

"Hilda settled." Georgia smiles softly. "I am no longer the owner of Reynolds Oil."

"What does that mean?" Mom asks.

We all wanted to be with Georgia, to support her, but her attorney felt it was best for only her and our dad to go. He managed to fast track it, and he didn't want Hilda to feel like she was being ganged up on and, in turn, create more problems. So, we've been waiting all morning at my parents' house to find out how it went.

"It means your sister is a millionaire," Dad says with a laugh.

"What?" I screech. "She bought it for a million dollars?"

"Way more than that," Georgia says. "But based on what the attorney said, she still got it for a lot less than I could've sold it for. And it turns out, Justin left me a trust fund as well."

"She should be thankful Georgia is so generous," Dad says, kissing Georgia on her temple.

"Wow, congratulations!" I hug her. "I'm glad this is all past you now." I know she's been stressed out over it, wanting to get it all settled. "So, what are you going to do now that you're a mega wealthy millionaire?"

Georgia snorts. "I don't even know. It's all so weird... and I hate that it's all from a man who tried to keep me from our mom and then tried to kill her."

"Hey," Mom says. "That money is rightfully yours. Put it away, invest it... you have time to figure it out, but don't feel guilty for having it."

Georgia nods. "Okay."

"Congratulations," Alec says as Mila and Mason walk through the door with his sister, Anna. Since I'm officially twelve weeks today, we're planning to tell everyone that we're expecting. Alec went with me to my last appointment and the baby's heartbeat was strong. We got new pictures of the little bean and we're so excited to finally be able to share our news with everyone.

"Hey, sweetie," Mila says to Alec, kissing his cheek. "Lexi." She kisses my cheek as well, then has a seat on the couch next to her husband. Dad tells Mason and Mila how court went while we wait for Max and Chase to get here.

Once they both arrive, and everyone is seated, Mason says, "So, let's have it. Mila has been dying to know your news. You can't text your mother that you have something to tell us and leave her hanging. She's been driving me crazy."

"I agree," Mom says. "I've been going nuts."

"Oh, c'mon," Chase says. "Like you guys don't know." He scoffs.

"Know what?" Mila asks.

"I'll let them tell you," he says with a smirk.

"Since you think you know, tell us," I taunt. There's no way he—

"Fine, Alec knocked up Lexi."

Everyone gasps, and Alec grabs the magazine off the coffee table and smacks Chase with it.

"You're pregnant?" my dad asks, his eyes going wide and straight to my still flat belly. I've started to put on a little weight and my clothes are fitting differently, but I don't have a present baby bump yet.

"Yes," I tell everyone. "I'm twelve weeks pregnant."

"I knew it," Georgia says. "I can't believe you tried to keep it from me, though." She side-eyes me half-jokingly.

"We wanted to wait until the twelve-week mark," I explain.

"Yeah, yeah." She stands and gives me a hug. "Congratulations."

"Wow," Mom says. "I'm going to be a grandma!"

Everyone jumps up and hugs us... Well, everyone except my dad and Mason. They're now standing against the wall, next to each other, with their arms crossed over their chests.

"Are you mad?" I ask my dad nervously.

"No," he says, tears pricking his eyes. "I'm just trying to figure out how the hell you went from my little girl, the one who colored all over the walls and hated boys, to being a wife and now a mother."

Mason huffs. "If I didn't love Alec as much as I do, I'd threaten to kick his ass for knocking up my goddaughter."

Both guys step forward and envelop me in a hug, each congratulating me. "We're really excited," I tell them.

"Hey, Lex," Max says. "Lex, you gotta see this."

I pull away from my dad and Mason and go to Max, who has his phone out. He hands it to me, and when I read what it says, I stumble back in shock.

"What's wrong?" Alec asks, taking the phone from me. "Holy shit," he murmurs, when he reads what it says.

"What is it?" my dad asks.

"Jason was found dead under the pier and Aiden has been arrested," I tell him. "We have to go to the station."

"Lex, you're pregnant," Alec says. "You can't be getting stressed out. Please, baby, calm down. We'll figure this out."

"Aiden saved me," I snap, grabbing my purse and heading to the door. "Had he not found me, I could've died. He needs us. Now."

"He needs an attorney," Dad says. "I'll call mine. Let's go."

We get to the station at the same time the attorney that my dad called does. We explain to him about Aiden and how he's homeless and it's likely he's autistic and has no one.

"I want to make sure he's protected," I tell him.

The attorney speaks to the authorities, who then agree to let us go back and see Aiden.

"He's not under arrest," the officer says as we walk down the hallway. "The woman who was attacked has confirmed that Aiden saved her, but we need him to walk us through what happened, so we have it on record. Then we can let him go."

I sigh in relief, thankful Aiden's not in trouble. "I'll go talk to him."

"Lexi," Aiden says when I walk through the door. "I want to go home. I need to go home. The nice man who brings me my tacos will be there soon." He's wearing his green glasses, but when I enter, he removes them.

"I'll make sure you get your tacos. Can you tell me what happened?"

"If I'm not there, he won't know where I am," he insists, only concerned with his tacos.

"I promise you, I'll make sure he knows, but I need you to tell me what happened, so you can go home."

Aiden sighs in frustration. "The mean surfer man didn't love her. He wasn't loving the girl," he says, shaking his head. "I told him he had to love the girl, like how your husband loves you, but he didn't listen. He yelled at me and hit me, like how my mom's boyfriend used to hit me. I told him it's not nice to hit, but he kept hitting me. He hurt me, Lexi." Aiden frowns and points to the black eye forming on his left eye, and my heart breaks. If Jason were still alive, I swear I would find a way to kill him myself.

"Then the police officer yelled at me and told me I had to leave my house and come here. I told him I didn't hurt her," Aiden continues. "I told him I had to be home for my tacos. Can I go home now and have my tacos?"

A part of me was hoping somehow Aiden would imply, through his words, whether Jason actually raped me, but to Aiden it's all the same. He doesn't actually understand the sexual act, only whether you're nice or mean. He might be an adult, but he sees things as a child does.

"Yeah," I tell him. "You can go home and get your tacos."

Aiden smiles. "Thank you, Lexi." He throws his arms around me in a bear hug. "I love tacos."

"I know you do."

He stands and puts his glasses back on, having no clue that he not only saved me but saved another woman. I'll never know how far Jason went, but what I do know is that had Aiden not been there, it could've been worse. Jason would've left me for dead, and had Aiden not been there last night, that woman could've been left for dead as well. Instead, she's safe at the hospital and Jason will never lay his hands on another woman without her permission again.

Aiden gets in the car with my dad, Alec, and me. He talks the entire way to the beach about wanting to go home and get his tacos, not caring that his home is a fucking tent under the pier. Not understanding that he's a hero.

When we get to the beach, he walks with me to the taco stand.

"Hey, Aiden," Greg, the taco stand owner, says. "I brought you your tacos, but you weren't there." He hands him a brown bag of food.

"The police made me leave," Aiden says. "I won't leave again unless they make me leave again. Will you bring me my tacos tomorrow?"

"Yeah," he says. "I'll bring you your tacos tomorrow."

Greg smiles sadly at me, obviously knowing what happened since it's been all over the news.

I walk with Aiden to his tent, and he sits in the same spot he always sits and starts to eat his tacos. I hate that I have to leave him here, but I still have no idea how to help him.

"I'll see you soon, okay?" I tell him, not wanting to leave, but knowing my dad and Alec are waiting for me.

"Okay, bye, Lexi."

Thirty Two

LEXI

One Week Later

"What are you doing?" Alec yells over the smoke alarm as I pull the burnt to a crisp bread out of the toaster and toss it into the garbage can.

"I was trying to make toast!" I yell back, swiping my tears off my face.

Alec reaches up and presses the button, turning the alarm off. "Lex, we've talked about this. You're going to burn the place down if you keep trying to cook shit."

He turns around and when he sees I'm crying, he pulls me into his arms. "Baby, what's wrong? It's just burnt toast."

"It's not *just* burnt toast," I cry out. "How am I supposed to feed my own baby if I can't even toast bread?"

Alec laughs. "We have a long time before you need to cook for the baby. Plus, don't babies take bottles until they're like four?"

"Four?" I glare at him. "I'm pretty sure that's not accurate. RJ doesn't take a bottle anymore and he's only one. But I don't know," I hiccup through a sob, "because I have no idea about babies, and apparently neither do you. How the hell are we going to raise a baby if neither of us knows anything?"

Alec almost laughs again, but quickly stifles it. "We have our family and friends. We'll read up on it all. Every new parent has to start somewhere, but, Lex... no more cooking, please. If I have to, I'll hire someone to cook for us."

"Fine," I huff.

"I love you," he says, giving me a kiss. "I'll see tomorrow morning."

"Love you too."

* * *

One Week After the Burnt Toast

"WHAT ARE YOU DOING LYING IN BED?" GEORGIA accuses.

"What else am I supposed to be doing?" I flip through the shows, trying to find one I haven't watched yet. "I can't surf because I'm pregnant. I'm not allowed to cook or bake anything. Alec forbade me from going out and graffitiing the walls..." I roll my eyes as I recall the fight that ensued. I know he was right, and had I gotten caught, being pregnant and in jail would've been a bad thing, but I'm fucking bored.

Aside from visiting Aiden every day, I have nothing else to do. "I'm a college drop-out... I can't figure out how to help Aiden..." I've tried calling several organizations but none of them were helpful because Aiden is an adult. The only thing I can do is report him, which would get him arrested. I looked into assisted living for him, but it's more than I can afford. I would use up my entire trust fund in three years, and then what? "Pretty much, I'm a loser."

Georgia grabs the remote and turns the TV off. "It's your birthday. I'm taking you to lunch."

"Fine." I can always eat. At fourteen weeks pregnant, the morning sickness is gone and my appetite is plentiful. Since Alec is working and couldn't get off, we're planning to celebrate my birthday this weekend.

We arrive in the Arts District and walk to my favorite deli. I haven't been here since Alec took me on our first date. The walls are filled with art, and it makes my heart both full and sad.

"I miss this," I tell her, when we walk past one of my drawings.

"Well, maybe instead of creating illegally, create *legally*."

I roll my eyes. "Have you ever searched my hashtag?" I pull my phone out and type it in, then show her. "Four million tags. Four million people took pictures of my art."

"And imagine how many would buy it if you created it on actual canvases instead of on the side of buildings."

"It's not about the money. It's about the purpose of the art.

Using it to make a difference. I just... I want to make a difference."

I continue walking down the sidewalk when I notice Georgia is no longer next to me. "What are you doing?" I ask, looking back and seeing her standing in front of the abandoned building.

"You said you want your art to make a difference," she says.

"Yeah..."

"And you want to help Aiden..."

"Uh-huh."

"I have an idea."

"Well, don't be all suspenseful. Tell me."

"An art gallery, here. It can be a non-profit organization to help autistic children and adults. We could create an entire program that allows them to create, and the pieces we sell can help fund the program."

I stare at the large, empty building and can picture everything she's saying. Aiden could come here and have a safe place to draw. I could paint and teach and help others like Aiden. There's only one problem...

"How would I afford this?"

"I said 'we'," Georgia says. "In case you forgot, I have money, and I met with my financial advisor the other day, who told me I should consider making donations to help with the tax write-offs at the end of the year."

"This would be more than a donation. This would cost a lot and it would be time-consuming."

"I have the money," she says, "and you have the time. You

would be in charge. Our grandparents run the rec center in Las Vegas. They would know what to do. How to set it all up."

She's right. Years ago, before we were born, our grandparents started a recreational center for kids to get them off the streets because Micaela's dad, Marco, was one of those kids on the street. They've been successfully running it for years and would gladly help us.

"And if Aiden agrees, we can pay him to work here, to help us..."

"Which would pay for him to live in assisted living." I throw my arms around Georgia. "You're a freaking genius, and the best sister ever! Thank you! Thank you! This is the best birthday ever. I can't wait to get started and tell Aiden..." I hug her tighter. "I love you, Georgia, thank you."

"You don't have to thank me, Lex. I'm your sister. I just want you to be happy."

I pull away from her and glance back at the building. "This is it, Georgia. I can feel it... This is my path."

Epilogue

LEXI

Seven Months Later

"Is that everything?" I ask, taking a look around the place one last time.

"I think so," Alec says, coming up behind me and wrapping his arms around me. "And if it's not, it's not like we can't get whatever we forgot... Your sister and Chase are still living here."

I groan. "I can't believe she'd rather live here than with us in our new house." Two months ago we closed on our first home. It was days before I was due to give birth, and we thought we would have time to fix up the small things we needed to fix up and then move in. Only our daughter surprised us by coming early. We stayed in the condo for two months, which was actually great since Georgia was around to help. Since I had a C-section, I couldn't lift anything for six weeks. Now, Abigail is two months old, sleeping almost through the night, and we're moving out.

"She wants us to have our own space," Alec says for the millionth time.

"Yeah, I know." I pout. "But she's staying here with Chase? She can't even stand him..."

"I own the condo," I remind her. "Instead of them having to find another place to live, I told them they can continue to live here. It saves me the hassle of having to find new tenants or sell the place."

"Umm... in case you forgot, my sister is rich. She can afford to live anywhere she wants."

Alec laughs. "Maybe she doesn't want to live alone." He shrugs. "Chase stopped bringing women around a while ago, and they haven't fought in a long time."

"I guess." I huff. "I'm just going to miss her."

"We'll only be ten minutes away," he points out, kissing me. I sigh into him and thread my fingers through his hair.

"Lexi," Aiden says, ending the moment. "Lexi's baby, Abigail, is crying."

"I'll go get her," I tell Alec. "You make sure we have everything."

I walk into the living room and find Aiden rocking Abigail's car seat. She's barely whining, but to Aiden that's crying. Any time she makes any noise that isn't happy, he wants us to make her happy. The moment she was born and he came to visit, he became attached to her.

"Here you go, sweet girl." I put her pacifier into her mouth that fell out and her eyes roll backward, as she instantly falls back asleep.

"Can we go paint now?" Aiden asks, referring to Through Their Eyes, the non-profit art gallery that's set to open soon. Right now, we're painting the inside. Georgia and I have contacted dozens of artists and celebrities and have gotten many donations. When it's done, it will be an art gallery people can visit and buy from, as well as an educational center. We're planning to run yearlong programs, where kids can come to learn how to create, and all the proceeds will go to help support autistic children and adults.

"Go ahead," Alec says, walking over and kissing my temple. "I'll handle the rest."

"You sure?"

"Yeah."

Twenty minutes later, we arrive at the gallery and Aiden goes right to work, painting his masterpiece. He spends the afternoon painting while I work on the business side of things. When it's time to go, I take him out front where the private bus from his assisted living center picks him up.

"I'll see you tomorrow?" he asks, like he does every day, Monday through Thursday.

"Yes, I'll see you tomorrow."

"And baby Abigail, too," he says.

I laugh under my breath, realizing I said I instead of we. "Yes, we will both be here."

"At nine o'clock, right?" It's taken a little bit of time for Aiden to adjust to living in a new place and having a new routine. At first, it was rough. We even had to bring his blue tent with him and set it up in his room. But he's slowly adjusting, and the most important thing is he's happy and safe. The assisted living center provides a private bus that drops him off and picks him up every day during the week. I would love to take him myself, but they said he needs consistency, so it's best to let him ride the bus every day.

"Nine o'clock," I assure him.

"Okay," he says. "Bye, baby Abigail." He gives her a kiss on her cheek. "Bye, Lexi."

He steps onto the bus, and once he's seated, waves to us.

"All right, sweet girl, you ready to go home?"

She doesn't respond, fast asleep, but I take it as a yes.

A little while later, we arrive at our new home. It's a beautiful four-bedroom, three-bath, two-story house near the beach. As much as we wanted to be on the beach, those houses were ridiculously priced. But we found the perfect house, that's in a cute gated neighborhood and is only walking distance to the beach. It's not too far from Alec's fire station or from our parents. It's perfect.

When I walk inside, I'm amazed by what I see. Alec must've been busy because everything is put away and organized. The boxes that were everywhere are gone.

I set Abigail down, who's still sleeping in her car seat, and walk over to the fireplace, where he set up several photos in frames. One is from our wedding day. We're both smiling at each other with such love, I can still feel it as if it were yesterday. The next photo is of the day I gave birth to Abigail. She's all wrinkly and frowning, but Alec and I are grinning like fools. I'm looking at Alec, and he's looking at our daughter. *Our daughter.* We made the decision not to get them tested. Alec said he doesn't want to know because as far as he's concerned, she's his and always will be. He's listed as the dad on her birth certificate and the three of us share the same last name. They also share the same blood type, which isn't the same as mine. That means, either Jason had the same one as them, or she's Alec's biological daughter.

"Hey, you're home," Alec says, walking down the stairs. "I put away most of the stuff, but there are a couple boxes left for you to go through. I put them in our closet."

"Thank you." I wrap my arms around his neck. "I can't believe this place is ours."

"Well, you better believe it," he says. "This is our home..." He kisses the tip of my nose. "Our daughter." He kisses my chin. "Our life." His mouth connects with mine. "And it's damn beautiful."

ALEC

The Next Day

Georgia: Thought you should know Lexi is out graffitiing the walls.

I CLICK ON THE PICTURE ACCOMPANYING THE TEXT and see Lexi stuffing spray cans into a backpack, unaware that her sister is taking a picture of her. I left them in the box for her to either keep or get rid of. I guess she's putting them to use.

Me: Did she mention where she was going?

Georgia: No, but she did say she needed to go finish something she started...

Me: How long ago did she leave?

Georgia: About thirty minutes ago. I figured I'd give her a head start.

Me: And I take it you have Abigail?

A moment later, a picture comes through of my beautiful daughter sleeping soundly in her crib—her belly up and her bottom popped up in the air.

Me: Give my daughter a kiss for me.

Georgia: Will do. Try to keep my sister out of jail...

Me: Will do.

I exit out of our conversation and pull the tracker app up, clicking on Lexi's name to see where exactly she is. When I zoom in on her location, I can't help but laugh to myself.

"Hey, Chase, you mind covering me for a little bit?"

"Sure." He shrugs. "Everything okay?"

"Yeah, I just need to run a quick errand."

A few minutes later, I pull up to the abandoned building I haven't been to since the night I was here with Lexi. Her jeep is parked along the side, and when I walk around the corner, I find her, with her back to me, spray painting the wall.

She doesn't know I'm here, so I stay quiet and watch her as she creates, lost in her own world. When she finishes and backs up to check out her work, I clear my throat, startling her.

She spins around, her eyes wide at having been caught. But when she sees it's only me, her shoulders sag in relief. "You scared me!"

"Shouldn't be doing bad stuff..."

She rolls her eyes. "My sister rat on me?"

I laugh, not answering her question, and walk over to her. "It feels like forever ago since we were here and I was watching you paint." I tug on the bottom of her tank top and pull her toward me, connecting our mouths for a brief moment. It's only been twelve hours since I last tasted her, but I'm already missing the hell out of her.

"A lot has happened since we were here," she murmurs against my lips.

"Very true," I agree. "We've gotten married, had a baby, bought a home... We've created a life together since that night."

Her lips curl into a mesmerizing smile, and I capture her mouth again. Her lips are soft and she tastes like her favorite raspberry drink from Jumpin' Java.

"I needed to paint one last time," she says when we break apart.

"One last time?" I quirk a brow in disbelief.

"I'm a mom now," she says with a shrug. "I can't be graffitiing the walls of LA... But I needed to complete the painting."

I glance at the work of art in front of us, really looking at it for the first time tonight. Earlier, my eyes were only on Lexi... The painting is the same one from before: of a couple facing each other with the backdrop of the night sky and twinkling lights. Next to them is the quote my mom said: *You don't find love... it finds you.*

But when I look closer, I see the addition she's made. In the middle of the couple is a tiny baby—our baby.

"Love found us," she says softly, wrapping her arms around my waist. "That dark, scary path... it led us here. To our baby girl. I feel like I've finally found my place in this world—with you and our daughter. As a mom and a wife. Our picture..." She looks up at me, her blue eyes twinkling from the hue of the streetlamp. "It's complete."

The End

ABOUT THE AUTHOR

Reading is like breathing in, writing is like breathing out.– Pam Allyn

Nikki Ash resides in South Florida where she is an English teacher by day and a writer by night. When she's not writing, you can find her with a book in her hand. From the Boxcar Children, to Wuthering Heights, to the latest single parent romance, she has lived and breathed every type of book. While reading and writing are her passions, her two children are her entire world. You can probably find them at a Disney park before you would find them at home on the weekends!

Made in the USA
Middletown, DE
23 July 2021